SHIBBOLETH

D J MALLMAN

PROLOGUE

"Are you an Ephraimite?" If he replied, 'No,' they said, 'All right, say Shibboleth.' If he said 'Sibboleth,' because he couldn't pronounce the word correctly, they seized him and killed him at the fords of the Jordan." Judges 12:5b-6 NIV

ACRONYMS

AQAP: Al-Qaeda in the Arabian Peninsula
CCM: Combat Craft Medium
CTI2: Cryptologic Technician Interpretive 2nd class
DEA: Drug Enforcement Agency
FBI: Federal Bureau of Investigation
JTTF: Joint Terrorism Task Force
KFFC: Kentland Farms Flight Center
MCADS: Maritime Craft Aerial Deployment System
NCS: National Clandestine Service
NSA: National Security Agency
NSC: National Security Council
NSOC: National Security Operations Center
POTUS: President Of The United States
RAAF: Royal Australian Air Force
SASR: Special Air Service Regiment
SEALs: Sea and Land Special Forces

PROLOGUE

Tehran, Iran

Hamid Hashemi fastened his seat belt as Lufthansa Flight 346 made its final approach to Imam Khomeini International Airport. He could just make out the Alborz Mountains through the heavy smog enveloping Tehran. Hamid heard the landing gear going down but couldn't see the ground. The yellowish-brown smog was inescapable, giving Hamid a creepy feeling. His shoulders tightened as his grip did the same on the armrests of his seat prompting him to consider, *was it a mistake to come back to Tehran?* He'd abandoned his life in Iran when Ayatollah Khomeini took charge in 1979, electing to seek asylum in the United States where he was attending graduate school. Now, moments from touchdown, he feared it was a bad choice to return.

Hamid was left to his thoughts, *"Hamid, your mother is dying,"* his cousin blurted out over the telephone. *"She wants to talk to you,"* he said passing the phone to the dying woman. *"Assure me you have not lost faith,"* was all she managed to say before sinking into the bed, exhausted by the effort. *What son could stay away and not comfort his mother as she died? His mother had pleaded on the phone in a voice hardly able to speak. Hamid knew he could only give her peace by making the trip.*

The airport was a busy place, far busier than Hamid had expected. The starkness, cold steel arches and bright piercing lights attached to the tops of concrete pillars did not offer Hamid any comfort. Watching American news coverage of Middle Eastern conflicts hadn't prepared him for the immediate shock of seeing older women dressed in the all-engulfing chador, juxtaposed with younger women attempting to push the limits of the law, their heads barely covered by a shawl and wearing skin-tight jeans.

Standing at the baggage carousel, Hamid reflected on his past for a moment. *I departed Tehran from Mehrabad airport in 1977. That airport was on the south side of Tehran and slowly becoming engulfed by neighborhoods of poor Iranians. This new airport was 30 kilometers away ... what was that, about 20 miles? Not far from his boyhood home.* He was jolted back to the present when he heard his name announced over the loud speaker, "Mr. Hashemi, Mr. Hamid Hashemi, please come to the baggage attendants office." Walking across the terminal his first thought was, *did they lose my bags?*

As Hamid entered the claims office, he clutched the handle of his carry-on bag and held it close to his body. Suddenly, someone with poor personal hygiene gruffly pushed him past the counter and into a back room. Sitting at a small table was a man in a Revolutionary Guards uniform smoking a cigarette. Hamid coughed as he was pushed into a chair. He looked up and saw the contents of his small suitcase strewn on the table. The official stubbed out his cigarette, reached into the pile of clothes and pulled out a small copy of the New Testament.

"It is against the law to bring a Bible into Iran," the man said as he slammed it on the table.

Against his better judgment but knowing Iranian laws concerning religions other than Islam, Hamid spoke up with confidence, "I must correct you, Sir. Bibles and other religious reading material for personal use are allowed. Preaching or proselytizing is forbidden." The severity and quickness of the blow to his head caught him off guard. He barely managed to remain in the chair. Hamid lowered his head, avoiding eye contact, trying to make himself a smaller target.

"Gohe sag!" the official bellowed, like a cobra spitting its venom. "For your own good, you should remain silent."

Hamid's head buzzed from the blow. Two more uniformed men entered the small room. Grabbing his arms, they made him stand up and then pulled his arms behind him. Plastic zip-ties were pulled tightly around his wrists. Hamid took one quick glance around the room. The man in uniform behind the table had three stars on his shoulder epaulets and collar devices displaying a prominent anchor. That was all he saw. He panicked when a dark cloth bag was pulled over his head. He was dragged out a back door and tossed into a waiting van. The official smiled and said, "Welcome back to Iran, Pastor Hamid."

Pulling out his cellphone, the official hit speed dial. An aide answered the private line at Bandar Abbas Naval Base and handed it to his boss. Taking the phone, he asked, "Success?"

"As you planned. The infidel is in custody."

"Praise be to Allah. He blesses our plans."

"The Saberin are at your command," responded the official as he came to attention.

"We have much to do. Put the infidel dog in a safe place. Then return to your duties."

"Yes, sir."

CHAPTER ONE

ONE YEAR later

September 6, (Wednesday)

National Security Agency (NSA)

Navy Lt. Davis picked up his tray and headed for the scullery belt, hesitated, then turned back to the table. Leaning down so his face was inches away from Sam's, he said louder than necessary, "Petty Officer, they are saying '*kill the presidents*,' not '*destroy the presidents*.' I don't want any more arguments. I'm releasing the translation as an EYES ONLY message to the restricted list as soon as I get back to my office."

Davis' outburst was louder than expected and nearby cafeteria patrons looked at him. He knew the rules, 'No Classified Talk in the Cafeteria,' but his anger had gotten the best of him. *No petty officer was going to question his interpretations.*

Navy Petty Officer Second-Class Sam Ives was a Cryptologic Technician Interpretive (CTI2) who knew it was unproductive to argue with the Lieutenant but felt it was necessary to explain his concern. Unconsciously pushing his tray between himself and the lieutenant, Sam steadied himself and said, "Lt. Davis, I agree the intercepted conversation clearly uses the Farsi word *'Kashteen'*, which normally means kill; however, other options are assassinate, destroy and annihilate. But it's more than that. I heard an attempt to draw out the word as if trying to give it emphasis."

"Kill, destroy, annihilate, assassinate; none of those changes the threat to the presidents," Lt. Davis snapped.

"True, but I think we should be open to other possible meanings. Maybe the caller is referring to a plan to destroy the reputations of the presidents?"

"That's crazy. How could anyone do that?"

"I don't know. Maybe provide proof of a government cover-up that's been perpetrated over the years."

"To what end?"

"I don't know. I just think we should keep our options open."

Lt. Davis stared at Sam for a long time. Sam was an excellent hard-working "I-brancher," as interpreters were called in the Navy. This hesitancy just didn't fit. Ives was fluent in Farsi and there was no questioning the Farsi word used by the caller. The intercept clearly indicated someone was planning to kill the presidents. The message had to go out to the various Directors and it had to go now. Returning to his desk and signing onto his computer, he pressed the send button with a feeling of self-gratification.

WITHIN 40 MINUTES, the National Security Operations Center was inundated with requests. All of the recipients demanded additional information. Lt. Davis was called to report immediately to the 6th floor Executive Conference Room. On several previous visits, Lt. Davis always found the room feeling like a refrigerator. It wasn't just the cold temperature of the room; the décor seemed to enhance the cold. The huge smoked-glass confer- ence table, metal picture frames displaying photographs of the Enigma machine and the original NSA building, steel-gray wallpaper and matching gray rug all added to the sensation. Chet Nelson, Director of NSA, his Chief of Staff and six other principals were sitting around one end of the glass table while several staffers were occupying perimeter seats.

"Let's cut to the chase, folks," growled the Director. "I've got to brief the National Security Council in an hour. Lt. Davis, give me the background on the alert message you released."

"Director Nelson, there's not much to say at this time. Station Caliber intercepted and recorded the call based on Dial Number Recognition protocols. Keyword filters automatically pushed it to a high priority in our department's queue." Lt. Davis paused, cleared his throat and continued, "The computer generated a translation but, because of the possible threat context, it was flagged for human review. My team and I reviewed the recording and agreed it represented a valid threat." Lt. Davis was not willing to append Petty Officer Ives' concerns about Farsi word definitions with this group. It wasn't of significance anyway.

"And we're sure it's a threat to the presidents – plural?"

"That's affirmative, sir. We believe the text clearly indicated more than one president and clarified the United States as the target when they said, 'The Great Satan'."

"Thank you, Lieutenant. What do we know about the caller and recipient?"

"Mukhtar al-Bayruti has been on and off the network for over 20 years. He was a low-level aide to Osama Bin Laden, slowly climbing the ranks before dropping out of sight six years ago. He was identified in a call to a friend the day after Bin Laden was killed. CIA shared a report last year that suggested he was working as one of several close aides to Ayman Al-Zawahiri."

"And what about this Sami guy? What do we know about him?" asked the Director.

"Not much. He's a mid-level operative for Al Qa'ida in the Arabian Peninsula based in Qatar. We only have a few recordings linked to him and all are related to acquiring material for AQAP operations – transportation and passports. He owns several Internet cafes in Qatar. Some AQAP message traffic transits his IP servers."

"Is he Qatari?"

"No, he's Iranian."

"How about al-Bayruti?"

"While his name implies that he is from Lebanon, our profile suggests he might have spent time in Iran, Esfahan specifically, in his early childhood."

"Why is that?"

"In some of our past recordings he speaks mostly in Persian. When he gets in a hurry, he sometimes pronounces Farsi words with a Levant Arabic accent."

"This exchange was in Farsi, right?"

"That is correct, sir."

"What do you think this exchange means, Lieutenant?"

"We do believe that the threat encompasses all four living presidents. There's too little information to go beyond that at this time, sir."

"Yet you released it as an Eyes Only to the bigot list," a backbencher said in a hushed voice.

Lt. Davis turned toward the staffer. Maintaining his composure he said, "Protocols dictate that anytime we have an intercept suggesting an attack on the President Of The United States, it goes Eyes Only to a select number of Cabinet and Intelligence Directors."

"Thank you, Lieutenant. Please have your team dig through those previous recordings for any associated or supporting information. All requests and responses to outside agencies must go through NSOC." Looking down the table, Director Nelson caught the NSOC duty officer's eye and continued, "I don't need to tell you the sensitivity of this intercept and the potential for a screw-up. Maintain control and keep me posted of any developments."

Lt. Davis was the last to leave the conference room, indulging in thoughts of how well the meeting went and how it would look on his next performance review.

CHAPTER TWO

***

SEPTEMBER 6, (Wednesday)

Kentland Farms Flight Center, VA.

Calm, placid even, was how most people described Zak Hashemi when he was flying his hover drones. Not tonight though. If he got caught doing this, he would spend the rest of his life in a Federal prison. If he didn't do it, those men would never release his father from prison. Instead, the Iranian Mullahs would hang him. Before they killed him, the regime would slowly torture his dad. Zak was convinced of this. He was in a terrible predicament and wondered how he might get out of it without deadly consequences. Sleepless nights and the thought he might be developing an ulcer tormented him. For the moment, he would continue with their plan but still not lose hope of seeing his father again. He prayed there would be a way out of this mess. Right now he had to put those thoughts out of his mind.

Zak turned his attention to the drone as it got close to the pickup location. He was glad that he didn't need any relay aircraft for this task. Transmitting signals to his drone through a relay always inserted a slight time delay. That delay could mean missing or poorly securing the package left for him behind the dumpster.

This wasn't the first time he picked up a package from behind the dumpster. *This had to be number six or seven,* he thought. He only missed one and that wasn't his fault. After that item was placed, the trash company came earlier than expected. They emptied the dumpster, repositioning the bin closer to the building than before, denying Zak enough room to maneuver his drone.

So much planning went into each pickup that it was a good thing Virginia Tech's Aerospace Engineering Department's Drone Support Center at the Kentland Farms Flight Center was across the river from the Radford Army Ammunitions Plant. The distance to any location on the Army compound was normally only a few minutes of flying time. Zak spent many nights conducting laser survey flights over the entire base; mapping it in 3D detail so he could preprogram his drones to fly to a specific spot without hitting wires, lightning arrestors or other obstacles. The short hop across the New River meant he could conduct numerous flights in a short period of time and, to all observers, it looked like he was just working on his master's project. The KFFC was open 24/7 with little activity, other than his, after dusk. Most of the other students were working with fixed-wing drones - scale models of those either currently in service with the US military or prototypes.

THE US GOVERNMENT selected Virginia Tech's Aerospace Department as one of six drone research centers in the US. Virginia Tech was specifically tasked to conduct research on drone survivability. The selections were announced in December 2015 and, as an afterthought, Zak attached a small tag to each of his drones saying, Property of VATech Aerospace Department Call (540) 555-8112 if found. He hadn't anticipated that Army helicopter swooping in to land as he was conducting one of the survey flights. His drone got caught in the helicopter's downwash, smashing it against the ground with such force that a circuit board cracked and short-circuited Zak's control functions. This resulted in an investigation by the Army base.

The intercom buzzed on the dean's desk. "This is Dean Walters," he said.

"Good morning Dean Walters. This is Staff Sergeant Boudreau with the Radford Base Security."

A puzzled look came across the Dean's face as he replied, "What can I do for you, Sergeant?"

"We discovered what we believe is a hover drone on our property this morning. There is a tag attached to the drone with a phone number for the Aerospace Department. Your receptionist answered and passed us along to you."

"What can I do for you then?" the Dean said, still a bit mystified.

"We are a sensitive installation and all of the area above the facility is restricted airspace. Your model airplanes are not authorized to overfly the base."

"I will look into the matter and find out who was flying over the base and impress upon them the restrictions."

"I'm sorry, sir." Trying to remain civil, Sgt. Boudreau thought to himself, *didn't these college types know the seriousness of this security breach?* With a calm voice he continued, "We would like to go further than that, Dean. We need to talk to the perpetrator ourselves to investigate why the aircraft was flying over the base. We request that both you and whoever you determine is the culprit come to the base and talk with the Chief of Security."

"As soon as I discover who is at fault, I will call for an appointment. Do you mind if we change the venue and have the meeting here? I'm sure the Chief of Security is equally busy but I'm in the middle of budget negotiations with the state comptrollers. I see little chance of free time for at least two weeks. My deputy could take my place if that would suffice?" offered Dean Walters.

"I think my chief would welcome a trip to the campus. Just call or send me an email when you find out who was trespassing. Your deputy's presence will be good enough for my chief."

Later that day, Zak was called into the Assistant Deans' office to explain why his drone was found on the base. Since he was the only student conducting research with hover drones, it wasn't hard to make the connection.

Mr. Seton explained the severity of the situation to Zak and the requirement to meet with the Radford Chief of Security.

Zak had prepared a story for just such an occasion and was surprised at how easily he was able to lie about the incident. "Mr. Seton, I can explain. I was using one of the hover drones to spot illegal deer poachers along the river at night. A helicopter appeared outside of established flight lanes and the rotor-wash made me lose control. I never regained control and thought the craft had crashed. I spent time the next day looking along the river and couldn't find anything."

"Why didn't you let either the Dean or me know about this incident?"

"I didn't think anyone would care about a broken drone. I didn't know it drifted into the base's territory."

"Well, the Chief of Base Security is scheduled to visit with us this afternoon. I hope they accept your story and won't press any trespassing charges," cautioned Mr. Seton.

The issue was quickly resolved after Zak told his story. The Radford security officer accepted Zak's explanation and returned his drone making sure he understood the no-fly restrictions over the base. Zak thanked them and told them he was aware of the rules and would conduct his flights within those restrictions.

A THREE-TONE BEEP in Zak's earpiece told him the hover drone was at the staging location and time for him to take command. Excitedly, he reached over for his cup, took a sip of his favorite tea and then switched over to manual control. The aircraft he was using tonight was a modification of an earlier craft. After the dumpster incident, he improved the hover drone with a lift hook he called *The Claw,* after the arcade machines where you try to maneuver a claw to pick up stuffed animals. His was far more sophisticated. The purpose was to improve every chance of succeeding and not dropping his prize.

As Zak viewed the area and package placement with the onboard video sensor, he slowly hovered to within one foot of the package. Extending the claw at the center of the package, he made contact. With careful deliberations he commanded the drone to secure the bundle, then tested its weight with a slight upward movement. The parcel was secure and it was time to fly it out. A weather front was predicted to come through the area in one hour with wind gusts in the 10-15 knot range. Zak could maneuver with wind gusts of 20 knots but a three-pound packet dangling below the drone might pose insurmountable problems. He wasn't sure what this oncoming storm would bring, but knew he needed to finish quickly.

Less than 20 minutes later the package was in his trunk and he was headed to a storage locker in Christiansburg.

CHAPTER THREE

SEPTEMBER 6, (Wednesday)
Karl's Home
An anomaly? Yes, an anomaly. That's the only way Karl could describe what he saw on the image. He would send a request to the technical geeks in the morning, asking them to review the image for possible pixel-smear or other processing errors. The dark-toned fuzzy oval, with an accompanying shadow, visible on satellite imagery acquired over the KFFC, troubled Karl. Two months earlier, he identified a similar oddity at Seidir airfield, east of Tehran, in Iran.

Seidir was Iran's principal 'show-n-tell' facility. Its close proximity to Tehran made it an ideal location for Iranian VIP's to review new equipment developments. New designs were brought here from other research and development centers. In 2013, the Iranians reverse-engineered the United States' RX-70, an Unmanned Aerial Vehicle (UAV) they claimed to have lured into Iranian airspace using a false homing signal, forcing the UAV to land at an airbase near the Afghanistan border. The company Karl worked for, GlobalWatch, observed and reported the presence of the first Iranian copy of the RX-70. Over the years other unusual craft were seen at Seidir, including drones designed to skim over the sea acting as a poor man's cruise missile. An Iranian opposition group recently identified Seidir airfield as an Al-Quds Force facility within the larger military compound known as Qasr-e-Firuzeh. Karl feared that anything appearing unusual at or in the vicinity of the airfield could only be intended for nefarious purposes.

Pausing to re-examine the unknown object, Karl wondered if the two sightings could be related or just coincidences. He hoped it was just a pixel processing error but, to ease his mind, he made a copy of the object and put it in his 'rainy day' file along with the example he already had from Seidir. He planned to come back to this file soon and spend time trying to make sense of the anomaly. Right now he had too much imagery to review before the end of the week.

KARL MATTINGLY WORKED for the CIA for 25 years as an Imagery Analyst, retiring when he was 55 to work for a 'beltway bandit' in order to put his kids through college. After eight more years of commuting in Washington D.C's horrendous and life-threatening traffic, he landed the job he had been praying for all those years.

He loved analyzing satellite imagery and when a friend offered him a job with GlobalWatch, he accepted without hesitation. Not only could he continue doing what he valued, but he could also work from an office in his house, eliminating the dreadful commute.

GlobalWatch used his varied skills to mentor analysts working on customer requests for information related to oilfield security, elephant poaching, genocide documentation and military force balances. Karl prized the diverse nature of his tasks but it was the search -- old-fashioned searching of every square kilometer of imagery -- that was his forte. He compared it to another passion, kayaking. You never really knew what was going to be around that next bend in the river, just as you couldn't predict what might show up on the next square kilometer of imagery. It didn't matter what the issue was for

Karl, he just loved looking at imagery and the detective work involved in making sense of what he saw.

Karl just finished a search task in Iran for an international customer interested in the status of Iran's airfields. Now he was putting together a training aid for the US Army on identifying UAVs or drones on commercial satellite imagery. He was starting with U.S. manufacturers and working through all the other builders. Recent expansion in the possible uses for these unmanned aircraft significantly increased the number of models he had to document for the Army's Friend-or-Foe Guide.

LESS THAN AN HOUR LATER, Karl's thoughts went back to the anomaly. He knew he couldn't wait until tomorrow for resolution. Karl picked up the phone and called the system support team at GlobalWatch. "Afternoon, Todd. I've got an image I need you to check for a possible processing error. Any chance you can take a look before tomorrow?"

"Tell me about the problem and I'll fit it into my schedule," answered Todd.

"I made a copy of the area and I'll send it to you as an attachment with the latitude and longitude. If you look at that location, you'll see a small dark spot on the runway and next to it is a slightly darker-toned spot. I think it's the shadow of the first object. I want to rule out the possibility of processing errors before I get too worried."

"I think I can get that done before the end of the day. Today's downloads are already completed."

"That would be great. Thanks, Todd. I might need to adjust my collection plan based on the outcome."

"We're here to help," offered Todd.

TRUE TO HIS WORD, Todd provided results within an hour. Unfortunately, the outcome only made the matter more of a mystery.

"Sorry, Karl. No pixel smear was detected for the images you sent," said Todd.

"Are you sure?" asked Karl, his mind beginning to contemplate other options.

"Positive Karl. I had the lab run several checks, even checked them myself."

"Then it's got to be some peculiar object without much bulk. It looks like a ball of chicken wire hanging in the air. I'll have to go back and check the sun angle. That could account for the darker shadow."

"Based on the lab's calculations, the chicken wire object is about ten feet off the ground," added Todd.

"I got the same results but I don't see any supporting structure," responded Karl as he ran his hand through what little hair remained on his head. "I'll go back and give it another review. Thanks for you help, Todd."

"You've got my interest. Let me know what you finally decide."

CHAPTER FOUR

SEPTEMBER 6, (Wednesday)
White House
"Mister President?" "Mister President?" Marcia asked timidly.
Chester didn't respond at first. Even after eight months in office, he still hadn't acclimated to being called Mr. President. Too many years of responding to Admiral was taking time to recognize the change to Mr. President.

Catching the president's eye, Marcia continued, "The National Security Council is in the Situation Room and ready whenever you are, sir."

"Thank you, Marcia. I'll be down shortly."

CHESTER NIMITZ WOLTON, President of the United States and retired Vice Admiral, sat behind his desk in the Oval Office contemplating how odd it was to be president. Two years ago he took orders from the Commander-in-Chief, now he was that person; a huge accomplishment for the great-grandson of the famous World War II Admiral. His great-grandpa had significantly influenced his decision to join the Navy. Many times he wondered if he had earned the quick movement up the ranks or if he was fast-tracked because of his great-grandfather. He entered the Naval Academy in 1978, was deep-selected for Commander after only 16 years. The selection board picked him before more senior candidates for Captain after only six years. He pinned on his first star five years later, with his third star coming very quickly at 30 years of service.

Those 30 years were packed with adventures and challenges. The most demanding duty was Commander-in-Chief European Command (CINC EUCOM) during the Ukraine crisis. Several times it looked like the US could go to war with the Russians as Putin tried to bully Obama, NATO and the European Union. Obama's divisive cabinet nearly caused WW III when a weak consensus professed a need for a show of force. Obama pleaded with NATO to move ground forces into the western part of the Ukraine. Had it not been for Chester's personal relationship with Russian Admiral Kirov and a plan acceptable to all the actors -- a cooling down period and removal of all foreign troops from the immediate area -- perhaps Chester would be fighting a war instead of sitting in the White House. Learning from Obama's problems, Chester very carefully picked the cabinet members who were waiting for him in the Situation Room.

CHESTER TOOK the short cut from the Oval Office down through the kitchen and back up three stairs to the Situation Room. As he entered, everyone rose from his or her seat. He quickly raised his hand and motioned them back down.

"Let's keep this meeting informal, please," said the president. Staff members settled into their backbench positions as the president took his seat.

"Let's get to business. I understand that NSA asked for this meeting to discuss a threat against my life?"

"Mister President," said NSA Director Nelson, "we have reason to believe that terrorist operatives are targeting you and the other living presidents. An intercept from a sensitive source mentions a determination to kill the presidents. We have very little information other than the two individuals identified from the phone intercept. One is a member of al Qa'ida on the Arab Peninsula and the other has an association with Ayman al-Zawahiri. NSA is currently scrubbing all archived records that match the voiceprints for these individuals for any pertinent information. All the other agencies are aware of the intercept and are reviewing records and sources."

"Thanks, Chet. Anyone have any amplifying information?"

"We have some background information, sir." the Director of Central Intelligence (DCI) Mark Baker, quickly responded. Since the amount of data available was slim, he wanted to give the CIA first voice before anyone could present similar information. "The CIA is also in the process of reviewing files on both individuals. We can confirm NSA findings that al-Bayruti has an association with Zawahiri and a history of targeting Americans. We believe he was instrumental in planning car bombings in Iraq. We also have reason to believe he was associated with Imad Mughniyah, the Marine Barracks bomber in Lebanon. We are still applying a rigorous review of available information."

National Security Advisor, Paul Albrecht, wanted more details. "Is this threat based on multiple intercepts, chatter as you guys like to call it, or just this one incident?"

"At the moment we have just the one intercept. We've made some filter modifications and are searching through the last two years of collection for any links to today's intercept," answered Chet, directing his response toward the president.

Rubbing his lower lip, Paul took a moment to speak and then asked, "Could this threat be a trick to make us commit resources better used to monitor other threats in the domestic arena?"

The Director of Homeland Security, Angela Kohlstead, hoping to get a word in edgewise stated, "Unfortunately, we have too little to go on at this moment. Even though resources are limited, this is a threat against POTUS and his predecessors." Leaning forward and glancing around the table, she continued, "This is serious. We can't afford to let it go to the back burner."

"I'll try to make this easier," the president stated. "Go full force for a week. If nothing of significance surfaces, drop the threat alert and get back to normal business. I'm in favor of short meetings so, unless there's other pressing business that we all need to discuss, keep me and Mark apprised of the situation."

"Mr. President, we need to discuss your upcoming public appearances in light of this threat," said Angela.

"Fine, but set up a separate meeting with Marcia to include FBI and Secret Service. A memo of that meeting can be sent to the NSC to keep them in the loop. Meeting adjourned," the president announced.

CHAPTER FIVE

PREVIOUSLY

Strait of Sunda, Indonesia

A slight wind blew over a calm sea state. An occasional star peeked through an otherwise occluded sky. An old scow idled as it rode the small ocean swells at the rendezvous point. Mohammed could just barely discern the outlines of the volcanoes Krakatau to the West and Pulosari to the East. He anxiously awaited a merchant ship that would dump shipping containers over the side as it passed the rendezvous spot. The hand-delivered message indicated that Allah was providing four 'gifts'.

Standing on the open bridge, Mohammed and Junaedi surveyed the scow. Anyone taking a casual glance would question its seaworthiness. Mohammed knew better. Months of repairs and modifications equipped it for the task at hand. Eight crewmembers lounged on the deck dressed in rubber suits, scuba diving tanks at the ready. Four more men sat in a tight circle smoking and chatting. Several short boarding ladders and coiled rope lay near the bow.

Louder than necessary, Mohammed hollered, "Keep watching the horizon, my brothers. I do not want to miss the ship."

MOHAMMED CHAUNDHRY WAS a senior operative in Jamaah Islamiyah (JI), an Indonesian terrorist group intent on establishing an Islamic Caliphate in Indonesia and the Philippines. Mohammed, orphaned in his teenage years, came under the care and tutelage of a small fanatical madrassa (Islamic school) in Ache, Sumatra. Arrested and convicted for his part in the Bali bombings as the person who assembled the suicide vests, he was sentenced to 18 years. In May 2014, along with 11 others involved in the bombings, he was released.

Junaedi Kusnadhy, who was released with Mohammed and now sitting with him on the scow's bridge, contemplated his past. Unknown to Indonesian authorities, Junaedi was the deputy commander of JI. During the time he fought the infidel in Afghanistan, Junaedi came to the attention of an Iranian Revolutionary Guards Corps (IRGC) recruiter. For the next two years, he received special training in setting up intelligence cells, assembling explosives, secret communications and other nefarious tasks at a camp outside of Tehran. Upon returning to Indonesia, he got swept up in the police dragnet that arrested the other Bali bombers. While in prison, he assembled a team to complete the task given him by the Iranians.

THE *SHAHR-E-KORD,* an Iranian containerized cargo ship, 30 minutes late, was finally observed on the horizon. From a small platform halfway way up the scow's mast came an excited cry from a crewman, "I see letters, 'I R I S L."

Good, thought Mohammed. IRISL stood for the Islamic Republic of Iran Shipping Lines. A quick glance in the starlight scope confirmed the letters, visible on the side of the ship. As it approached, Mohammed saw a crane maneuvering a six-meter-long shipping container towards the side of the ship and then drop it overboard, followed quickly by three more. Within 15 minutes, the ship steamed out of the area as if nothing had happened.

Mohammed quickly steered to the location of each container. Divers slipped into the water as crewmembers dropped flotation gear and ropes to secure the containers. It took almost a half hour to attach the floats that kept the containers just partially above water and the cargo from sinking.

Making a return pass, he exhorted each team, "This is precious cargo. We must not lose any of the containers!" Mohammed and his crew attached towlines and pulled the containers for 10 km to get them away from the sea-lanes. Twice the scow had to stop and put divers back into the water as flotation gear broke loose.

"Brothers!" Junaedi yelled at the divers in the water, "We've practiced this over and over. What is the problem?"

A muffled but unintelligible reply was returned.

As they reached the new rendezvous point, smaller boats awaited the cargo. Their crews hastily unloaded the containers. As dawn lightened the sky around them, Mohammed and Junaedi exchanged glances of accomplishment.

Two of the shipping containers held a cargo of heavy-machine guns and Rocket Propelled Grenades (RPGs). Off-loading the bulky crates created some moments of tension as each item found a resting place in the fishing boats' holds. Those boats would travel for several more hours to reach the Tegalpapak River. Navigating the 8-kilometer trip up the river, to a smaller stream and then into an oxbow, demanded careful attention. A cache site was carefully prepared for future use. The other two containers each held six of the newest version of an Iranian naval mine. Mohammed's boat hauled the mines aboard and carefully secured them on the deck, covering them with a large piece of canvas. The shipping containers were then scuttled in the 50-meter deep water.

Junaedi looked at Mohammed, both were beaming with excitement. "Mohammed, my brother," Junaedi exclaimed as he hugged his friend, "Allah has blessed us with an early success. Now we must pray for his continued blessing as we complete our mission."

"You are right. We have much to do and only a year to prepare the mines for the mission. We already have the tramp steamer and a location to conceal our activities."

Turning to address the crew, Junaedi cautioned those onboard, "We must prepare better than we did for the activities tonight. I will not tolerate weakness or shoddy work. Mohammed and I have a plan and we will practice and practice again until we exceed perfection. Our plan comprises a delivery method that will catch the Americans off-guard and ensure maximum destruction and loss of life. Inshallah!"

CHAPTER SIX

Previously

Virginia Tech's Kelly Hall

Dean Walters introduced Zak to the two U.S. Naval Criminal Investigations Service (NCIS) agents sitting in his office.

"With your permission, Dean Walters, we would like to speak with Mr. Hashemi in private regarding this sensitive subject," requested one of the agents.

"By all means. Use the conference room two doors down on the right. I'll have my assistant make it available. How long will you need it?"

"Not more than an hour, thank you. We're sorry to keep the details from you. We appreciate your assistance and the recommendation of Mr. Hashemi for the program."

"Your welcome. Zak is our brightest and most experienced UAV operator. He can do things with a drone never believed possible."

"That's what we've heard."

Zak led the two officers to the conference room, grabbed some waters from the small refrigerator and sat down. Both agents sat across the table.

Pulling wallets from their coat pockets, they flashed badges and identification cards in front of Zak. "Mr. Hashemi, just to reiterate Dean Walter's introduction, I'm Agent Baxter and this is Agent Reynolds."

Shaking the outstretched hands again, Zak asked, "What can I do for you gentlemen?"

"We have a proposition for you but, before getting to that, we're interested in how you like it here at Virginia Tech?"

"I love it. The aerospace graduate program is one of the best in the country and they give me considerable latitude in my research program," Zak offered with enthusiasm. "The only thing that's missing is the ocean."

"Not a fan of the mountains?" Agent Reynolds probed.

"Oh, I like the mountains. The hiking trails around here are plentiful and the scenery is beautiful. During my undergrad days at Old Dominion University, I fell in love with the ocean."

"Bikinis versus hiking shorts?"

""Those factor in but I just feel relaxed at the ocean. I can decompress much faster listening to the waves than I can to the rustle of the wind through the leaves."

"Maybe we can help you spend some time on the beach."

"How's that?"

"I'm sure you're curious why we wish to speak with you in private."

Nodding his head in agreement, Zak waited for one of the agents to speak.

Prompted by the visual signal, Agent Baxter continued, "The Chief of Naval Operations has given us permission to discuss a very sensitive topic with you. You came to the attention of the Navy when you were hospitalized after the beating you received from some drunken sailors. One of the nurses at the hospital told a colleague about your fantastic abilities with a hover drone. By the way, we did arrest and convict those sailors and you should know that you have every right to refuse to deal with us. We ask that you look beyond that terrible incident and consider the lives you could save."

"That was a very tough time for me," interjected Zak. "I couldn't walk for over six months and an infection kept me in the hospital for most of it. At first I wanted to see those sailors suffer for what they did to me, but then I forgave them and it's all in the past. All told, it was probably another God-incidence."

"I don't understand. A God-incidence?" asked Baxter.

"Yeah, when something we thought was terrible is used by God for something good. While I was lying in bed, paralyzed from the waist down, someone bought me a Traxxas hover drone toy. I drove the nursing staff crazy for weeks. I fell in love with the aerodynamics of hovercraft and changed my undergraduate program to aerospace engineering. I've been happy ever since."

"Zak, before we go any further, we will need you to sign some papers that act as an official record of this briefing. The papers will hold you legally responsible if you disclose this information to anyone other than those we will designate. Are you willing to proceed?"

Confused and hearing the threatening words, '*legally responsible*', Zak tried to reclaim his usual placid composure, asking, "Do I get any idea of what this is about before signing any legal papers?"

"I'm only at liberty to tell you that your skills as a hover drone pilot, programmer and aerospace engineer will greatly assist the U.S. Navy and our country."

Still uncertain, Zak shifted in his chair, "I would really like to talk to the dean and my mother before I sign anything."

"I'm sorry, Zak. Because of the sensitivity of this project, we have to limit awareness to a very small number of people. Should a leak occur, we believe the Navy would be left vulnerable to an attack."

Zak folded his hands and placed them on the table. A long moment passed before he asked, "How long do you need my assistance and how much time will it take away from my studies?" He already had a full plate of classes, drone competitions and independent research. He needed to know how anything these guys asked would fit into his schedule.

"We need your assistance for about one year. We estimate 3-4 hours a week of preparation and a few days each month in the Norfolk area for operational work."

"Norfolk? Operational work? Can you expand on that?" inquired Zak.

"Hopefully that will become clearer in a few moments. Dean Walters agreed that you would get ten credit hours for the work you do for us. An additional incentive, a stipend of $500 cash per month for the whole year is offered. Any expenses incurred by you will also be reimbursed."

Smiling a little too much, Agent Baxter attempted to sweeten the deal; "There's a $20,000 bonus if you succeed."

Sitting back in his chair, Zak twiddled his thumbs for about a minute trying to think this through and what impact it might have on his studies. He knew he could keep a secret and the thought of $500 each month would lessen the burden on his parents. In his own mind he didn't think he would fail to achieve the ultimate goal ... $20,000 *could make a nice nest egg.*

"Do you mind if I sleep on this?"

"Sorry, Zak. The clock is already ticking and we need to catch up. You are a significant part of this study. We would hate to have someone of less caliber take the job."

A multitude of thoughts raced and ricocheted around Zak's brain. *What do they mean I can't tell anyone? The money could really help. I've always wanted to work with the Navy.* The intrigue finally got the best of him. "OK, I'll sign. If this gets to be too much and my studies start to suffer, can I back away without serious penalties?"

"Zak, you have every right to back out at anytime. Additional paperwork is necessary if that happens, but we won't harbor any ill feelings."

"Fine. When do I start?"

"Today," said Agent Baxter as he reached into his jacket pocket and pulled out several sheets of paper, pointing out where Zak needed to sign.

The bureaucratic nature of the documents overwhelmed Zak and he found it difficult to concentrate after the first two paragraphs. Instead of reading any further, he concentrated on the bold print. A Top Secret project code-named *Atomize*. Any unauthorized disclosure of the project could result in 20 years or more in jail. Zak's hand shook as he signed the papers.

Officer Baxter scooped up the papers as Zak finished signing each one. "Do I get copies of these documents?"

"We will keep them in a file for you." At that point, Officer Reynolds leaned forward and, in a very soft voice said, "Zak, welcome to Project Atomize. You will be helping us make our naval ships, especially our aircraft carriers, safer from the threat of unmanned aerial attacks."

Letting that sink in a little, he added, "We want you, over the course of the next nine months, to try and infiltrate the USS George H. W. Bush, CVN-77's defenses, with the ultimate prize being access to the nuclear reactor control room. The CNO and his planning staff conducted several war game studies over the past year. The latest one suggested that US Navy ships are vulnerable to drone attacks while in port.

"Zak, your special skills are what we want to employ," continued Reynolds. "Using the UAV's you've designed, we want you to penetrate the defenses of the USS Bush. You will conduct your attempts when she's in port at Norfolk, eventually gaining access to the nuclear reactor control room. You can use whatever is at your disposal. We have a budget for new equipment so all you need to do is contact either of us with a request. Here are our business cards. We will get your requests procured as quickly as possible. Do not, repeat, do not under any circumstances contact anyone other than the two of us. No one else in our field office or our headquarters is aware of this project. It comes directly from the CNO."

Agent Baxter sipped from his water bottle, leaned back in his chair and said, "We want you to keep a record of everything, including any preplanning and brainstorming ideas you have on this project. Keep that information on this computer." Baxter leaned down and pulled a new MacBook Pro Air from his case and handed it to Zak. "Our email addresses are the only ones in your contacts lists. Keep it that way! Keep this laptop secured and in your possession at all times. Do not let anyone else use it. We will conduct most of our discussions with you via the laptop. Here's the password. Memorize it and then shred this piece of paper.

"You are to conduct yourself as if you have no protection from the law. Everything possible will be done to clear you and any record created but it may take several days. So, be extremely cautious."

"What do you mean it might take several days?" blurted Zak.

"We won't be checking on you on a regular basis, so if something happens, like someone reports suspicious activity near the Norfolk piers and they pick you up, we might not hear about it for a day or two as the report goes through channels. Do not and, I can't emphasize this enough, do not call us or reveal Project Atomize. The need for secrecy is paramount. If word leaked out and terrorists knew the vulnerabilities of our naval vessels, they would quickly exploit those weaknesses before we could bolster our defenses. People's lives are at stake. Are we understood?"

Agent Reynolds got up from his chair and walked toward Zak. "Other than the CNO, the three of us and a few other senior officials, no one knows about the project. Expect the USS Bush to have an action plan against drone attacks so use your imagination and don't get caught."

Zak nodded his head. Baxter rose from his chair and shook Zak's hand. "When is the next time you're going to be at the Kentland Farms Flight Center?"

"I'll be there on Wednesday night after 6:00 PM. Why?"

"One of us will bring some schematics of the USS Bush to help you get acquainted with your target."

"I don't have a place to store large sheets of schematics, especially a secure location? Can't you just send me a digitized file?"

"I like the way you are thinking, Zak. Shows good tradecraft."

"Tradecraft?"

"Yes. You are already thinking of situations that could affect the security of this project and taking action to mitigate any problems. We'll send you digitized files after we get back to our office. At some point we'd like to see where you work."

"I'm usually the only one around after 6:00 pm. Just call my cell and I'll make arrangements."

"Thank you, Zak. We appreciate your acceptance of this tasking and wish you the best of luck. I want to emphasize two things before we leave. First, security is paramount. Don't share what you are doing with anyone. Second, use the laptop as a journal. Document every step you take in preparation and operation. This will be invaluable to our analysts at the end of the project."

Agents Baxter and Reynolds turned and walked out the door leaving Zak, still a little stunned, standing in the conference room.

Zak watched the agents walk down the hall. His heart was beating a little faster as the thought of doing Top Secret work for the government raced through his mind. He was also excited to show off his talents. He grabbed the laptop and headed for his next class as his mind started grasping the complexities of getting a hover drone into the interior of an aircraft carrier. Something nagged at him. Something about the agents seemed familiar. A faint accent, a mannerism or was he just being paranoid?

CHAPTER SEVEN

SEPTEMBER 7, (Thursday)

Department of Homeland Security (DHS) Headquarters

Alexander Garfield Mumford was a hard working agent who came from a middle-class background, graduating with honors from the University of North Carolina and consistently voted Democrat. He already had two tours of duty in Iraq under his belt. Now he was a team leader for an analytic group watching domestic terrorist threats. When his department chief asked for volunteers to work on a temporary threat assessment team dealing with the new threat against POTUS, Alex jumped at the chance and lobbied for the manager position to showcase his management talents. This would help him toward promotion to GS-15 and position him nicely for the Senior Executive Service.

That was yesterday. He was selected for the manager position. Up most of the night sending e-mails to other members of the team, deluging them with requests for immediate information, Alexander was taking a quick break, sitting in his cubical watching as other team members assembled in the conference room for the meeting he had scheduled.

"Good morning everyone," Alexander said as he entered the room. "Thank you all for coming on such short notice. I hope you cleared your calendars because we need to move quickly on this threat notice. Most of you know each other but there are a few new faces. Let's go around the room and give your first name and what office you represent. Let's start with you, Morgan."

"Hi, I'm Morgan, analyst with Current Intelligence."

A burly man who looked out of place in the office, responded gruffly, "Frank, ICE."

"Hi, I'm Samantha from Border Security," sheepishly looking at the rest of the team, she added, "and I've only been here three months."

"I'm Colleen, but you can call me Kelly from Public Affairs."

"Hi, I'm Nooradin from Production."

A grumpy looking older man, sitting a few chairs further down the table than anyone else, piped in, "I'm Kris from Cyber, and before you ask, I don't fix crashed hard drives on your personal computer."

"My name is Denny. I'm from Homeland CT, that's Counter-terrorism."

Looking somewhat lost and disheveled, Carmella answers, "I'm Carmella, working for Information Sharing."

"Molly, Secret Service."

"Again, thanks to everyone for coming. I assume everyone has read the alert message, the memo from the NSC meeting and the National Security Advisor's review of the president's schedule. I've requested additional information from various groups and responses are starting to trickle in. I've asked you here to accomplish the following."

The large flat-screen TV clicked on and a power point slide opened on the display.

1.Review the president's schedule and make recommendations for changes or cancellation.

2.Dig into the archives for any record of entry/departure of the individuals in question.

3.Contact all your Intelligence Community colleagues, discreetly, for information related to the individuals.

4.Review all threats against POTUS for the past six months.

"Mr. Mumford," interrupted Samantha.

"Please, call me Alexander."

"Alexander, will we be moving to the pit or staying at our desks?"

"The pit is under renovation so we will remain at our desks and use Instant Messaging and e-mail. Please copy me on all correspondence. Molly, are you prepared to cover the president's schedule for the next month?"

Molly moved to the front of the room and stood by the TV. She pushed the remote and a calendar page for September appeared on the screen.

"As you can see, President Wolton is very busy. Because the threat said "presidents," I've highlighted all those events where at least one former president is in attendance. From the threat alert message, we can't tell if the intention is an attempt to kill all the presidents at one location or individually.

"It looks like the only time all of them are together is on September 28th at the change-of-command ceremony aboard the USS Bush at Norfolk Naval Base. The president and the three former presidents have accepted the invitation. President Wolton insists on going because it's his academy roommate that is getting his second star.

"Secret Service is trying to convince the president to cancel this appearance and we've recommended that the other presidents follow suit. No takers at this point," said Molly.

"September 18th shows three of them together at a fund raiser for the Red Cross in Ann Arbor, Michigan. The venue is at the University of Michigan's Wolverine Golf Course. Presidents Wolton and Bush II will play in the Pro-Am tournament on the first day and join Bush 1 at the Ann Arbor Country Club for the Red Cross Gala

Dinner. It will be hard to get the president to cancel his appearance since the First Lady has taken the Red Cross as her pet project.

FBI had some chatter in the Ann Arbor area last month related to the acquisition of a truck for something spectacular. They've continued to monitor that intercept and are looking at the local Fundamentalist's Websites. Nothing specifically attributed to a threat against POTUS is identified but the FBI and Homeland are concerned enough to increase surveillance."

"Thanks, Molly. Folks, we've got one week to convince the president to cancel these appearances. Any suggestions on how to do that with the minimal information we have available at the moment are most welcome. Let's head back to our desks and get to work on the other items. Please keep me cc'd on all emails. We will convene here at 5 PM unless something breaks earlier," Alexander stated.

CHAPTER EIGHT

SEPTEMBER 7, (Thursday)

Mattingly's Home

Amanda Mattingly was already through the front door before it dawned on her that she should have knocked. It was just natural to walk in; after all, it had been her home for most of her life until joining the CIA after college. She never tired of the jolt she got walking into her parent's home. The open concept of the main floor just dramatized the view through the huge picture window in the living room. The water view looked more like a bend in a river instead of a small lake. Two muted swans were slowly paddling across the lake where a neighbor was spreading some food for them by his dock. It was too early for the leaves to have any autumn colors but it was still a gorgeous, relaxing view. As a young girl, Maddie and her family would watch the thunderstorms through that window with popcorn and soda. That's probably why she never developed a fear of storms.

Maddie followed her dad into *The Company* as an all-source analyst specializing in link-analysis for the Directorate of Intelligence. She spoke German, Arabic and Farsi at near fluency. She already had a good reputation because she saw linkages in information that a computer didn't always consider. It was a gift from God. Her language skills got her sent to GITMO to debrief several al-Qa'ida operatives. She liked to call it talking rather than debriefing because that is what she did. It made them more comfortable especially after they got over the whole talking to a woman issue. Like most men, they always ended up trying to impress her.

Her mom came around the corner of the kitchen. "Maddie, you startled me," she said stepping back and bringing her hand to her mouth. "When did you get here? I thought you were still in Jakarta."

"I was able to leave early. I got in late last night, stopped and saw Philip and then crashed at home. I told Philip I was coming down here to relax for a few days and told him to come too. I hope you don't mind the unscheduled invasion?"

"Of course not. You know Philip is always welcome. We're going to see your brother tomorrow for the Virginia Tech – UVA football game on Saturday. Dan says he has a big surprise for us at the pep rally on Friday night. We can change plans and stick around or you two can join us. I think I can get hotel rooms for you."

"Don't change your plans for me, mom. Flip and I need some time to talk anyway. I also want some time to just vegetate." Maddie's family was notorious for using nicknames. Phillip was called Flip. They always tried to shorten names. A cousin whose nickname was D.J. was shortened even further to Deej.

"Did you set a wedding date yet?"

"Mom, we're lucky if we can even coordinate a date. That's one of the items we need to discuss over the weekend."

"We'll be back early-evening on Saturday."

Maddie lifted her nose, took a deep breath and was rewarded with the delightful smell of bacon. "What's cooking mom?"

"You're in luck. We're having Budget Spaghetti for dinner."

"Fantastic. By the way, is dad ok?"

"He seems to be. Why?"

"When I came into the house, I heard *Victory at Sea* playing in the basement. That usually means he's stuck on some analytical problem."

"You're right. It could even be worse. He took his kayak out fishing about 20 minutes ago."

"*Victory at Sea* and fishing? Oh my! He's working on something big.

"Do you need any help Mom?"

"No. Why don't you pour a glass of wine and go sit on the dock and wait for him. Maybe you can cheer him up. You go relax. I'll come join you in a few minutes."

MADDIE MADE her way down to the dock, setting her wine glass on the patio table before getting a cushion out of the storage chest. She loved her parents' home. There were several decks to sit on, each offering a slightly different view of the lake. When she and her brother were real young, a switchback path went from the basement door to the lake. Her mom would pack them a lunch and make Maddie and her brother go to the bathroom before they went down the hill to go swimming. Now that path was replaced with 44 stairs from the lake to the basement door.

Maddie settled into the chair, lifted her feet onto one of the other chairs, closed her eyes and said a short Thank You prayer. When she opened her eyes, she caught sight of her dad all the way down in the 14th green cove, swishing his fly rod back and forth. Karl had tried to teach the kids the art of fly-fishing but they could never get the hang of it, especially while sitting in a kayak.

Maddie's phone rang. She thought she had left it in her purse up in the house but instead it was ringing in her sweater pocket. She wanted to ignore it but it was the office ringtone. "This is Maddie. I'm not available at the moment. Please leave a message and ... "

"Nice try, Maddie," said Ken, the Deputy DI. "I know you got in last night, stopped at the office this morning and you're at your parents, probably sitting down at the lake."

"All true. Did you guys plant a tracker bug in me while I was at the Farm?"

"No, but that's probably not a bad idea. I'll be quick. We need you in the office ASAP."

"I can't, Ken. I really need a few days to decompress. I haven't seen my parents or my fiancé in two weeks."

"I feel your pain but I still need you here."

"Can you give me any hint as to why you are ruining my weekend?"

"NSA published a threat on POTUS. NSC, Homeland, FBI and others are up in arms. We need you to look over some past reports."

"Must be a serious threat if it can't wait until Monday."

"We don't assess it that way but the others have a bee in their shorts and want answers yesterday."

"Ok, is tomorrow morning early enough?"

Ken sighed, "I'll live with that. Make it early though."

"After that I'm coming back here to spend time with my family," she implored but the connection was already broken.

Maddie hung up. She heard her dad calling as he maneuvered the kayak next to the dock. "Maddie, my girl. What a treat. Does your mom know you're here?"

"Hi Dad. Yes, mom knows I'm here. She should be down soon to join us." Holding up her phone she asked, "Want me to text her and ask her to bring you a glass of wine?"

"No need. I'm sure she already has it covered. How was your trip?"

"Long as always. Overall it was good. I had a productive session. "

"Anything you can share?"

"Not really. The big question though is what's up with you?"

"What do you mean?"

"Well, I walk into a house where *Victory at Sea* is playing and you are out fishing. Care to explain?"

"Just having trouble understanding some activity. No big deal."

"Dad, I recognize the significance of the music and fishing. I've known it ever since I was a young girl. Something has you worried. Come on, come clean."

"Alright. I never could hide anything from you or your mom. You know my procedure for chipping out suspicious activity when I see it on imagery and then, when I get a chance, I'll review the chips and maybe spend some additional time researching for an answer or clue?"

"I've had a few of your old colleagues tell me about this process and how it's produced both amazing discoveries and also a lot of dry holes. Which is it this time?"

"Not sure. Earlier today, I reviewed two separate images of an anomaly I might have at two airfields."

"What kind of anomaly?"

"Well that's part of the issue. I initially thought what I was seeing was just a pixel-smear or blur which is like a computer burp. But as I looked at both images closer, I could see that what I thought was a pixel issue had created a shadow on the ground. By itself, no big deal, except that one image is in the United States and the other is in Iran. Nearly identical presentation."

"What do you think it is?"

"I wanted to think that it was just a flock of birds in a tight formation flying over the two airfields, but what are the odds of that? The shape of the fuzzy oval, the tonal quality and the size, on each image, is very similar. Both images were taken about one month apart."

"You said you 'wanted to think' it was birds. What do you think now?"

" Crazy as it may sound and possibly weighted by the fact that I'm doing a research project on drone identification, I think it might be a drone swarm."

"You need to educate me,, Dad. What is a drone swarm?"

"For a number of years now drone enthusiasts and researchers have tried to amass drones, mostly hover drones, to accomplish tasks not possible by a single drone. You remember the ads by UPS and FedEx delivering packages by hover drone to your doorstep?"

"Didn't one of them drop a package and cause a major accident?"

"Yes. Those drones were usually restricted to no more than a three-pound package. Otherwise the drones would be enormous. You might as well build a small helicopter.

"Some aerospace techy decided that you could fly drones in tandem with a net or tether between them carrying a larger load. That just opened the door for enthusiasts to try for a place in Guinness Book of World Records for the heaviest load and most drones together. Then the mathematicians got into the act. Seems that almost 10 years ago a bunch of number crunchers took lots of video of birds flying in large flocks. They analyzed the flight patterns of each bird and determined that a large flock operates on the Rule of Seven."

"What's the Rule of Seven?" asked Maddie, "and don't go Sheldon on me." Her family was huge fans of the Big Bang Theory. The character, Sheldon, was always going into excruciating detail when asked a question. Karl sometimes suffered the same affliction.

"Each bird watches the movements of the seven birds closest to it and moves accordingly. That's why you get an undulating movement of the flock as it passes overhead. You can visit YouTube and see competitions where hover drone teams try to navigate an obstacle course with multiple drones."

"Could that be what you are seeing, a competition or practice?"

"That might be the case for the activity at KFFC which is Virginia Tech's Drone Research Center, but the airfield in Iran is just east of Tehran and it's controlled by the Quds Force and IRGC."

"Dad, do you mind if I mention this to a few people at work?"

"Not at all. Just remember to preface it with being an anomaly and early-stage analysis that is packed with a lot of guessing."

"I will. Look, here comes mom with wine and cheese."

Conversation stopped for a moment while they all selected from the cheese board and took a sip of wine. Karl and Liz liked taking an early evening break by sitting on one of the decks with wine and cheese. It was relaxing. It normally didn't take long for the resident Muted-swans to show up looking for a handout.

Maddie sat back and took another sip of her wine, turning the glass and admiring the honey color. "Mom, what are we drinking?"

"It's my new favorite, Sauvignon Blanc from New Zealand. It's from the Marlborough area. I love the citrus finish, smooth but with a little tartness.

"I like it too." Maddie glanced at the bottle and said out loud, "Oyster Bay. I'll try to remember that, better yet I'll add it to my phone notes. I'm always looking for a refreshing white wine."

"Dad, what was the other issue you had from your review?" Maddie asked as she put her phone on the table.

"Let's talk about your plans instead of work. Your mom's here and I'm sure she doesn't want to waste precious time talking shop."

Liz smiled at Karl and said, "That's ok. You two will sit here and stew until you get to talk. Go ahead. I'll savor the sunset."

After a little more back-and-forth, Karl relented. "About eight months ago, I was doing a research project for World Bank to evaluate the recovery process on Sumatra, Indonesia from the tsunami in 2004. I came across what I think is a small tramp steamer that someone is taking special efforts to conceal."

Maddie spilled white wine down the front of her sweater and her right arm. Both her mom and dad saw the look on her face.

"What's wrong, Shug? You look like you've seen a ghost," asked her mother using a family nickname, Shug, short for Sugar.

"It's nothing, mom."

"Now it's your turn to come clean. That look on your face was shock. Was it something I said?" asked Karl.

"Yes, Dad, it's something you said but I can't talk about it."

"Classified?"

"Yes, and rather sensitive."

"Your mom and I certainly understand that situation. Maybe I can put you at ease. Was it the tramp steamer?"

"Dad, I can't go into it. I'm sorry. I know you still hold your clearances for some of the side research you do for the CIA but this is on a need-to-know basis only."

"Karl, Shug," said Liz, "let's just let it drop and enjoy the sunset. You came to relax so let's relax."

"Okay but I've got to cut my visit short and leave early tomorrow morning. I just got a call from the office and they want me back now. I negotiated for early tomorrow morning. Flip is due to arrive here shortly and stay through weekend. Do you mind entertaining him tomorrow until I get back?"

"No problem, Shug. We were going to Virginia Tech for the pep rally. He can join us."

"Thanks, Mom. Now it seems I need more wine in my glass."

CHAPTER NINE

SEPTEMBER 8, (Friday)

CIA Headquarters

Maddie drove through the front gate at CIA headquarters and marveled at the number of open parking spaces so close to the building, for a second, until she realized it was just 5:00 in morning. During the hour and a half drive from her parents she kicked herself for not telling Ken to just wait until Monday; other members on her team could handle White House inquiries. What was it Ken had said? *We don't assess it that way, meaning it wasn't a big deal. So why was it a big deal?*

She parked in row D spot 21 of West lot since the northwest entrance was the only one open 24/7. She couldn't remember the last time she was able to park this close. Maddie badged through the turnstile, waved to the Special Protective Officer, and headed for the Green elevators in the OHB. Employees, to denote which building they worked in or where a meeting would convene, used OHB and NHB. Lots of folks thought it stood for Old Headquarters Building and New Headquarters Building. The NHB was correct but OHB referred to the Original Headquarters Building.

Maddie went up to the 4th floor E corridor and entered the Far East Division front office where Ken was sitting with Yasha Bahmini, the chief. Ever since 9/11, the Company had worked hard to keep the flow of information moving to the right people. The days of 'information is power' were waning but not totally gone. Yasha was a State Department employee on rotation to CIA.

"Have a seat, Maddie," offered Yasha. "Thank you for coming in so early this morning. We wanted to let you have some time at home but the Secret Service and DHS are pushing for information about this threat to the president and possibly the former presidents."

Ken handed Maddie the threat cable and a summary of the National Security Advisors memo. Maddie took a moment to review them and asked, "This is it, Ken? No other supporting data?"

"What you see is all that we have to go on. I already assembled some analysts in your spaces to work the issue. I want you as the lead. At the moment keep just the chief and me on distribution. The Secret Service doesn't want to start alarming more people than necessary. Please use your discretion when reaching out to others in the IC," said Ken.

"Do I have flexibility to change team members?"

"Of course. Just give me a heads up of any changes so I can anticipate any hurt feelings but I think you will approve of the team. Get them started and then get back to the lake unless you feel the need to stay and monitor the progress."

"Maddie, I do appreciate your coming in. I asked specifically for you so I'm the one who ruined your time off. Ken protested but I want your skills on this," the chief said.

KEN AND MADDIE stood and left the chief's office. As they were walking down the corridor Ken asked, "Anything come from the Jakarta debriefing of that walk-in ?"

"Yes. He mentioned that he was coerced by a gang of men he

thought belonged to Jamaah Islamiyah (JI) to transport guns from southern Sumatra to the Ache area. They threatened to kill his family if he didn't help them. He did this for two years until he could arrange to visit his brother in Jakarta. He took his whole family and fled. He came to the embassy hoping to obtain visas to the United States in exchange for the information he had on the terrorists. COS Jakarta is working on getting him to return to Ache as our eyes and ears. The salary being offered might make him accept. I think it's just a matter of time until what little money he has runs out and he becomes a burden to his brother. His risk is low and COS has his best officer working the case."

"That's good news. We've been trying to get someone into JI for over a year. I'm not sure how much we will get from the Ache group but it is a start."

"I did get a small piece of information from him that didn't sound too exciting until I talked with my dad."

"You told your dad about the walk-in?"

"Ken, my dad spent over 25 years in this building and overseas. It's a bit hard to keep much from him. However, I did not tell him about the walk-in, only that the trip went well."

"What did you tell your dad?"

"Nothing. It's what he told me. I must say I didn't cover myself very well. He caught me so off guard."

"You? Caught off guard?"

"The walk-in told me that the JI guys in Ache were bragging about pirating a small cargo ship. He didn't know anything more but said their leader was excited about being famous soon. I didn't think much of it because we've had other reports of JI pirating ships, mostly to offload the fuel that they then sell on the black market to fund their operations. One coastal tanker can net over a quarter of a million dollars for these guys."

"What does this have to do with what your dad said?"

"Apparently my dad found a tramp steamer parked up a small estuary in the Ache East area of Sumatra that someone is trying to hide. He said it was covered with camouflaged netting and natural material."

"Sounds interesting. Go ahead and reach out to the DI and NGA analysts to see if they have anything about a pirated ship hiding in Ache."

They both reached for the door handle at the same time but Ken opened it and motioned Maddie inside. They parted company as Maddie walked down the inner corridor toward the conference room.

"GOOD MORNING EVERYONE. Thank you all for coming in so early this morning. Like you, I have plans for today. Let's get down to work quickly," said Maddie. "Unless I'm reading the message traffic and the atmosphere from the 7th floor incorrectly, the pressure is on to provide background for the two mentioned plotters. Everyone, please review your holdings, then think about possible sources that might have even peripheral access.

"Jane, please arrange a working group meeting for Monday morning that includes all the team leads of the various IC members. I especially want NSA to either send an MP3 chip of the raw intercept or send someone with it to the meeting.

"Everyone else, don't kill yourselves but I want a thorough review of our records before Monday morning. If something comes up, call me," added Maddie.

"Maddie," asked Richard, "do you want a product or will this just be informal discussion?"

"Informal discussion. I want just a roundtable dialogue of what we have in our holdings and outline our next steps before the meeting Jane is arranging. Let's shoot for 9 AM. If there are no more questions, let's get started," sighed Maddie, knowing it wouldn't be until later afternoon that she got back to Flip.

CHAPTER TEN

PREVIOUSLY IN JUNE
Off the coast of West Ache, Indonesia
Light from a full moon slowly diminished as a squall line developed. Mohammad and Junaedi stood on the flying bridge of the *Fatimah*, formerly identified as *Warapi*, about 20 km offshore from their hideout. The gentle ocean swells and faint breeze that had characterized the last five hours now shifted to torrents of rain.

THE *WARAPI* WAS like thousands of other small cargo vessels constantly transiting the Malacca Strait and coastal waters. Most carried rice, cooking oil, farm tractors and other small items to distant islands whose harbors could not accommodate larger vessels. Mohammed's crew captured her at the pier in Sabang Port, boarding her from a small boat in the middle of night. The vessel was topping off her fuel tanks for the return trip to Singapore and would not be missed for five days. Junaedi's source said the ship normally steamed directly back to Singapore without picking up any cargo.

The *Warapi* was 55 meters long and 8.5 meters wide with a free-board of only 3 meters when fully fueled and without cargo. The ship's draft was only 2.5 meters when loaded making it possible to navigate portions of many of the rivers in the Archipelago. The ship only required a crew of five: Captain, Engineer, 1st Officer and two deck hands. Mohammed transferred the hijacked crew to a local contact as they passed Banda Ache. That contact held the crew for ransom at least four months before releasing them.

Mohammed and his crew brought the vessel, renamed *Fatimah*, to a small inlet near Suak Seumaseh, maneuvering it into a bayou where the trees on either side almost touched overhead. They stretched several sections of camouflage netting, pilfered from an Indonesian Army base in Jakarta, over the ship to make it invisible to the prying eyes of satellites and military aircraft. With considerable effort, Mohammed's team learned how to use the onboard cranes. The cranes were a critical piece of equipment needed to position the shipping containers designed to carry their special cargo.

Over the next three months, they experimented with the placement of four shipping containers on the deck so the special cargo could easily and quickly be dumped over the side. Their plans called for only two minutes to discharge the cargo in the designated location. Any longer and they might be seen by passing ships and the whole operation would be blown.

They finally decided that placing the containers perpendicular to the keel and slightly elevated on the port side would facilitate the quick discharge of cargo. They then spent the next 30 days practicing loading the containers and the cargo, sailing from their hiding place and simulating the delivery. Mohammed's crew of seven trusted fighters felt confidant and thanked Allah for his blessings.

———

"ARE all of the mines secured with tow lines?" Junaedi hollered at the three teams standing on the forward deck.

Each team leader gave a thumbs-up signal toward the bridge.

"This is the last practice tonight," Junaedi yelled once more into the bullhorn, trying to be heard over the increasing wind gusts. "On my call and the drop of my hand, team one will deploy mines from the first container, followed in sequence by team two and team three."

Lightning struck nearby followed by a horrendous roar and crackle a few seconds later.

"It's not safe for us or the men to be exposed to this weather," Mohammad said as he grasped the ships wheel to hold the small vessel steady. "We might lose one of the mines. I'm stopping the exercise," he yelled, hoping that Junaedi could hear.

"We have to practice in bad weather as well as good. Only Allah knows what will be in store for us," replied Junaedi, steeling his eyes to watch the activity on the deck.

Junaedi dropped his hand. The teams sprang into action. First the container doors on the starboard side of the ship were opened and latched. Next the rail extensions were quickly attached to the rails mounted inside the containers. The extensions allowed the mines to slide past the side of the ship and fall into the water. The lines secured to each mine were only attached during practice as a means to retrieve the weapons. On a signal from the team leader, crewmembers pushed a mine along its rail until it fell toward the sea, repeating the action for all four mines in each container.

Container one was emptied in 30 seconds. 'Allah be praised,' thought Junaedi looking up from his stopwatch. Peering through the rain and darkness, he could barely see the second team begin deploying the mines. Fumbling with the button on his watch, Junaedi's attention was diverted from the deck as a huge wave struck the small vessel at the forward quarter and engulfed the deck half way up the sides of the containers.

Mohammad and Junaedi heard a scream – a blood-curdling scream followed by a second one. Staring across the deck, Mohammed saw that the doors on the forward container had slammed shut and the container partially ripped from its holding brackets.

"We must secure that container or we will lose the mines and maybe the whole ship," screamed Mohammed.

Junaedi slid down the forward ladder and headed toward the bow. He grabbed a coil of thick rope and approached the container from the port side of the ship. Four crewmembers joined him as he ran the rope through a mounting bracket and then secured it to the steel framework. Another crewman did the same thing at a separate bracket.

Satisfied that the container was temporarily held in place, Junaedi moved to the starboard side, slipping in a puddle of blood and losing his balance. He kept from banging his head on the deck by grasping a handrail. He could see the container had shifted almost a meter towards the starboard side of the ship. Looking closer, he saw legs protruding from the closed doors.

The little ship started to roll as another wave attacked the bow. Not as big as the one before, but it still set the deck awash, dragging a stream of blood with it.

"Brothers," he yelled, "we have to recover the mines." He had a rush of guilty thoughts, *Why did I insist on using the real mines ... I should have filled some pipes with concrete and used them for practice ... if we lose the mines our mission will fail.*

"We will be killed!" one of the crew shouted back.

Junaedi ignored him and started hauling on the towrope.

It took two hours to get the mines onboard and secured. They finished as the storm passed permitting the crew a chance to exam the damage.

Returning to his position on the bridge, Junaedi gave the grim news to Mohammad, "We lost Sami when the doors crushed him. Hopefully he didn't suffer. Faoud and Khalid got banged up as the container was tossed by the wave. They all have bruises but no broken bones. All the mines look okay on the outside."

"It gives me no pleasure to tell you I wanted to stop the exercise,"

Mohammad replied, trying to quell his anger and thinking, *we lost our best crewmember. He was the most skillful of the group in using an acetylene torch. Now we have repairs to accomplish. Who will reattach the framework?*

Knowing Sami's death affected the crew and the potential it had to ruin their mission, Mohammad struggled to lift the crew's spirits. "Sami's death is unfortunate. No one could have anticipated that rogue wave. We must accept what Allah gives us," he exhorted. "We have some repairs to make but I believe we are ready to accomplish our mission. We must complete our task and honor Sami with our dedication."

"Allah Akbar, Allah Akbar," came the unified cry from the crew.

Junaedi, in an attempt to keep the men's minds on track, addressed the group, "My brothers, you were exceptional. You had the best times for unloading the mines – less than two minutes for all the containers. We have accomplished much since last year.

"When we return to camp we must be ever vigilant not to let the prying eyes of the satellites find us. Much still needs to be done before we can leave on our mission.

"Each team needs to clean, inspect and re-lubricate the mine launching rails. We can't afford having a mine get stuck on the rail and fail to deploy. All the containers are to be spotless," demanded Junaedi. "Faoud, you will replace Sami. When we return to the cove, all of the mines will go to the test shed. Make sure to do this only at night. I will run the diagnostic checks, remove the flotation pods and schedule the reloading of the rails."

Junaedi got to his feet, placed his hands on his hips and surveyed the assembled men. "Get some rest, brothers. The next month will be busy as we wait for news. Inshallah."

"Inshallah."

CHAPTER ELEVEN

SEPTEMBER 8, (Friday)

White House Situation Room

National Security Advisor Paul Albrecht was sitting at the conference table with his laptop trying to capture the gist of the morning's council meeting. President Wolton had popped his head in for only a few seconds to encourage the group to find more concrete evidence of the threat against him and the other presidents. The posturing by other agencies that followed his departure was nearly unbearable. The United States Secret Service chief was trying every ploy possible to take over as lead on the investigation while the FBI was fighting for control. The Secret Service had suffered several embarrassments over the last few years, the use of prostitutes in Mexico and the multiple security breaches at the White House. Even after its transfer to DHS, a worse episode was the White House Tour member who drifted from the tour and wasn't missed until he was discovered in the kitchen as the president came in for a snack. POTUS nearly sacked the entire force and reached out to both DHS and FBI for proposals to revamp the service. DHS lobbied hard to retain them but was having difficulty showing improvement. The FBI focused on the budget money available to the Secret Service that would come into its coffers. The Congressional Budget Office wanted a complete review of all budgets before signing off on a transfer.

Meanwhile, none of the NSC members had any new leads. Everyone reported that they had teams digging through back reports that mentioned or alluded to the two terrorists identified in the intercept. Maybe there would be more by Monday morning.

Paul stared at the flat-screen monitors in the cabinet along the wall. Al Jazeera was broadcasting from Donetsk, Ukraine about the latest round of discussions to divide the country. POTUS was acutely aware of the need for a resolution on the issue. Plans were already being made to include him in any formal treaty signing. The President and Secretary of State worked their contacts and influence with a passion to get the parties to the conference table. Ukraine had been quiet for the past 3 months and it looked like a deal could go through. Al Jazeera's reporter was saying that not all was quiet on the eastern front. Several rock-throwing incidents and the detention of a rebel soldier by Ukrainian police threatened the fragile tranquility.

As the National Security Advisor to the president, Paul was constantly catching up. Everything was a reaction to global events with little time to think strategically. This was true for many of the other departments and a sad state-of-affairs for the country. Ever since the demise of the Soviet Union and the current cycle of terrorist related incidents, very little forecasting or strategic intelligence was getting produced. Granted, some of the think tanks still did some excellent work but even their focus was narrowed to what was current. They too followed the money, whether it was to the War-Fighter or the Global War Against Terrorism. Getting analysts to conduct research further back than two years was a chore. Seems all these new kids were conditioned by constant software upgrades, 3.0 this month and 6.1.2 point whatever every few months, that anything older than two years was ancient history and not applicable.

CHAPTER TWELVE

DECEMBER, previous year

Zak's Room at Virginia Tech

The lights were dimmed; WVTF radio was on in the background playing some Easy Jazz. There was a hint of garlic in the air. It could be the setting of a romantic dinner. Instead, Zak was sitting at the computer, given to him by the NCIS officers, compiling his list of accomplishments. Zak typed ... the following are accomplishments through December:

1.Located two secure launch sites for drones along James River – upstream of naval base.

2.Reviewed provided schematics for access routes to control room.

3.Purchased 3D printer.

4.Sent two laser-mapping drones into the hangar bay of CVN-77.

5.Two video drones emplaced to monitor hatch activity for ammunition elevator and hatch #1-150-0-T.

6.Two video drones emplaced to monitor hatch activity on 2nd and 3rd deck (Frame #2-185-0-Q and #3-206-1-C)

7.Prepositioned 2 laser-mapping drones near hatches identified in line 5 above.

8.Prepositioned 3 interrogate/download drones to relay collected information via cellular phone network.

9.Preparing for the first flight of drone swarm.

Amplifying notes:

To date I've mapped the hangar bay and access routes from the 1st deck to the 3rd deck and have determined with some reliability the times when hatches are open. Longest 'hold' time was 3 minutes between hatches. Once a month, normally between midnight and 4 AM on a Friday, all hatches on this route are open while sailors strip the deck and wax the passageway. The only other occasion when the hatches remained open with clear access from hangar bay to 3rd deck was on Thanksgiving. I correlated this with a Family Open House event.

The leave-behind video drones are all parked in the morass of power cables in the ship's overhead and are drawing a trickle charge through the special clamp I designed. They can stay where they are indefinitely. I send an information recovery drone into the hangar bay each time the carrier is in port, usually in the very early morning hours, to recover data. I can also pull information from the 2nd and 3rd deck monitors by calling them on the cellular network whenever the ship is near shore.

Surveyed drone launch sites are:

1.King-Lincoln Park 36-58-02.89N/076-24-39.98W and is 4.5 miles (7.3km) from the carrier docking piers at Norfolk Naval Base.

2.Tidewater Community College Campus – Commercial Drivers License training area 36-54-25.79N/076-26-30.18W and is 7.16 miles (11.5km) to the piers.

Over the New Year's holiday, I will conduct my first outdoors flight test of drone swarm using forty drones. I will restrict the flight zone to just KFFC property until I have more confidence in my algorithms.

An hour after posting the email Zak got a reply from Baxter.

"Zak – thanks for the update. We would like to join you for the drone swarm test. Please give us date and time and confirm that it will be at KFFC. Baxter"

"New Years Day, 2PM Kentland," Zak responded.

CHAPTER THIRTEEN

JULY 13, Current year

Northern Tip of Sumatra Island, Indonesian Archipelago

Mohammed and Junaedi were on the flying bridge of the *Fatimah*. In the distance they could see Sabang Port on Palau We, where they had pirated the ship almost a year ago.

After passing Sabang, Mohammed calculated they still had 4-5 days before they arrived at the target location. Mohamed and Junaedi decided to travel only during darkness and avoid the normal shipping channels to reduce the chances someone might recognize *Fatimah* as the missing *Warapi*. Mohammed didn't think anyone could because he had changed the appearance of the deckhouse with scrap metal to make it look longer and higher. It would suffice to confuse someone at a distance but would create serious issues if boarded. Junaedi said that his sources knew the previous owner had already collected the insurance on the vessel and wouldn't be looking for it. Beside, the various maritime police services had much bigger ships to find.

CHAPTER FOURTEEN

SEPTEMBER 8, (Friday)

Virginia Tech University –Blacksburg, VA

Dan Mattingly was in the Aerospace masters program at Virginia Tech working on a thesis program with Zak related to controlling swarms of drones. He invited his parents to come for the pep rally on Friday night and got them tickets for the UVA – Virginia Tech football game on Saturday. Dan mentioned to Karl that there would be a really cool finale at the pep rally. Dan said his colleague and friend was a genius when it came to drones. They both planned on using over a 100 drones in a spectacular show. Karl was intrigued, especially since seeing the anomaly at KFFC.

KARL AND LIZ cancelled early morning hiking plans but still left their house early on Friday morning and made a day of traveling the back roads that drifted back-and-forth across the Virginia and West Virginia borders. A favorite route was heading southwest out of Staunton, over to Covington, down to New Castle and finally into

Blacksburg. There were times when the roads paralleled the Blue Ridge Parkway. At this time of the year, the Parkway would be a parking lot as tourists would crowd the overlooks and stop to photograph each deer eating alongside the road with their iPhones. A few of the trees, at the higher elevations in the Shenandoah Mountains, were just starting to show color but everything in the valley was still in various shades of green.

They stopped for lunch at a quaint tavern in Clifton Forge where Karl had an excellent smoked sausage and German sauerkraut plate. Liz settled for a lighter course of soup and a small salad. They both decided to come back in October for another drive to enjoy the colors and take advantage of the large fireplace at the tavern after a morning hike.

Karl and Liz arrived in Blacksburg by dinnertime and met their son Dan at *Top Of The Stairs*, locally referred to as *"TOTS"*, his favorite restaurant in Blacksburg. Karl was very familiar with *TOTS* since he was a Virginia Tech alumnus. Liz graduated from Liberty University in Lynchburg but became acquainted with Blacksburg while dating Karl. As an undergrad, Liz was a member of the Ethereals, an *a cappella* group. At a VATech sponsored competition, Karl was in the audience and became mesmerized by her voice, like Ulysses to the Sirens. He made every effort to contact Liz after the competition. He nearly missed her but managed a quick introduction and a request for coffee before she boarded the bus back to Liberty.

After dinner and the chance to catch up on Dan's latest adventures, they dropped him at the Fieldhouse before they indulged in a leisurely walk through the campus. It brought back both good and bad memories. Good memories about how Karl and Liz enjoyed numerous picnics on the Quad, making guesses about when it would become one big sinkhole. The few bad memories were Karl's and related to underage drinking, attempting to survive "The Rail", a concoction of nine liquors mixed with Sprite. The Rail was the signature drink at *TOTS*.

DAN SCORED some choice seats for his parents, midway up the bleachers on the 50-yard line, not far from the band. The crowd was still streaming in for the pep rally. The UVA-VATech game was the Redskins-Cowboys contest for Atlantic Coast Conference football. Both teams were having good seasons and the tension could be felt throughout Lane Stadium.

When Karl attended Virginia Tech, pep rallies were nearly non-existent. With the arrival of Coach McHenry three years ago, all that changed. The Coach had a talent for motivating not only athletes but getting the students excited about the games. Nowadays the stadium was almost as packed for a pep rally as it would be for the game. Cheerleaders kept up a constant chant that got the crowd doing the Wave and shaking the stadium. Karl was sure that you could hear the "Go, TECH! Go TECH! Hokies, Hokies!" cheering a mile away because it was thunderous in the stadium.

The stadium lights were not to the highest brightness, which left the upper seats in the dark and a soft light shining on the field. The *Highty-Tighties*, VATech's Regimental Band, finished a great performance followed by a stirring pep talk by Coach McHenry. After the Coach finished his talk the crowd went wild. The cheering would have gone on for five minutes except the crowd became captivated when illuminated ball-shaped objects entered the stadium from the four corners of the field at a high rate of speed. There were a hundred balls, 10 inches in diameter, hovering about 10 feet above the field. Each object was aglow and flickering through a series of colors. The objects formed into a huge football-shape in the middle of the field and began to move toward the goal line in a spiraling motion. As it crossed the goal line the crowd cheered and the drones separated and formed the word GOAL, flashing in the school's maroon and burnt orange colors.

No sooner did the word GOAL form than it appeared to fade and all the drones returned to the center field. They formed a column about 20 feet high and two feet in diameter with a cone-shaped top. The drones at the base started to glow bright yellow, transitioning to a flashing yellow as the whole column began lift-off. When the whole thing was about 100 feet above the field it appeared to explode. Each drone flashed yellow, blue and red lights as they blew away from the center, falling toward the ground just like the cinders from Roman candle fireworks. The crowd went wild and Karl couldn't believe his eyes. His mind was racing as he tried to grasp the tremendous amount of control and practice this display represented. For the next ten minutes the crowd was treated to even more sophisticated explosions, accompanied by a sound track booming from the stadium sound system. The last explosion formed the letters HOKIES. Each letter formed by the drones then settled onto the field and almost immediately switched backwards so the other side of the stadium could read it clearly. As the drones went dark the crowd was up and stomping their feet, chanting "Encore! Encore!" The crowd was in for a final surprise as the noise subsided. The hover drones went dark and moved to the center of the field before breaking into the outline of the *Hokiebird* and each drone flashed like lightning. The crowd went crazy. As they departed the stadium, Karl and Liz overheard the students talking excitedly about the show. They agreed it was fantastic.

Karl and Liz agreed to meet up with Dan at *Sharkies* after the rally. Karl quickly texted Dan and asked him to invite his friend. He was interested in talking to the young man about this remarkable light show.

SHARKIES WAS CROWDED AND BOISTEROUS. Karl was having a hard time hearing the answers to questions he posed to both Dan and Zak. Finally, he gave up trying and asked to meet before the game tomorrow. Zak said he wouldn't be going to the game but instead would be at KFFC evaluating the condition of all his drones used in the pep rally display. He agreed to meet at one PM. Dan would not go because his mother insisted on taking him shopping in Christiansburg to replace some of his, as Liz called them, "disgusting T-shirts". He looked forward to the morning with his mom and it would give him a chance to ask her about some relationship issues with his girlfriend. Liz had a God-given talent to see through much of the bull in a relationship. As Dan and his sister Maddie matured, they realized how smart their mother was and sought her opinions.

CHAPTER FIFTEEN

SEPTEMBER 9, (Saturday)
Virginia Tech's Drone Facility
The drive out to the KFFC was beautiful. Just the slight elevation increase from Blacksburg had caused the leaves to start showing some color. Somehow Karl missed his turn at McCoy Road, finally turning right onto Norris Run thinking it would circle back to McCoy. The road started out surfaced with asphalt but soon turned to gravel. Karl was so wrapped up in the beauty he didn't mind the two miles he had to backtrack to the main road. He should have recognized he was off track because he had researched the whole area on satellite imagery. He seldom used his GPS, much to Liz's chagrin. It wasn't because he was a proud man. He just didn't like being told where to drive. Yes, he disabled the voice but that purple line still bothered him. Maybe a shrink could make sense of it.

Karl pulled up to the large pole building that served as a workshop and hangar for VATech's Aerospace department at KFFC and parking for the Agriculture Department's tractors. The area around the hangar had several small outbuildings for lubricants and gasoline container storage. A 90-meter long asphalt runway was just east of the hangar.

Karl knocked on the door several times without any answer. He walked around the building and found the door on the north side propped open. He entered and stood in the hangar area. One scaled-down version of the military's Global Hawk drone sat in a far corner with a slightly damaged port wing. In another corner was a stealthy looking drone. As Karl walked through the hangar, he heard classical music coming through an open door at the far end. He walked over to the door and saw Zak standing next to a large workbench covered with the ball-shaped drones he had seen last night.

"Hi, Zak," said Karl.

"Oh! You startled me, Mr. Mattingly."

"Please. Call me Karl."

"OK. Just give me a few seconds to finish up with this drone."

"Sure, Zak. Take your time."

Karl watched as Zak pulled a small wire connector from the drone, plugged it into a small box which was in turn connected to a laptop. The screen displayed an oscilloscope and several other diagnostic tools. Zak tweaked a couple of settings and then unplugged the drone. He turned to Karl and said, "Mr. uh I'm sorry, Karl. I'm a bit short on time. I have to get all 100 drones recalibrated for a completion on Thursday. What can I do for you?"

"For starters, congratulations on that fantastic show you and Dan put on last night. I've never seen anything like it."

"Thank you. It was Dan's idea to make the drones act like fireworks. We've been working on swarm theory and thought a fireworks display would showcase what can be done. We're considering starting a business to provide indoor pseudo-pyrotechnics."

"Wow! That sounds like you could make enough money to cover tuition costs."

"We've discussed getting it up and running, to prove the concept, and then presenting it to the Shark Tank either to get investment or be purchased."

"Where do you buy these drones?"

"Right now we make them all right here in the lab. Except for wiring and a few generic metal pieces, all of it is made with a 3-D printer. Once the parts are printed, it takes about 30-minutes to assemble each drone."

"How many people were involved in flying these drones for the show last night?"

"Just Dan and me."

"You're kidding?"

"No, sir. Dan and I spent about a month putting together the flight path sequences for the lead drones then slaved the rest to the leads."

"So, just two people on the controls?"

"Nope. Just me. Dan was following the whole show on a backup system in the event we had a signal malfunction. If something like that did happen, all the drones would form into a ball at the center of the field and maintain position until the leads received commands through a new link."

"I'm truly amazed that one person can manipulate 100 drones at one time. Do you mind telling me how that works?"

"The simple answer is starlings."

"Starlings? Ah ha – the Rule of Seven."

"Yes, the ugly black bird that to most people is a pest. So you are familiar with the Rule of Seven?"

"Just on the surface. Feel free to add some background."

"Several studies have shown that flocks of starlings maneuver through the sky by watching the seven birds nearest to themselves. That's why you see the undulations as they fly in mass. The nearest birds start to react to those near them and it transfers down the flock, which accounts for the slight lag time. We took that action and applied it to the drone swarm, adding an ability we don't think the birds have – memory."

"So, if I understand this correctly, you only need to communicate with one lead drone which the others follow based on what's stored in their memory?"

"As a simple explanation, yes. A huge amount of number crunching to calculate the 3-dimensional nature of flight is required. Your son is a whiz at those calculations."

"Thanks for working with him. I know he's very excited about this project. He was keeping it secret until the show last night."

"We both were. Our final grade is based on how successful the performance was last night."

"How long have you been practicing this?"

"We began the actual flight sequences last month."

"Did you do any swarm work with the drones before that?"

Hesitating for just a moment, Zak answered, "No." He hoped Mr. Mattingly didn't notice. He had to protect his involvement in the project for the CNO.

"Is anyone else doing this kind of work with drones at Virginia Tech, especially here at KFFC?"

Zak fidgeted before answering, "Not to my knowledge. Why?"

Karl noticed Zak's hesitation but didn't press any further. "I'm an imagery analyst that looks at commercial satellite imagery for various organizations. I'm currently working on a project for the Department of Defense to compile a global drone identification guide. I've been getting images taken over KFFC for the past seven months. During that time I've seen both the scaled-down version of the Global Hawk and the stealth drone you have in the hangar. I also think I've seen your drones in tight swarm formation from about 4 months ago."

"I'm not sure who that could be. Dan and I are the only ones working with hover drones."

"You're sure?"

"Uh, yes I'm sure. I told you we only started practicing last month and only went outside to the field for one or two sessions," Zak replied nervously, feeling a small trickle of sweat drip from his armpit.

Karl could see that Zak was unsettled and displaying several triggers that made him believe Zak wasn't telling the whole truth. Part of Karl's training as an Operations Officer with the CIA involved Behavioral Analysis. His kids hated it because Karl had learned to look for the prompts and question his kids in a manner that revealed if they were lying. His biggest difficulty was selecting which incidents to let pass and which to confront. That's where he and Liz worked well as a team. But now, Karl was confident Zak was hiding something and not sure why.

Karl changed the subject by asking Zak who was sponsoring the drone competition.

"UVA. They hold a regional competition every year. VATech has taken the trophy for the past three years."

"Do you fly any drones other than the hover drones?"

"I do, but I like the extreme acrobatics I can do with the hover drones."

Karl started to walk around the workbench in the direction of the scaled-down version of the Global Hawk when he saw the first page of some schematics for a hover drone on the table. From the brief glance it appeared to be for a larger diameter drone than the ones Zak had been fixing. Zak's face went pale and he made a feeble attempt to move the schematic under some other papers.

"So, what happened to the Global Hawk?" asked Karl in an attempt to put Zak at ease.

"One of our first-year students took it for a joy ride and clipped a telephone line on approach. We are waiting for some sheets of polycarbonate to make the repairs."

"Trying to impress a girl or alcohol?"

"A little bit of both. He's on suspension at the moment and will probably have to wait until his Junior or Senior year before the Dean lets him at the controls again."

Karl took another look at the hangar just to visualize the inside when he looked at it from Space. He turned toward Zak and asked, "Are there limitations for your hover drones?"

"What do you mean?"

"Well, are there weight or weather restrictions?"

"The hover drones we used in the show can't lift more than 10 ounces. Others can lift 2-3 pound packages and carry them for short distances. Like the UPS drones.

"Weather conditions are a concern. A five mph breeze will toss the drones around and getting them wet can cause power problems. We are working on waterproof models but keep running into weight issues."

"Zak, thanks so much for your time and giving me the tour. I hope I can come back or get your email address if I have more questions?"

"Dan has my email and cell number. Thanks for your interest and for enjoying the show last night."

"If you don't mind, I'll take a stroll around the outside to help me with spatial relationships. When you spend your time looking at things from space, you forget that they are several feet long and not just millimeters as they appear on the computer screen. I can let myself out."

"Sure Mr. uh, Karl. Just watch out for the ground hog holes if you stray off the paths toward the river."

CHAPTER SIXTEEN

SEPTEMBER 11, (Monday)

CIA Headquarters

Maddie's meeting of the Intelligence Community representatives didn't go well. Sitting at the conference room table, one hand supporting her head as she jotted notes on a yellow legal pad, she tried to capture the highlights from the meeting. She would have preferred her iPad but they weren't allowed in the building. Attendees were still leaving, some stopping briefly to thank her for hosting the meeting. The DHS representative, who tried to overtake the meeting by stating his organization had the lead, was still trying to make his points with an FBI representative as they left the conference room.

Deep in thought about how to diplomatically compose a memorandum for the record, Maddie didn't see Petty Officer Ives sit down next to her. "Petty Officer Ives, did you need something?"

"Ms. Mattingly, you may not remember me," was as far as Ives got when Maddie interrupted.

"Sam, I do remember you and please call me Maddie. If you recall, I tried to convince you to join us at the CIA when your tour was completed. Your language skills and analytic talent are sorely needed here."

"Thank you, Maddie. Would you have a few minutes to discuss something related to this case in private?"

"I've got some time before my next meeting. Do we need a secure space or can we talk over coffee in the Starbucks lounge?" The CIA, in an attempt to offer new hires that *Google-feel* added a Starbucks café to the cafeteria, improved the fitness centers and started offering healthy meal choices well before the other government offices followed suit.

"I think this would be best discussed in secure spaces."

Maddie gathered her legal pad, pen, coffee cup and company Blackberry from the table and told Sam to follow her. After two minutes of walking down hallways, between file cabinets and cubicles, Sam asked if he needed to start dropping breadcrumbs. Maddie laughed as she pulled a spare chair into her cubical.

"Do you want some coffee or water before we start?" asked Maddie.

"No. I don't have a lot of time if I'm going to avoid traffic on the trip back to the Fort."

"I understand that concern. What's on your mind?"

"I didn't want to bring this up during your meeting because I knew my boss, Lt. Davis, would get into an argument about the official NSA stance. Can we keep this between us?"

"Of course," assured Maddie.

"To put it simply, I think NSA's official translation of the intercept is wrong. Instead of emphasis on targeting the presidents for assassination, I think they intend to destroy the presidents."

"Sam, you're going to have to give me more than a simple presentation because I see little difference between assassinate and destroy in the context of the threat message."

"I understand. Please remember that this is my analysis and not from the NSA. I did the initial translation of the intercept and unconsciously translated *kashteen* as 'to destroy' instead of its normal meaning 'to kill'. When I reviewed the intercept, I couldn't explain why I used that translation other than a gut feeling that I was right. When Lt. Davis pushed for the 'kill the presidents' translation, I couldn't back up my choice with hard evidence to the contrary."

"This still doesn't seem to matter. The threat against the presidents is still valid regardless of word translation."

"Maddie, please give me just a little more time to explain. I went back over that intercept several times until I noticed the inflection given to kashteen. I even factored in that it was an Arab speaking Farsi but still came to the conclusion that Bayruti is intentionally elongating the word. He is sounding out every syllable, *ka-sh-teen* instead of a short clipped *kash-teen*. Most folks aren't going to hear the inflection change because it is very subtle but I'm positive it's there, almost like a stutter. "

"So?"

"I asked myself the same question. I then ran a search in our archives for any use of that word by either of these guys. This resulted in several other occasions but in independent conversations. The Qatari merchant, Sami, only used it once in a sentence that clearly indicted he wanted his houseboy to kill a chicken for dinner. His houseboy comes from the Bandar Abbas area of Iran and only speaks Farsi.

"The ten intercepts we have on Mukhtar al Bayruti that popped up in a search going back two years reveal him using the normal and modulated versions of the word. At least three uses can be positively translated as 'kill' and three are positive for 'destroy'. Quality of intercept or ambiguity of the sentence or conversation hampers positive usage either way for the remaining four intercepts. Of interest, the three positive 'destroy' conversations were all with Ayman al-Zawahiri."

"That is intriguing, Sam. I'm not sure it's enough for me to make any statements to my bosses at this point."

"Maddie, one of those intercepts when al Bayruti was talking to Zawahiri, he uses the inflected *ka-sh-teen* in relation to destroying some secret documents. I'm going out on a limb here but I think al Bayruti is talking about destroying something rather than killing. The reference to the presidents could be about attacking US Navy aircraft carriers or even buildings named after the presidents."

"What? That seems like a gigantic leap from anything you've told me."

"I know. If I'm correct in my analysis and *kashteen* is being used to mean destroy rather than kill, I only come up with one meaning for the message. Several of the Navy's aircraft carriers are named after presidents. For example – Teddy Roosevelt, Lincoln, and Reagan. I think the threat alert should at least be expanded to include all the carriers with presidential names."

"What about presidential buildings, libraries and the like?" asked Maddie.

Sam clasped his hands together for a second and then stuck his hands in his jacket pockets. "I don't think the buildings should be ruled out. I just don't think they represent the spectacular targets normally chosen by terrorists. The carriers symbolize the might of America, the ability to project power around the globe. The cost of each one is far greater than all the presidential buildings together."

"Let's not forget the number of people serving onboard," added Maddie. "Sam, that is interesting but lacking in some solid evidence. What do you see as your next step? As you saw during the meeting, DHS is adamant that the threat is against the living presidents and will not take lightly to changing that focus."

"I wanted you to understand because I've read your analytical reports and have seen several of your briefings. You speak Farsi and Arabic and I believe you would detect the subtle inflection. I want to dig deeper into our archives but need some sponsorship to account for the time spent on research. I've been doing this at night on my off time but a deeper dig would require a lot more time. Would you make a formal request to NSA for the search?"

"I'm going to have to run this by my boss. I have that gut feeling too that you might be on to something. If I don't email you by tomorrow afternoon, please call me for an update."

"Thanks for listening, Maddie."

"You're welcome, Sam. Thanks for the research effort and bringing it to my attention. Since you didn't put down any bread-crumbs, let me get you back out to E-corridor. Will you be able to find your way out from there?"

"Yes," said Sam as they wove their way through the rabbit warren of cubicles.

CHAPTER SEVENTEEN

AUGUST 5, (Saturday)

Borders Bookstore, Fair Oaks Mall, Fairfax, Virginia

The drive from Blacksburg to Fair Oaks Mall took Zak 3 hours and 30 minutes; Google Maps said it should take 3 hours and 47 minutes. Either way it was a lot of time on the highway and way too much on Interstate-81. The number of trucks along the route was at times overwhelming and fearful. Having a semi-trailer less than 40 feet behind you doing 75-80 miles an hour, weighing who knows how much, scared Zak almost as much as the two Iranian lawyers he was going to see. Zak had to meet them in Fairfax because US State Department regulations restricted them to a 50- mile radius from the Washington Capitol building.

THE LAWYERS CALLED the meeting to discuss new information regarding Zak's dad, Pastor Hashemi. Zak's dad was born and raised in Tehran and was on a student visa in the United States in 1979, when the Revolution took place. He was married with one daughter, applied for and was granted political asylum. Zak's grandfather, a colonel in the Iranian Army, was arrested, tortured and killed by the revolutionaries. Other family members fled but Zak's grandmother refused to leave, saying she was too old to move.

His grandmother was one of a small number of Christians still living in the Islamic Republic. Over the years she was pressured to accept Islam as the true religion, sometimes through coercion. Her family sent her money that tended to get "lost" in the mail or "taxed" to nearly nothing. She survived with the help of her Christian friends and longtime neighbors who did not agree with the revolutionaries' tactics. Her health had finally deteriorated to the point she knew she didn't have much time. She asked that her son come to reassure her that he was holding strong to his faith in the land of the Great Satan.

Pastor Hashemi was arrested at Khomeini International Airport upon arrival for carrying a Bible. He was thrown into prison without any outside contact. Zak, his mother and sisters didn't comprehend what had happened for over a month until an official looking envelope arrived, addressed to Zak, from the Ministry of Justice. It informed Zak of his father's arrest and the charge of proselytizing that carried a death sentence. The letter further stated that two lawyers, assigned by the Iranian government, would assist Zak in any legal matters pertaining to his father.

Zak immediately went to the Board of Elders at their church asking for guidance. Many in the congregation were immigrants from Islamic countries whose policies of persecuting Christians had become too threatening. The Board agreed to help financially and with prayers.

Three long weeks after receiving the letter and a worthless trip to the US State Department, Zak received a phone call from a man claiming to be one of the lawyers assigned by the Iranian Ministry of Justice. The lawyer told Zak he would only talk to the oldest male member of the family. Since that was Zak, he agreed to a meeting at the Iranian Embassy in Washington DC. It was fortunate that Zak was on Easter break from school and visiting his mother in the Countryside Development just inside Loudon County. He wouldn't have to make the long drive from Blacksburg.

THAT FIRST ENCOUNTER was ineffaceable in Zak's mind. He still had nightmares. The Iranian Embassy, upgraded from an Interests Section by the former administration in an attempt to reopen negotiations on nuclear proliferation issues, was near the US Naval Observatory and off of Wisconsin Avenue. The quiet neighborhood contradicted the evil Zak felt oozing out of the compound.

He was taken to a small second floor conference room with an oversized portrait of Ayatollah Khomeini that would make anyone have hallucinations. He was left alone with the sinister painting 45 minutes before two bearded young men with ill-fitting suits entered the room and sat across the conference table from Zak. They explained that they would be Zak's father's legal representation in Iran. They further stated that his father's trial date had not been set, but could happen at any time. Zak left the Embassy close to tears. How could he and those lawyers prepare a defense for his father with such short notice?

When Zak told his mother and sisters what had transpired he broke down, feeling so very helpless. His mother, wiping her tears away, pulled them all close and prayed for God's guidance and comfort. Zak recalled how strong his mother seemed to be even though her husband was sentenced to die in a country that hated them for their religious beliefs.

Later that same week, Zak was summoned to the Embassy for another meeting with the lawyers. It was at this meeting that Zak's life turned from bad to worse. During a long session on how the lawyers planned to defend his dad, one of the lawyers left the room on the pretext of finding some additional documents. The other lawyer, Mohammed Najjar, came around the table and sat in the chair right next to Zak. Up until this point, both lawyers always sat on the opposite side of the table, keeping as much distance as possible. Zak joked in his mind that they probably were afraid of touching a Christian and getting converted. Mr. Najjar leaned toward Zak and in a very conspiratorial tone said, "I can help you with your father but you must help me." At first Zak thought he might want a bribe, but he continued, "We need your skills with hover drones to accomplish several tasks for us. You may not tell anyone, not your family, not the American authorities, not anyone. If you do, we will torture your father and then hang him." Zak was stunned and speechless. He had no idea where the strength came from to answer, "What tasks do you want me to do?"

Over the next 20 minutes, Mr. Najjar told Zak what was needed. The most important item seemed to be transferring packages from Radford Army Ammunition Plant to a storage locker in Christiansburg. They also wanted the algorithms that he and Dan were working on for swarm theory and any practical lessons learned. Zak had protested that he didn't have access and didn't know anyone who could get into the plant. Mr. Najjar said that Zak had the best access - - his drones. He would fly his drone, on a specific date and time, to pick up a package weighing no more than three pounds from an identified location within the plant's open area. He would then take the package to the storage locker. He was, under no circumstances, to open the package. Again, Zak protested. If he were caught doing this, he could spend the rest of his life in a Federal prison. Mr. Najjar had told Zak, "You hold your father's life in your hands. We will send him home after you accomplish these tasks."

ZAK WAS HOPING that this meeting at Borders with the lawyers would be his last and that his father would be coming home soon. He did everything they wanted. They weren't very far into the conversation when Mr. Najjar placed a document on the table, pushing it toward Zak. As Zak read the first few paragraphs he realized they weren't done with him yet. Now they wanted him to build five hover drones like the one he used to get the packages from the ammunition plant, but with a five-pound lift capability. He had to place them in the storage locker by September 15th.

"I don't know if I can get them done by the middle of September," Zak said.

"Then we can no longer guarantee the safety of your father," stated Mr. Najjar.

"You realize, and I have proven, that I want my father to come home. This latest task is not as easy as you might think. Besides, calculating new designs to accommodate for the increased weight will be difficult. I still have to work on my school projects. If I fail my classes I will no longer have access to the places needed to fulfill your requirements."

"This is our last request. By the end of September your father will be free."

AS ZAK DROVE BACK to Blacksburg, he was depressed and elated at the same time. Depressed that they still required more from him – *why did they need hover drones with that much lifting weight*; elated because he would finally see his dad again.

By the time he got to Blacksburg he was back to being mostly depressed. For six months he had provided everything the lawyers had asked. He was feeling guilty about his actions. Actions that he knew were against the law. If he turned himself in to the local authorities then his father would be killed, he would go to jail and his mother and sisters wouldn't have any male member in the family. All his dreams would come to an end. He sat in the car contemplating his next move. He bowed his head in prayer asking for the peace that comes without understanding and for guidance and strength to do what was right.

CHAPTER EIGHTEEN

AUGUST 6, (Sunday)

FBI Field Office, Alexandria, Virginia

'*Poor kid,*' thought Agent Thomsen as he sat completing the paperwork on his surveillance of the two Iranian lawyers. He wondered how much ransom money they would try to get from the kid's family. Even if the FBI found evidence of coercion, the Iranians could not be prosecuted. Declaring the lawyers *persona non grata* and kick them out of the US was the most the FBI could do.

FBI Agent Thomsen was tasked with keeping tabs on the two Iranian lawyers since they arrived in the United States. Although they had diplomatic passports and were restricted to the 50-mile radius from the Capitol Building, it was always possible they had other plans. Thomsen didn't care about a 'thaw' in relations between Iran and the US; he had to make sure the lawyers were really lawyers and not intelligence officers. So far, they maintained the outward appearance of what the embassy stated were their intentions.

'*That poor Hashemi kid,*' thought Thomsen again. The Iranians had his father locked up in prison. Thomsen had seen a couple of CIA reports saying the treatment in Iranian prisons was brutal. The father was arrested for proselytizing during a visit to Tehran. Apparently the father, a pastor at a Christian Church in the US, was also an advocate for reforms in the religious laws in Iran on several websites. It didn't look good, if history was any indicator. At least three other Christian pastors had been hanged for the same charge.

The FBI ran background checks on the kid and his family just to make sure they didn't have connections with anti-Iranian militants or some terrorist organization. A clean report came back on all of them. The FBI got a court order to put Zak under surveillance following the first encounter with the lawyers to make sure he wasn't some middleman. After two weeks of scrutiny, it was determined he was as he appeared – a student at Virginia Tech.

Agent Thomsen finished the last part of the standardized surveillance report form with a few remarks, '*subjects met with US Citizen Zakari Hashemi for one hour at the Borders Book Store in Fairfax, VA. No untoward activity noted. No audio of meeting ordered or undertaken. Interactions observed between subjects and Hashemi appeared formal and calm.*'

CHAPTER NINETEEN

SEPTEMBER 11, (Monday)

Jacoby Jackson took off his hairnet cap, booties and unzipped the one-piece yellow clean-suit required of all workers in Radford Army Ammunitions Plant, or the RAP, as most employees called it. He knew he had to put it all back on in 30 minutes when he finished his lunch, but he just couldn't sit in the small lunchroom on such a beautiful autumn day. He walked up the eight steps from the main floor of the partially buried building. Many of the buildings at the RAP were either partially or fully buried and separated by over 50 yards to minimize damage if an accident occurred while mixing or moving volatile chemicals or explosives. Some of the old timers talked about the big accident in January 1978, when five thousand pounds of nitroglycerine exploded, killing one worker. Thankfully no accidents had happened during Jacoby's employment. Right now all he wanted was some fresh air, air that hadn't been filtered 10 times and had no odor. Autumn was the time he loved because folks fired up woodstoves and he could smell the hickory or oak logs burning. There was still a lingering scent from those morning fires, started to take the chill out of the houses. A small picnic table sat adjacent to the building.

From Jacoby's viewpoint, he could see the dumpster where he had placed many packages of the new explosive scraps he purloined while servicing the cutting machines. He hoped this next placement would be his last. He didn't think his nerve would last much longer.

Jacoby had started 20 years ago as a janitor for the RAP, slowly moving up the pay scale to become one of several plant stewards. Along the way he learned how to operate and fix almost every machine in the plant. Some of the new digitally controlled robotic machines were still under warranty so his boss wouldn't let him tinker with them. 'Tinkerin' was how he learned. He took every opportunity to look over the shoulder of the factory representatives when they came to repair or tweak those machines. He knew he could do the same thing, even went back to trade school to learn about robotics.

His life had changed two years ago. A steel cross member fell across his shoulder while he was dismantling an old machine to make room for a new one. The doctor said he had broken his clavicle, tore his rotator cuff and dislocated the shoulder. He spent eight weeks out of work and got addicted to Percocet. His workman's compensation barely provided enough to put food on the table. When the physical therapy technician told him he might be able to help, Jacoby never thought it would involve stealing explosives from the US Government.

He must have been high on Percocet when the tech told him all he had to do was bring him a few scraps from the new explosive material. The RAP was a manufacturing plant for propellants and explosives, not a research center. However, several BAE chemists that normally conducted batch tests got bored and started playing with the formula for C-4. They stumbled upon a mixture that was several times more explosive than the original C-4 and they jokingly called it C-4++. For the past year they were making small batches, usually 10-20 pounds and running tests on the product. Since it wasn't covered under any of the other manufactured explosives, the accounting process for the material was non-existent. The scraps that Jacoby picked up were never missed. This was the logic that the tech used to convince Jacoby that no one would ever realize any of the material was gone.

During a therapy session, Jacoby said he could no longer bring out the scraps. It made him too nervous and one of the gate guards had noticed. He was able to pass it off as feeling ill and even took a sick day the next day. The therapist told him to keep collecting scraps but keep them at the site while he worked out another way to get them out of the plant.

A month went by before Jacoby was told to wrap the scraps together in a bundle no heavier than three pounds and to place it behind the dumpster at his building. Complying with this request eased Jacoby's mind. He checked the location after his first deposit not knowing how or who had picked it up. The therapist told him the new system worked well. Now all he had to do was send a text message saying "deposit schedule such-and-such a date" to a number the therapist gave him and all would go well.

Jacoby had enough hidden under his workbench in an old lunchbox to send in the next shipment. He would stop by for physical therapy tonight and tell the tech this was his last shipment. He had to break his habit and considered telling his boss. The RAP, he discovered, had a good program to help people with drug and alcohol addictions. As much as he feared losing his job, he feared losing his life more.

CHAPTER TWENTY

JULY 18, Current year
Onboard *Fatimah* in the Malacca Strait
Mohammad and Junaedi completed inspection and diagnostic tests on the last of the Iranian naval mines. Exiting the container, they closed the makeshift access hatch. Everything checked out. The mines were the latest developments from the Iranians but Junaedi was sure they either came from the Chinese or were reverse-engineered from Chinese samples.

They were called rocket mines and were feared by most navies. They could be deposited in deep water for up to one year and activated by either remote control or by an acoustic signature. The mines that Mohammad and Junaedi had were already programmed with the acoustic signatures of several American aircraft carriers. Junaedi remembered the serious look on one of his Iranian handlers when he discussed the acquisition of the acoustic information for the mines. It seems several Iranian submariners had lost their lives getting the data. Years of planning had gone into collecting the specific acoustic signals given off by the carriers.

The American ships normally operated in the Arabian Sea, more commonly called the Persian Gulf. The IRGC-Navy's Ghadir-class mini-sub unit stationed at Bandar Abbas was given the mission to collect against the Americans. After watching the operational patterns of the American Navy, it was determined that a mini-sub could deploy to the southern end of the Gulf, near Abu Musa Island, settle to the bottom and wait for a carrier to start operating in the area. They had to remain silent so the Americans wouldn't detect their presence. If discovered, the Americans would consider them an active threat and probably destroy them. Faulty mechanical systems on one of the submarines caused a catastrophic failure. Two crew members died but not before they were able to transmit the collected data.

As Junaedi understood from his training by the Iranians, each ship makes its own unique sounds, recognized as its acoustic signature or fingerprint. Every piece of mechanical equipment, engine, pump, valves, etc. makes noise. These sounds are picked up by a hydrophone. Different speeds will produce different specific signatures and harmonics. Buried in all that noise are sounds specific to each vessel, sometimes caused by how a ship's propellers are tuned or the efficiency of support pumps. The only time these signature sounds change is when the parts are replaced during an overhaul. The US Navy has collected acoustic information on Russian and Chinese submarines for years and can identify individual units by their sound.

The rocket mines have an ability to store the acoustic information for up to five vessels. The data loaded on the mines in Junaedi's possession had information on three of the carriers that normally rotated duty in the Oman Basin and the Persian Gulf: USS George Washington – CVN-73, USS Nimitz – CVN-68 and USS Ronald Reagan – CVN-76. With testing completed, all that was left was getting the mines into position in the Malacca Strait; then, wait for information from his Iranian contact.

Mohammad glanced at the GPS again to make sure he was at the right point for his turn. He praised Allah for the smoke that covered the Strait. He knew that illegal clear-cut timber operations on Sumatra and the subsequent brush fires caused the smoke that blanketed the narrow waterway. Conditions on some days threatened to close transit operations in the Strait. The heavy smoke made navigation treacherous in this busy water highway but would help hide his activities as he turned to cross the constricted navigation channel's limits. As he traversed the westbound channel, the crew opened the doors on of all four of the shipping containers. One-by-one the mines were pushed out the doors and into the sea. All twelve mines would sink to the bottom and remain submerged until remotely activated.

He couldn't believe how smoothly everything went. Junaedi wrestled each day of the transit from their hiding place with his paranoia. He expected the authorities to surround his vessel, board it and arrest them for terrorism. Now, with the task completed he felt an overwhelming calm. Praise be to Allah.

CHAPTER TWENTY-ONE

SEPTEMBER 12, (Tuesday)

NSA

Ever since Maddie called Sam with approval for an official archive search, he had been busy. He requested that all records associated with Mukhtar al Bayruti be reviewed for words translated as kill, destroy or assassinate in either Arabic or Farsi going back 20 years. Sam utilized some software programs that helped to create a picture of all the links to Bayruti. Most were associates, friends, family and unknowns. Limited contact was noted between Bayruti and Zawahiri. This didn't alarm Sam because he knew these guys tried to stay away from electronic communications and instead arranged personal meetings or used couriers.

Sam felt a personal satisfaction that his initial instinct to place the emphasis on destroy rather than kill was being revealed as he reviewed the old intercepts. On several intercepts, al Bayruti slowed down his pronunciation of the word *kashteen* enough to clearly indicate he was placing some significance on the word. He was making a point. Most telling was an intercept recorded three days before the USS Cole was attacked by a suicide team and nearly sunk in Aden harbor in 2000. Al Bayruti received a phone call at his mother's house in Baalbek, Lebanon, from a number traced to a previously unknown contact in Iran. The message was very short, *Kill the Great Satan.* Al Bayruti almost immediately made a call requesting a meeting with Zawahiri who was also in Baalbek for meetings with Hezbollah leaders. The use of *kashteen* had that elongated inflection. Sam knew it was a reach because threats to kill the Great Satan were all too common in both Farsi and Arabic. However, the inflection that Sam heard convinced him he had discovered a Shibboleth. Al Bayruti meant *Destroy the Great Satan.*

He immediately called Maddie's cell number before he even looked at the time. It was 2:34 AM and Sam was ready to disconnect the call after the second ring but Maddie answered in a slightly drained voice, "This is Maddie."

"Maddie, this is Sam. I'm so sorry to call you so late. I didn't look at the time. Please forgive me. Please call me in the morning."

"That's OK. I'm waking up. Are you still at work?"

" Yes. Please, I think this can wait until morning."

"Sam, too late. It is morning. Must be something important for you to call me. Give me about 5 minutes to shake off the sleep and get a few sips of coffee, then I'll call you back. OK?"

"Sure, you can call me back on this number. They're using a Shibboleth," he blurted.

"A Shibbo what?"

Sam realized that to talk any further he would be close to talking about sensitive information over the phone. He might be able to talk around the specific details but might not be able to convince Maddie of the importance of his discovery. "I really can't fill you in anymore on the phone. I was calling to arrange a meeting as early as possible to go over my findings with you."

"Do we need to meet at Langley?"

"I think that would be the best place. Traffic shouldn't be an issue at this time. It will start getting nasty in about two hours. "

"OK. I'm waking up. I can be at Langley by 3:30 AM. Do you have an IC badge or do I need to call you into the compound?"

"I have a badge but my after hours entrance might raise some concerns. Might be best if you call me in."

"I'll do that right away. In return, you can stop at PamE K's and pick up some chocolate-covered glazed donuts."

"I thought they closed back in 2001."

"They closed the store in Fairfax City but the original location in Alexandria is still open."

"Are they open at this time of night?"

"This is the best time. They only close from midnight to 1:00 AM. The donuts are just coming off the line, like at Krispy Kreme only better."

"OK. See you at Langley's Northeast entrance at 3:30 AM."

CHAPTER TWENTY-TWO

SEPTEMBER 12, (Tuesday)

CIA HQ

Where had summer gone, thought Maddie as she exited her car in the northwest parking lot. The wind had picked up; a few leaves were being blown into small tornadoes as she crossed the lot. She thought about parking in one of the reserved spots near the entrance with the intention of returning before 6:00 AM to move her car to an unrestricted spot. Instead, she parked with the other early arrivals in the open parking lane to avoid being towed and fined. She was glad she had a windbreaker in the car and put it on as she trekked toward the entrance.

Sam was standing by one of the potted plants that acted as anti-vehicle barriers with a box from PamE K's under his arm, his other stuffed into the pocket of his jeans. They walked through the double doors. Maddie processed through the turnstile as Sam went to the guard desk. He set the donuts on the counter as the guard ran a check on his IC badge. After the guard gave him the go ahead, Sam opened the box and offered him a donut.

"You OK with stairs, Sam?" asked Maddie.

"By all means. Maybe the exercise will get my blood moving again. Where did summer go?" He replied.

They both munched on a donut as they climbed the stairs to the fourth floor and took a convoluted route toward Maddie's cubical. Sam was surprised to see several people already in the office, busy at their computers. Maddie told him that they ran a 24-hour operation and rotated the duties a month at a time. Since most of the stations were in the Middle East and six to seven hours ahead of the East Coast Time, much of the message traffic generated from case officers and chiefs could be addressed or flagged for immediate action when the group chiefs arrived. Sam said that this was what NSOC did at NSA.

"We have an Operations Room that is open 24/7 but they are dedicated to the faster breaking events. We handle the more mundane messages coming from the stations," Maddie mentioned.

They stopped by at the small coffee break room, selecting Star-bucks K-cups and then headed to Maddie's cubical.

"I'm really sorry for getting you out of bed, Maddie."

"Damage already done and forgotten. On my drive in I searched my mind for the word Shibboleth. It finally came to me that it is a Hebrew word. Maybe I am learning more than I think from my Small Group Bible Study. It's from Judges, isn't it?"

"I'm impressed. Yes, it is from Judges. It was a password used by the Hebrews to uncover escaping Ephraimites. Seems the Ephraimites couldn't pronounce the word Shibboleth correctly, instead saying Sibboleth. US military forces in World War II did the same thing to the Japanese. The Japanese couldn't pronounce the letter L, so passwords always contained one or more L's ... Cinderella, Balloon, Ballerina and so on. Most dictionaries I looked at indicate *shibboleth* is a linguistic password. It's a pronunciation or the use of a particular expression used by one set of people to identify another person as a member or a non-member of a particular group."

"So you think *kashteen* is a code word?"

"In a way, yes. I see it more as an authenticator."

"Explain for the uninitiated please," Maddie said between bites of her second donut.

"When you sign on to your computer, the system requires a password and then an authentication from a randomly generated key fob that's been assigned just to you. That way, if your password is compromised, someone still needs your key fob to get into the system. That's just the first line of defense."

"Tell me about it. I've got more passwords than a teenage girl has twitter followers."

"I think Bayruti and his contacts use an elongated inflection of *kashteen* to authenticate each message with the meaning 'to destroy', rather than the more common meaning, to kill."

"What do you mean by elongated inflection?"

"Each time Bayruti uses the word as destroy, he slows his speech. I compare it to Jeff Dunham's dummy Achmed the Dead Terrorist, when he says "I k-e-e-e-l you! Maybe not to that extreme."

Maddie had to laugh at Sam's example. She loved that comedy act. "Alright, Sam. This is pretty significant and certainly gives more credence to your theory that aircraft carriers are the target."

"Just the aircraft carriers named after presidents," replied Sam.

"How many are there?"

"Nine active. CVN – 80 has been designated John F. Kennedy to replace the previous JFK removed from service in 2007, but its not due until the mid to late 2020s. The USS Nimitz should be considered a tenth since many of the president's close friends call him Admiral Nimitz. The press even picked that up during the campaign.
"

"Do you think we should inform the Navy?"

"At this point it's only a theory that makes sense to us. The threat could still be to the presidents. I need to do some additional research on the links uncovered to Bayruti. Can I send you some names I've generated and have you check your records?"

"Of course. I also think we should get the IC members together later today or tomorrow to discuss what you've discovered."

"Let's make it tomorrow. That will give me some time to look at these other folks linked to Bayruti."

"You have any names I can start checking now?"

"Zawahiri right now. I'm particularly interested in what you might have on his movements and contacts before and after the bombing of the USS Cole on 12 October 2000. The limited transcript I have indicates Bayruti received a possible heads-up to the Cole' bombing and he immediately reached out to Zawahiri. I wonder? Is anything traceable to Zawahiri? Or maybe anyone that Zawahiri contacted?"

Maddie typed some search parameters into her computer and got the file number for Zawahiri. A restricted message popped up on her screen stating she would have to get permission from the National Clandestine Service (NCS) Reports Officer.

"This could take awhile. Reports officers have a kingdom all their own and don't like outsiders rummaging through branch or division files. We might be in luck though. I know the lady who handles this account. We've worked a number of issues in the past and we have a good relationship. She comes in about 8:00 AM. I'll try to contact her shortly after that."

"Who brought PamE K's donuts?" asked Linda as she walked by Maddie's desk.

"Sam stopped on his way in. Care for one?"

"Please. These are the best. I'll have to spend a little more time on the elliptical today but it's worth it."

Sam got up and started to make preparations to leave.

"I'd invite you to breakfast but you did put a pretty good dent in that dozen."

"You did alright yourself," replied Sam.

"Are you going back to work or home?" asked Maddie.

"Home for a catnap and wait for the traffic to subside. Otherwise I'll just be sitting in traffic for two hours or more."

"Call me when you get to the office. Hopefully I'll have arrangements for a meeting by then. Do you remember how to get out?"

"I think so."

"Here, take the rest of the donuts. If you get lost you can either eat them to survive or bribe someone to get you to a recognized location."

CHAPTER TWENTY-THREE

SEPTEMBER 12, (Tuesday)

White House Situation Room

As the meeting came to an end, Paul Albrecht summarized the key points and reiterated the action items. "We still have limited information on both al-Bayruti and Sami. NSA archives hold several conversations conducted by both individuals but at the moment, nothing disquieting. The CIA is also reviewing their holdings and keeping in close coordination with NSA. The FBI and DHS/Secret Service have been unable to discourage the president from his two public appearances with former presidents, even though more chatter in the Ann Arbor area suggests a plan is imminent. POTUS refuses to cancel because the Red Cross Gala is very important to the First Lady. Actions: NSA and CIA will step up searches to include downstream links on both al-Bayruti and Sami. The Detroit field office will put pressure on all available assets to uncover information related to any possible threat. The CIA will also revisit sources with potential access based on their link analysis. The FBI and Secret Service will keep the president apprised of any change to the threat. At the moment, all we have is a single source threat. We have until Saturday," he paused for a second before adding, "three days folks, to flesh-out this threat or it will be dropped, per instructions from the president. POTUS and the First Lady will leave for Ann Arbor to attend the Red Cross outing at 6:00 AM on Saturday. Until then, this is still considered a high threat until resolved. Please thank your personnel for their attention to this matter."

"Paul, do you have a moment?" asked the Director of NSA.

"Of course. Do you mind walking back to my office in the event my secretary has some immediate requirement on my schedule?"

"Not at all."

As they left the Situation Room and walked up the stairs to the White House main floor, Chet filled Paul in on the close coordination going on between NSA and CIA. He needed Paul to understand that under his management, NSA would not 'stove-pipe' information like previous directors. The last thing he wanted was Congress calling him in front of yet another committee hearing.

"That's good to hear, Chet. Don't hesitate to call if CIA doesn't appear to be as forthcoming."

CHAPTER TWENTY-FOUR

SEPTEMBER 13, (Wednesday)

National Geospatial-Intelligence Agency

Karl stood in front of the visitor center desk at the National Geospatial-Intelligence Agency (NGA) waiting for the guard to check his security clearances. Maddie called the day before to tell Karl she arranged a meeting with some of the imagery analysts at NGA to discuss his discovery of the hidden ship in Sumatra. Karl hurriedly pulled together a short power point briefing highlighting the activity he observed at the small inlet and then sent it to his point-of-contact for the meeting. After just a few minutes, the guard handed him an Unescorted Visitor badge and gave him directions to the main lobby. During the time Karl was waiting for his badge, he determined it had been almost a year since his last visit to NGA. He had never worked in the new NGA building but served many years at Building 213 in the Washington Navy Yard. What a difference in the two neighborhoods. The National Photographic Interpretation Center, NPIC to everyone who worked there, was the US Government's premiere center for photographic reconnaissance. The entire product from national level collectors, U-2s, SR-71s, early drones and the early stages of reconnaissance satellites, was reviewed at Building 213. NPIC was considered a Secret Government facility. When the CIA first assigned Karl to the building, over half of the employees were CIA while the rest came from the Defense Intelligence Agency (DIA) and the military services.

The Washington Navy Yard neighborhood appeared down-trodden even before Karl started to work at Building 213. A Chinese restaurant was on one corner, a liquor store on another and a bar known for frequent fights on a third. It was not unusual to see police cars with lights flashing in front of any one of those places, day or night. The new NGA building, however, was set in a wooded ravine where you could forget that the I-95 mixing bowl was only a few hundred yards away.

AS KARL ENTERED THE LOBBY, he was glad to see Milo Cox. Milo was an old acquaintance of Karl's, both having worked African issues for a number of years. Milo progressed through the ranks and moved into the management side of NGA while Karl remained an analyst. Even though Milo was a good manager, his imagery skills were better.

"Karl, it's good to see you again," said Milo as he gave Karl a friendly man-hug.

"Same to you, Milo. I'm glad you met me down here in the atrium. I'd probably spend 20 minutes trying to find the conference room."

"A lot bigger than 213, isn't it?" Milo said as his hand made a sweeping gesture. "Don't worry. I know where we are going. Want some coffee before we head upstairs?"

"That would be nice. I only had my traveller cup on the commute. That's something I do not miss at all."

They walked down the stairs from the lobby into the food court. After the very limited choices of food at the old NGA cafeteria and sometimes-questionable food outside the gate, the variety of selections here were a bit daunting. Milo and Karl each picked up tall black coffees from *Starbucks* and headed for the elevators that took them to the 4th floor. After a series of turns, Milo passed his badge over the card reader and waited for the click before entering the conference room. They were the first to arrive. They had about 15 minutes before Karl's briefing. This was fine with Karl as he could make sure the attachment he sent in the email worked. The conference room was one of the few in the building that had a connection to the unclassified Internet. This had been part of the plan so contractors could present proposals and no outside digital data was loaded onto NGA systems.

As Milo signed into the Internet and selected the email attachment, Karl looked around the room. What a difference from the windowless offices and conference rooms at Building 213. Light streamed through a wall of glass that looked over the atrium. Ferns hung in the corner of the room, thriving in the light-soaked environment. Karl had tried his hardest over the years to keep a philodendron growing over his desk with limited success. "Milo, when are you going to retire?"

"I still have a daughter in med school for another year. After that I'm not sure what I will do. How are you enjoying retirement?"

"As you can see, immensely. I have a very flexible schedule with GlobalWatch and get to look at imagery. My wife and I can plan trips without the worry of being called up to travel to some forgotten part of the world. I'm blessed."

"I have to tell you, Karl. You guys at GlobalWatch are both respected and cursed by NGA analysts."

"How so?" asked Karl, although he had heard this comment from others.

"You may recall from your days at NGA how we responded to field imagery analysts publishing intelligence discoveries from imagery we had already reviewed. We didn't like being upstaged."

Karl did remember those events. "Our response wasn't always

professional," he replied. "Still that information needed reporting and, in the long run, it made us less complacent. No one likes to be caught unaware. They were all learning experiences. I know. I encouraged all the young analysts I mentored that less time talking about the Redskins and more time looking at imagery would significantly reduce those embarrassing moments."

"On the other hand," Milo interjected, "GlobalWatch's analyses are spot on. We've copied your reports and included them in our briefings. Just as a heads up, be prepared for a bit of negative atmospherics. Your discovery of this camouflaged ship has angered a couple of analysts. NGA still has a remnant of folks who don't think too highly of commercial satellite imagery and 'off the reservation' analysts."

"Point taken. Thanks, Milo."

At that moment three young analysts entered the room followed by a middle-aged woman. Karl thought he recognized the woman but could not quite make a connection between face and a name.

"Please take seats around the table. I've only invited a few of you to discuss this matter until we determine the sensitivity of the information," said Milo. "This gentleman is Karl Mattingly, a former CIA analyst and current employee of GlobalWatch. You've all seen the email I sent giving a bit of background on Karl and his discovery of the small ship in the Ache area of Sumatra." Turning toward Karl and indicating he was done speaking, Milo settled into his chair while steadying his coffee mug on his leg.

"Good morning. It is a pleasure to have this opportunity to visit NGA and have frank discussions with those that are on the front line. If Milo agrees, I would like to take a moment to get acquainted with my audience. First names are fine and a specialty if you wish to share."

Milo nodded in agreement. "I'm Milo, Division Chief for the Far East Division."

"I'm Nancy, Branch Chief for Far East Naval Forces."

"Hi, Karl. I'm Tara, a naval forces analyst."

"Good morning, Karl. I'm Robert, industrial analyst for Far East region," said a young man that didn't look like he was old enough to vote.

" Economic and political all-source analyst, uh, Anders."

"Thanks everyone. Nancy, you look familiar to me. Have we ever crossed paths?" asked Karl.

"We may have attended the same conferences when I worked on North African issues. I saw you at a couple of planning sessions during the Libyan Revolt of 2011."

"Thanks, Nancy."

Karl took a deep breath and checked over his shoulder that his first slide was on the screen. "What I hope we can accomplish today is discover who this ship belongs to and why they are taking such pains to hide it from overhead systems."

Karl proceeded to go through his prepared briefing. He walked through how he discovered the ship while searching for illegal logging on the island of Sumatra. He told them about the four 6-meter shipping containers and the on-load/offload activities he had observed. He showed panchromatic and near-infrared imagery of the camouflage netting pulled across the small channel to hide the ship and how he had used the shadows and radar imagery to watch the movement of the shipping containers. He finished his briefing by telling them he also thought portions of the ship's superstructure had been changed to mask its original profile.

"I think at this point we need to move this conversation from the unclassified realm into the classified," Milo said as he looked around the room. "Let's set the level at Top Secret for now. Karl is cleared for that level plus several compartmented programs."

Karl looked around the room and saw the normal reaction of people steeped in classified information, vacillating about sharing classified data with an outsider. He broke the silence, asking, "Have you had a chance to review your archives over this area?"

"Not at the moment," interjected Nancy. "Our management, sorry Milo, has us focused on China and North Korea, both of which keep us strapped for time. We don't have the luxury of looking under every rock," she added with edginess in her voice.

Karl ignored the slight but make a mental note that Nancy seemed to hold a grudge against non-NGA analysts.

Tara jumped in to save the moment, "I did a quick look at our imagery collection over the area for the past year. It is rather dismal. Most of the area is set to collect once a year with a 20% cloud free threshold. We only have two targets that we collect on a regular basis. You have far more imagery of the place than we do."

Cautiously, Anders leaned forward in his chair, placing both hands around his coffee mug, looking briefly at Milo and said, "About two years ago we had reports that one of the terrorist groups in Indonesia had established a camp in Ache East. We collected some imagery over the area but never found anything. The search task was passed to the Counter-Terrorism Division (CT) but they also came up empty. A recent CIA report from a walk-in to the Jakarta embassy mentioned that a group affiliated with Jamaah Islamiyah was boasting of pirating a small ship and had plans for something big."

Karl smiled. "I think I know who produced that report. If possible, may I use the secure line to call my daughter after this meeting? I might be able to provide you with a little more background on that report."

"Any additional information will be helpful," replied Anders.

"That wraps up what I came to say. Any questions?"

"What are your plans for monitoring this ship?" asked Milo.

"Without a customer request, I will continue with some speculative collection and keep my own notes of unusual activity. We have a small budget for 'oddities', as my boss likes to call them. Any major collection effort would require an infusion of outside funding."

"The problem we have is manpower. I talked with Nancy before the meeting and her staff is inundated with keeping track of Chinese naval forces. Each year the Chinese Navy expands its operating range. In addition they produce new vessels with ever increasing lethality. We spend an inordinate amount of our time writing activity reports and not enough on assessments. Since this discovery appears to have a terrorist connection, I want to get the CT folks to hear your briefing. Do you have time today if I can make arrangements?" queried Milo.

"I made the 70-mile commute with the intention of being here as long as discussions were warranted."

"Nancy, you and your team are welcome to join in the conversations with the CT folks."

After a quick look at her team members, Nancy told Milo that they would be available if needed but had work piling up at the office. They all rose from their chairs and shook hands with Karl as they left the room.

Milo spent the next ten minutes on the phone arranging a meeting with CT representatives in 30 minutes. He then handed the phone to Karl so he could call his daughter.

"I THINK THAT WENT WELL, KARL," Milo said as he disconnected the video link to the CIA after most of the CT attendees left the conference room. Sheryl, Chief of the Far East Division's counter-terrorism branch, remained.

Before Milo could say anything, Sheryl interjected, "Karl, I know Milo and his team have indicated that they don't have time to spend on researching this ship. Unfortunately, that is the same for CT. Since you have a close connection with Maddie, it seems a logical connection to get you involved. I can quickly set up a contract requesting your assistance. Not to exceed 30 days. Would Global-Watch let you concentrate on trying to discover what's going on with this vessel?"

"If I could make a phone call to my boss, I'm sure I would have an answer before lunch."

"That would be great."

"Before I make that call, can we discuss parameters of the work being requested? I'd like to give my boss as much background as possible."

Milo interrupted and said he had another meeting to attend, one of many that took up his time. He thanked Karl for his discovery and hoped to see him in the building. "Some of the old guys are still around. Once you get a schedule in place, send me an email and we'll try a lunch meeting."

"I would like that," said Karl.

BEFORE LUNCH, Karl caught up with Sheryl and told her he had approval from his boss. Sheryl took Karl over to the Human Resources offices and got all the paperwork signed to bring Karl onboard. He would schedule time to review NGA's imagery holdings and work with the CT representative on a collection plan.

Sheryl reached out her hand to shake Karl's when he said; "I almost forgot to pass another item to you. Can we duck into a secured space for a minute?"

"Do you think it will take long?"

"Maybe a couple of minutes at most."

"Let's go back to the conference room since it's closer than my office," Sheryl said as she directed Karl around the corner.

Once in the conference room, Karl told Sheryl about the anomaly he had observed at the KFFC, Virginia and Seidir airfield in Iran. Sheryl said she would make the proper arrangements to give Karl access to NGA's imagery over Qasr-e-Firuzeh. She would create a separate imagery queue so he could review it and pass any findings to her analysts. She emphasized that any time he spent on the review would fall under the same contract. Karl agreed.

During the long commute back home, Karl was delighted to be contributing again.

CHAPTER TWENTY-FIVE

SEPTEMBER 13, (Wednesday)

White House Situation Room

"Mr. President, we believe that recently discovered information regarding the threat message of last week, indicates we should extend and expand the level of effort currently applied to discovering the validity and scope of the threat," reported the Director of CIA, Mark Baker.

"Let me hear what you have and I'll decide where we go from here," replied the president while scanning a file folder. He was used to multitasking, but the job as president at times could be overwhelming.

Mark laid out for the president the findings of NSA analyst Ives and CIA analyst Mattingly.

"What the heck is a Shibboleth?" demanded the Chairman of the Joint Chiefs of Staff.

"It's a Hebrew word. In the Bible it was used as a password because Israel's' enemies couldn't pronounce it." The DCI continued, "NSA's analyst reviewed almost twenty years of intercepts and believes the original callers, al-Bayruti and Sami, were using the word '*kashteen*' as a *shibboleth*. Not so much in the sense of a code word but as an authenticator."

"You'll need to explain that to us, Mark," said Angela Kolstead, Director of DHS.

Turning in his chair to look for Sam and Maddie, Mark swung back and made eye contact with the president. "I could pretend to understand all the nuances of what the analysts have discovered but I suggest we let them tell us, if that's agreeable Mr. President?

Maddie darted her eyes between the president and Sam. She could feel the sweat start to run down her ribs and wasn't sure she could get out of her chair. Sam wasn't in any better shape as he slowly walked up to the front of the conference table and took a laser pointer from the aide. He cleared his throat and started to speak but the words got caught in his throat.

"Petty Officer," said the president, "In my entire career, I never had the opportunity to brief the President of the United States. Now you're one up on me. Take a deep breath and just tell us what you've deduced."

Sam, with renewed confidence, wiped his hands against the side of his pants and said, "In the original intercept, the Persian or Farsi word 'kashteen' was translated as 'kill'. We now believe that 'kashteen' might have another meaning and use. Al-Bayruti and others use 'kashteen' to authenticate a message that means 'destroy' rather than the more common translation of 'kill'." Sam nodded for the next slide that displayed excerpts of previous intercepts. His hand was still shaking as he tried to get the laser pointer to fall on the first item but the dot just bounced around the slide. Unable to calm his nerves any further, he placed the pointer on the table. "I've reviewed a number of past intercepts attributed to al-Bayruti. Depending on the context of his sentence, he uses 'kashteen' in its normal translation for 'kill'. He elongates the enunciation of the word when he and a select group want it to mean 'destroy'." Sam paused, took a deep breath and continued, "We now believe that the original threat message isn't focused on you, Mr. President, or your predecessors. We think the reference is to US Navy aircraft carriers named after the presidents or possibly buildings bearing a president's name."

You could almost hear a pin drop in the conference room. Seconds later people were stirring in their seats and conferring with those in the adjacent chairs. All the while the president just stared at Sam. Finally, leaning forward in the chair he said, "Let me get this right. You believe that our aircraft carriers are in jeopardy?"

Sam gulped. He knew that he and Maddie didn't have a 'smoking-gun' but did have enough to feel confident about the analysis. He was just about to speak when Paul Albrecht interjected, "You base all of this on some subtle change in speaking one word? Looks to me like you are scraping the bottom of the barrel for connections to make a wild theory have credence."

"Mr. President," the DCI said as he stood up. "We do have more." Pointing to Maddie he continued, "Mr. President, this is Amanda Mattingly. She is our principal analyst on this threat alert and, along with Sam, has some interesting items. They both convinced me early this morning that several of our carriers are the targets of a planned attack. Maddie, please elaborate for the president."

Seeing the trouble that Sam had trying to keep his hand and the laser pointer still, she opted not to even pick it up. "May I have the next slide please? Mr. President, lady and gentlemen, I preface my remarks with the admission that these are preliminary assessments." Turning her head to the side and softly clearing her throat, Maddie continued, "We did a deep-dive into our records on al-Bayruti and discovered numerous links to the former Hezbollah intelligence officer, Imad Mughniyah. Noted here," her hand extending toward the screen, "are the links between al-Bayruti and Mughniyah. Imad was involved in the Marine barracks bombing in Lebanon, planned several kidnappings of foreigners in Beirut and was implicated in the early planning stages of the USS Cole bombing as was al-Bayruti. Mughniyah was killed by a car bomb in Damascus in 2008. We have numerous reports, with just as many names, mentioning his replacement. The name most often mentioned was al-Bayruti."

Looking around the room, Maddie could see her audience was putting two-and-two together. "Mr. President, our analysis, again preliminary, relies heavily on al-Bayruti's involvement with the USS Cole bombing and his position as Hezbollah's intelligence chief. We have requested our overseas partners, the Brits and Mossad, to conduct deep-dives as well and send us any relevant information."

Maddie caught the DCI's eye and indicated she was finished.

"Mr. President," cautioned the DCI, "this is preliminary and our efforts will continue to seek resolution. I believe, however, that an action message should be sent by the Department of Defense to notify all carriers named after presidents of a possible threat and that they should take appropriate action."

"You understand I'm scheduled to attend the change-of-command ceremony on the Bush on the 28th?" Turning to face the Director of Homeland Security he asked, "What do you recommend I do, Angela?"

"Mr. President. That ceremony is two-weeks away and, as these analysts keep telling us, the information is preliminary. I agree with notifying the ships but I don't think you need to change your schedule at this time. I will discuss options with the Secret Service."

"Thank you, Angela. Anyone else have anything to add?" No one moved or spoke up. "Good. I want you all to give this threat another week of effort. Let's get back to work." Standing up, the president reached out to shake the hands of Amanda and Sam saying, "Miss Mattingly, Petty Officer Ives, thank you for your briefings and hard work. Do you think there is more you can do?"

Without hesitating Maddie blurted, "We still have old records to review and sources to task."

"Good. Keep me posted. Nice job on connecting al-Bayruti and Mughniyah. I remember reading reports about him in the 1990's. He was a ruthless SOB. I'll be interested in getting your take on al-Bayruti."

CHAPTER TWENTY-SIX

S EPTEMBER 1 4, (Thursday)
DHS HQ

"She said what?" Alexander couldn't contain himself. *She can't take this away from me. This is my ticket to advancement,* he thought. Speaking into the secure phone he tried to remain calm. "Tell me what she said again." Alexander waited impatiently as the caller answered the request.

"She told POTUS that he could keep the change of command ceremony on his schedule? I just sent her a memo yesterday outlining why we needed to cancel that event. Who convinced her otherwise?" Alexander wanted to slam the receiver back in the cradle but he looked up and saw people in the outer cubicles staring at him. He just nodded as if nothing had happened and plunked down in his chair. *This can't be happening.* He took a breath and slowly exhaled but continued in his thoughts. *For the last week my team has been making every effort to keep DHS-Secret Service in the limelight of this threat notice. Now the Director shoots us in the foot.*

He needed to stay on track. Someone must have more information than this one phone call. Just then, Alexander's computer chimed notifying him he had an incoming internal chat message. He clicked on the message and read: *'Alexander- Quick notes from NSC meeting – NSA says, Farsi word kashteen elongated during enunciation, might be code word or authenticator for terrorist group. CIA claims Al-Bayruti implicated in USS Cole bombing and probably protégé of Mughniyah. Bayruti could be Mughniyah's replacement as Hezbollah operations chief. – Karen'* Alexander quickly responded, *'I owe you drinks!'* He wished he could talk her into more than drinks. Karen was the Director's assistant. She and Alex had a short fling about two years ago. They parted on good terms but she let him realize their intimate relationship was over. On the professional side, she continued to keep him abreast of developments she thought he should know.

Stepping outside his office door, he called across the cubicles, "Conference room in 10 minutes for all people working the threat against POTUS."

CHAPTER TWENTY-SEVEN

SEPTEMBER 14, (Thursday)
CIA HQ

When Maddie arrived at her cubicle in the morning she found a dusty records box sitting on her desk. Attached to the box was a disclosure form. She looked it over and saw that the last person to open the box was Herman Crawford or Crawfoot. It was hard to read the handwriting even though the form requested a printed name and signature. What surprised Maddie was the date – July 15, 2008. She couldn't believe it. Five months after Imad Mughniyah's death and all his records were packed up and sent to storage? Granted, much of what was probably in the box could be found on the Company's computer. The chance something was in the box that didn't make the computer was possible. Maddie had no intention of disparaging the crews of young college-age summer interns who had the underappreciated job of scanning these old documents. Maddie gained first hand knowledge of the process during the summer between her college freshman and sophomore years. She was a summer intern working in the bowels of the Agency's archives. Now she would painstakingly look at each piece of paper. Her dad taught her that. "Take the extra time. Learn your target. Look for the nuances and questions," he would say before expounding on other things.

She had to finish writing up her after-action report on the briefing to the president. On the ride back to Langley, the DCI told her he appreciated her work and would tell the Chief of the Far East Division to give her time to pursue any avenues that might arise relating to Bayruti and others regarding the threat. He encouraged her to stay in contact with Petty Officer Ives. She told him that she tried to recruit him for the Company. The DCI said she needed to try harder.

It was 11 PM. Maddie was tired and needed some sleep. It had been an exciting day and she wanted to share what she could with Phillip. He was probably already asleep. Maybe they could fit dinner into their plans this week or even do something fun over the weekend. That thought disappeared in an instant as Maddie looked at her whiteboard. Filled with circles and lines, bunches of colored notes and numbers, she knew she couldn't make the time. Maybe they could have lunch in the cafeteria tomorrow. She would call him in the morning and set it up.

CHAPTER TWENTY-EIGHT

SEPTEMBER 15, (Friday)

Department of Homeland Security – HQ

Still seething from the wrongheaded comments made by Director Kolstead to the president and the lackluster reactions from his team members, Alexander picked up the phone and punched in the numbers for CIA's Far East Division.

"I want to speak with Miss Mattingly," and then, remembering his manners, said, "please."

"Do you wish Miss Mattingly's open or secure extension, sir?" a gentle voice responded, one familiar with gruff requests.

"Her secure extension, please."

"Yes, sir. That is extension 65447. You will need to ... ,"

"I know the prefix," answered Alexander as he abruptly broke the connection.

Looking at the extension number on the scrap of paper, Alexander thought it wise to get a grip on his composure. *It probably won't do me any good attacking Miss Mattingly, even though she never did send me a courtesy copy of her notes for the meeting with the president. Should I just let that slide?* Just the thought of it ticked him off. He punched in the numbers and waited while the phone rang. After three rings, he was getting ready to sever the connection when he heard, "Good morning, this is Miss Mattingly."

"Miss Mattingly. This is Alexander Garfield Mumford at DHS," with as much sweetness in his voice as he could assemble at the moment.

What a pompous ass, thought Maddie. *Who makes an effort to tell you their middle name over the phone?'* "Hi Alex, what can I do for you?"

Alexander disliked being called Alex and weighed the situation. *Should he correct Miss Mattingly or let it go? He let it go.* "I've been told you were in attendance and briefed the NSC on Wednesday?"

"That's correct. The DCI grabbed me in the morning after I briefed him on our latest developments and told me I was to accompany him to the White House." Sensing a little hostility in Alex's voice and remembering how he tried to take over her meeting last week, she added, "I had no idea it would be the NSC."

Alexander thought on that for a second. *I should probably cut her some slack. Her time was probably spent getting briefing slides prepared and reviewed prior to the meeting.* "I'm sure you were busy. Would you consider sending me a cliff notes version in the future? I had to send my Director to the meeting unprepared for the information relating al-Bayruti with Mughniyah."

Wanting to make this interchange as brief as possible, Maddie said, "I'll do my best, Alex. Under the circumstances I barely had time to get my briefing bullets completed. I'm still writing up the after-action notes now."

"I understand you are trying to take the emphasis of the threat away from an attack against POTUS and FPOTUS ..." started Alexander, but was interrupted as Maddie asked him, "What is a FPOTUS?" Breathing through his clenched teeth and wondering how dense could this woman be, he continued in a harsher tone " ... to some harebrained idea about attacks against aircraft carriers."

"Excuse me." Maddie said raising her own voice. "First, you will not talk to me in that tone. Second, the possibility of a threat against the aircraft carriers is a suggested alternative." Taking an opportunity to achieve her own jab, she continued, "At the CIA's Directorate of Intelligence, we are taught to review all possible angles and run them through a series of analytic tools that highlight strengths and weaknesses in an argument. Our conclusion, with the information currently available, suggests the threat is against the ships and not the presidents."

"Well I think it's just obscuring the issue. The threat message clearly said the presidents were the targets. We even have threats ongoing in Michigan related to the president's upcoming visit. This weak connection you've made between Al-Bayruti and the former Hezbollah chief is tenuous at best and only clouds the issue."

Pulling strength from a seldom-tapped source, Maddie tried to diffuse the conversation. "Alexander, it appears we are going to disagree. We can schedule an Inter-Agency meeting on Monday and come to a consensus. We could serve the president better by fully scrubbing all options."

"Fine. Monday. I'll send the invitation and we'll hold the meeting at DHS. In the future," pausing to make sure Maddie would hear the rest of his statement, Alexander's voice dripped with revulsion, "make sure you send me any briefing notes you develop for an NSC meeting. Before the meeting!"

Maddie hung up, slamming the phone into the cradle so hard that it jumped back out. She sheepishly reached over and placed it gently into the cradle.

"Bitch," Alexander said out loud before sitting down in his chair.

CHAPTER TWENTY-NINE

SEPTEMBER 15, (Friday)

CIA HQ

The cafeteria was busier than normal. *Must be that Community Underground Facilities Conference,* thought Phillip. He talked with Maddie earlier and told her he would meet her on the upper level. Surveying the area, Phillip caught sight of an empty table against the railing in the back corner. Not romantic by any means but it would offer them a little privacy.

"Sorry I'm late, Flip," explained Maddie as she took the seat next to Phillip.

"I just got here myself. What a crowd! Must be a popular conference."

"It's the annual Non-Proliferation and Arms Control (NPAC) Technology Working Group. They've been here for three days. I see you get away from your desk as much as I do," she added sarcastically.

"Not really. Just saving my money to spend foolishly on you during our honeymoon."

"Have you stopped spending money on food?" Maddie asked when she noticed Phillip didn't have a tray.

"Heck no. I've been bringing leftovers," he said proudly, lifting an insulated lunch box to the table.

"Where are you getting leftovers? Pizza Hut?" laughed Maddie.

"I've been practicing. We can't have you be the only person in our marriage that knows how to burn water."

Maddie punched him in the arm and then gave him a hug. He was right; she could burn water. Her mom, a fantastic cook, tried many times to teach her. Unfortunately those were the years when her relationship with her mom was filled with friction and teenage angst.

Turning toward Maddie and taking her hand, Phillip smiled with that wide abandoned grin she loved and said, "I already knew you were special. Seems the DCI thinks so too."

"I wouldn't go that far," she responded while blushing and squeezing his hand. "That was my first occasion to brief the president and the NSC. I thought I was going to be tongue-tied. I'm so thankful that Sam went first. I admire the president for making us both feel at ease."

"What prompted the DCI to take you along?"

"As much as I want to believe he felt Sam and I could present the information more concisely than he could, it's probably more of an attempt to cover his behind."

"What do you mean?"

"I briefed him earlier in the morning and he grilled me pretty good on the connections we made between Mughniyah and al-Bayruti. He wasn't fully convinced." Leaning back in her chair as she nibbled at her carrot stick, she continued, "To tell you the truth, I'm not 100 percent sure myself. I think he just wanted to show the president that the CIA was taking the threat seriously and providing relevant intelligence." Looking over her shoulder before leaning closer to Phillip, she whispered, "The DCI took the first opportunity to talk, probably to overshadow or preempt any other agency from revealing what we discovered first."

"Are the egos that big?" Phillip asked with a feigned shocked look on his face.

"It's early in President Wolton's term and they are all trying to establish turf. I've heard the agency briefers tell stories about the machinations that take place to get their information in front of the president first. Some are quite funny."

"Enough of this talk. Are we going to get any time for ourselves this weekend?"

"I wish I could give a definitive answer, Flip. I've got a white-board full of questions and I haven't finished going through Mughniyah's records."

Looking at Maddie to catch her eyes he implored, "How about brunch after church on Sunday?"

"That would be wonderful, but it will have to be the early service. Think you can get your butt out of bed and meet me there?"

"As I recall, I'm usually waiting on you."

"Okay. I'll give you that one. Now I've got to get back to my quest." Maddie stood, picked up her wallet and gave Phillip a quick kiss on his lips. "See you in church. I love you."

"Love you more," whispered Phillip to Maddie's back.

CHAPTER THIRTY

SEPTEMBER 15, (Friday)

NGA HQ

Looking at his watch Karl couldn't believe it was already 11:30 AM. His stomach growled just to remind him breakfast was a long time ago. In thirty minutes he was having lunch with Milo to discuss his progress.

For the last two days, Karl arrived at 5:00 AM to find the offices already bustling at NGA. He wasn't surprised. NGA was a 24/7 operation. The helpful staff arranged for a place to camp and a quick tutorial on some procedures that were unfamiliar to Karl since he last worked on NGA's imagery exploitation systems. He only had limited access to those areas around the camouflaged ship in Indonesia and the Qasr-e-Firuzeh garrison in Iran.

A search through the historical imagery records for coverage over Indonesia proved disappointing but not unexpected. Since the tsunami in 2008, the lack of any intelligence about the area lowered the demand for imagery collection to infrequent updates. Competing issues in the countries to the north limited the number of satellite collections. The few collections Karl reviewed helped fill some gaps in the time line he had prepared from the commercial imagery at GlobalWatch. One selection in particular, a high-resolution shot, provided good details on the ship as it left the protective cover. The coverage over Qasr-e-Firuzeh was much more prolific.

Grabbing his coffee cup and smaller lunch cooler, Karl headed for Milo's office.

"Knock, knock," Karl said as he lightly tapped on the half open door. "Am I too early?"

"Not at all. Come on in, Karl." Sitting at a small conference table in Milo's office was Sheryl from the Counter-terrorism branch and Tara, the naval analyst. A cafeteria tray, holding lunch selections, was in front of each person on the table. "Hope you don't mind a few more for lunch?"

"It's a pleasure to see you all again. I thought a working lunch would be easier than trying to set up individual meetings," said Milo.

"Do you want to finish lunch or should I just start telling you what I've discovered?"

Milo, with his sandwich poised to enter his mouth, stopped short of biting down and answered Karl. "Let's make it a true working lunch to save time."

Karl took a small bite of his lunch, paused long enough to swallow and started. "The vessel is located on the west coast of Sumatra near Teupin Peuraho in the West Ache State. The vessel is approximately 90 meters long, 6 meters wide, with three 4x8 meter hatches. It has a cruiser stern and the upright sequence is Mast, Crane, Crane, Mast, Mast."

"Karl, you're taking me down memory lane. I can't recall the last time someone used the upright sequencing code to describe a vessel. Normally they just show me a photo."

"Sorry, old habits die hard." Looking at the flat screen monitor mounted on the wall in Milo's office, Karl asked if he could get his saved files displayed.

"Did you send me an email with the file attached?"

"I did, Milo, just before coming down here."

Pushing his chair toward his desk and in reach of his keyboard, Milo punched in his password, selected his emails, searched for the one from Karl and opened the attachment. With a few more clicks the monitor came alive and the first power point slide was displayed. "You can use the remote at the end of the table to control the slides, Karl."

Karl began anew, "I've pulled together some bullets related to the search. A total of twenty-two images were found in both commercial and classified archives. Five of those were thrown out because clouds covered the target area. Three of the images were radar coverage. The time period I selected is 2 February last year until three days ago.

Pausing for another bite of his grilled chicken salad and waiting until it was chewed, Karl noticed that his audience was doing the same thing. "The first image I located that shows the netting and probably the vessel hiding underneath was in November last year.

"Here is a representative photo of the type of vessel I see under the camouflage netting. Hundreds of these can be found working the waters of the Malacca Strait and Indonesian waters. I haven't spent any time trying to identify a specific vessel yet."

"Do you think that will be possible?" asked Sheryl with a look of astonishment.

"I'm not sure but I'll give it a try as I find time."

"As a naval analyst," interjected Tara, "I think that would be nearly impossible. As you said, hundreds if not thousands of very similar vessels ply the area."

"It's not a task I savor. I don't like puzzles left unfinished. It's an idiosyncrasy of mine."

Picking up the remote, Karl clicked for the next slide. "These before and after images show how the camouflage netting was stretched and incorporated with tree cover over the cove.

Karl continued as he eased into his briefing groove. "The cove and entrance to the sea were relocated and deepened by the Tsunami. That's evident on the right image. Multi-spectral imagery from 2014, revealed the entrance and cove depth were at least 8 meters, even at low tide. Deep enough for our suspect vessel to navigate without issue."

"How did you find this vessel again?" asked Tara.

"GlobalWatch had a customer that invested heavily in the reconstruction effort in Ache after the tsunami. That customer asked us to conduct a search and compile a report on the completion of reconstruction projects and to highlight areas still requiring work. I was looking at changes to the small river deltas to assess navigability. The livelihood of villages upstream is significantly affected by the ability to access the sea. Something caught my eye in that cove so I ordered another collection. Once I determined a vessel was under the netting, I put a tasking order in to DigitalGlobe and Airbus/Astrium, the two largest commercial imagery companies that GlobalWatch supports as an analysis center." Pausing, Karl looked at Milo. "I hope you don't mind. I need a couple more bites of lunch. My stomach is growling."

"Please. Take your time," uttered Milo. Looking at Tara he asked, "Do you have any idea what might be going on here?"

"Certainly looks suspicious. I haven't seen any reports, other than the CIA report last week that mentioned a group possibly associated with Jamaah Islamiyah and a pirated vessel. This could be that vessel," Tara said with some consternation.

"I think they are related," offered Karl. "My daughter conducted that debriefing in Jakarta. She mentioned that the source had been transporting materials to the West Ache area. I think we need to find what vessels of that class were pirated or just disappeared over the last 2 years. Insurance records will probably be the best place to start."

"I can work on that," added Tara with a touch of excitement. It would be a nice change from her normal duties.

"Thank you," Milo said.

Wiping his mouth with a napkin and placing the top back on his leftovers before placing it in the lunch cooler, Karl was ready to resume his briefing. "I reviewed one high resolution image from your files that was helpful and disturbing at the same time."

"Disturbing?" Karl's audience said in unison.

"Yes. In other words, it resulted in more questions than answers." Karl let that statement sink in for a second and added, "Here's that image," he said clicking the remote. "The three hatches on the ship have a framework attached to the surface of the hatch that prevents them from being opened. I have a theory about that framework which I believe is supported by another image."

"I assume you are sharing that theory?" Milo inquired.

"Of course. The framework doesn't make sense until we view a radar image from the archives."

A new slide pops up on the monitor and everyone takes a serious look at the image. Radar images, unlike standard photos, are much harder to interpret. They take additional training and skill sets to draw as much information as possible from the black and white scratchy-looking image. Karl's audience was or had been imagery analysts so he wouldn't need to walk them through the process of acquisition and interpretation. "There are three shipping containers sitting on shore under the netting. They are standard six-meter long containers. When I measured the size of the framework, it matches almost exactly the dimensions of the containers. The intent is probably to mount or at least secure the containers to the ship."

"Looks like they are just modifying the ship to carry containers rather than bulk cargo," Tara stated. "Might be something wrong with the vessels bulk cargo holds,' she added trying to offer other ideas.

"Those are all good thoughts," remarked Karl. "I don't think these pirates are trying to get into the cargo business. And if they are, why all the effort to conceal their activities?"

Milo stared at the image. His chin was propped up by his left hand and he appeared in deep thought. "I see what you mean by disturbing. Any idea what is going on?"

"I wish I knew. At the moment I have nothing."

"What do you suggest as our next steps?"

"Using the connections afforded to GlobalWatch, we can request

coverage from each satellite every time it matches the collection parameters. If you could mirror that collection on the government side,
lets say for 15 days, we might have a chance of making sense out of
the activity."

"Done," Milo said with little hesitation. Looking at Sheryl and
Tara he added, "We can revisit the collection strategy in two weeks.
This area has a lot of demand so we will be bumping up against other
priorities. I'll write the tasking request."

Karl fiddled with the remote before catching Milo's eye, "Do you
want me to move right into a discussion of activity at Qasr-e-
Firuzeh?"

"I've got a meeting coming up in 10 minutes. Will it take longer
than that?"

"It could as I expect there might be more discussion."

Moving to his desk, Milo checked his computer screen, found the
calendar icon and opened the file. "I have a 4 o'clock but I am free
between 2 and 4. Does 2 o'clock work for you, Sheryl? I don't think
we need to take up Tara's time on Iranian issues."

"I can start getting the collection for the boat processed," Tara
stated.

Sheryl replied, "Two o'clock will work for me. Do you want me to
invite any other team members?"

"Let's not make it a big event. Maybe at most two more analysts
and we'll meet back here." Picking up a leather bond folder and
heading for the door, Milo stopped, returned to his desk and prepared
to put his computer into sleep mode. "I will have your files ready to
go as soon as we reconvene."

"I'll see you here at 2 PM."

CHAPTER THIRTY-ONE

SEPTEMBER 15, (Friday)

NGA – Milo's Office

Karl bumped into Milo as he came around the corner. "Sorry, Milo. I wasn't paying attention."

"That's okay, I was doing the same."

Sheryl and two other analysts stood outside Milo's door.

"Go right in," Milo motioned toward the small conference table. I want to make a quick stop at the men's room. Too much coffee at the last meeting."

Reaching out his hand to one of the analysts, Karl introduced himself. "Hi, I'm Karl."

"Nice to meet you, Karl. I'm Peter and this is Trudy. We work for Sheryl."

"Pleasure to meet you both," Karl, said as he shook Trudy's hand.

"You used to work the terrorism issue from the North African and Middle Eastern angle, didn't you?" Peter asked.

Surprised these young people would know anything about him, Karl stumbled through a reply, "Many years ago, yes. How do you know that? Has Milo been talking out of school?"

"Milo didn't tell me. My father worked here for many of the same years you did but over in the WARSAW Pact division. He's over at Langley now and said to say hello."

"Let me guess. You are Peter Foster, Greg's son."

"That's right, Mr. Mattingly."

"Please, just call me Karl. You look just like him. Welcome to the business."

"Let's not get tied up in family stories," Milo hurriedly said as he reentered the office. "Give me a second and I'll have your file up on the monitor, Karl."

"Milo always ran a tight ship, " Karl said, as he looked around the room, but it didn't register with Milo who was busy typing in a series of passwords.

"There you go, Karl. Back in business."

Karl remained sitting at the table and reached for the remote before starting his briefing. "Shifting gears from the denial and deception problem to possible terrorism training activity, I draw your attention to this overview of the Qasr-e-Firuzeh military garrison." Sipping from his water bottle, Karl continued. "You all could tell me far more about this large complex so I'm going to concentrate on Seidir airbase and the area immediately to the north.

"At the end of July, I completed a detailed report for a customer who wanted to identify the status of all Iranian airfields over 1,000 meters long and hard-surfaced. The report detailed support facilities, fuel and ammunition storage, and other items of interest. If I found any interesting information while conducting Internet searches I would included it in the final report."

Switching to the next slide that depicted an enlargement of just Seidir airbase, Karl continued his briefing. "While reviewing open source reporting for this airbase, I found several mentions of Al-Quds Forces occupying or probably training at the base. You understand the nuances better than I do that Al-Quds is IRGC's Special Forces, responsible for external operations."

"We've read the same reports and make the same assumptions," Sheryl said as she nodded her head.

"I found occasions when one or more copies of the RX-70 drone and some experimental drones were on display. I assume this was for Army Day or some other major celebration. My assessment for the customer suggested it was either a VIP viewing center or a special research and development center for unmanned aerial vehicles of interest to the IRGC. Similar to the facility at Kashan near Natanz."

With a surprised look on her face, Sheryl asked, "How do you know about Kashan?"

"I mentioned earlier that I was doing an airfield study. This required identifying all airfields within the customers parameters and then looking at all images in our archives of each airfield."

"Just like the old days of baseline reporting," Milo interjected.

"Kashan airfield was bonus coverage because of its close proximity to Natanz Centrifuge Enrichment Facility. I noticed a number of occasions when small aircraft, to small for pilots, on the tarmac or in flight near the airfield. I had the collection parameters expanded to make sure Kashan got imaged every time Natanz was collected. This was a year ago."

Karl paused for a moment, "I was interested, from a curiosity stand point, what new drones were being developed and asked GlobalWatch to seek speculative collection on a rotating weekly basis."

"What do you mean by rotating weekly basis?" Trudy asked with genuine interest.

"I asked for the satellites to collect an image of the airbase once a week but never on the same day."

"Thank you," said Trudy as she scratched some notes on her legal pad.

Pointing to the monitor, Karl added, "This first image of Seidir in early July is from your systems. The strange object I observed on commercial coverage two months ago is the main focus for this briefing. I've indicated its location by an arrow. The object measures one-meter in diameter and is elevated three-meters above the ground."

Sheryl interrupted, "Is this the same object you mentioned you saw at Virginia Tech's center?"

"A similar object was seen a month earlier at Kentland Farms or KFFC as the University refers to it. My hunch is that we are seeing a hover-drone swarm." Karl let that sink in before continuing, "I visited KFFC a week ago and talked to a graduate student who is conducting research on drone swarms. Just as it sounds, swarms are multiple drones flying in close formation. In this case a small globe-shaped hover drone. I saw a display at Virginia Tech's pep rally last week that was stunning."

"Is that the pyrotechnic display that used drones with flashing lights?" Peter eagerly asked. "I saw a YouTube video of the event. Really impressive."

"It was impressive and, at the same time, frightening."

"How so?" Milo implored.

"Let me show you what I think is related activity," Karl said as he changed slides on the screen.

"I'm going to show you a series of slides of an open area just north of the airbase that is nestled in a ravine. I'll show you each one for about 10 seconds and then I want you to tell me what you think is going on. I want your assistance in making sense of the activity and assure myself that I'm not going crazy."

Karl selected the first slide depicting several peculiarly shaped black crescents on the ground. Each successive slide showed more of the same crescents that progressed to full circles. Some of the black circles appeared smeared while previous crescents appeared faded. When the series finished, Karl turned toward his audience finding them deep in thought.

"I've been away from the analysis side for too long," Milo said as he signaled for the others to take the lead.

"I'll make a stab at it," volunteered Peter. "Looks like we have a progression of activity. Something is making the black marks on the ground, almost like small explosions that aren't going off at the same time or failing to explode."

Trudy had a puzzled look on her face, bit her lip and settled back into her chair.

"Trudy, you look like you have an idea. Please don't feel threatened by this group. All ideas are welcome," Karl requested.

"If those are explosions, then the goal seems to be a timed explosion in the shape of a circle."

"I think you're all on the right track or, at least, in agreement with what I'm thinking. Let me show you a few more images that I find even more worrisome."

"These next images are in the same area but a little more to the east. Three pits, two-meters wide by two-meters long by about one-meter deep, were dug in late August. Large pieces of material were placed over the pits and circles similar to those seen in the sand were noted on the material. By last week, sheets of steel, confirmed with multi-spectral imagery, were placed over the pits. At least one is now sitting off to the side in a trash heap with a one-meter hole near the center."

Again Karl stopped and let that information sink in. "I think the Iranians have developed a way to arm small hover-drones with explosives and program them to cut holes, probably through at least three-inches of steel."

"Crap," exploded Milo. "Just what we don't need. Another threat that's hard to detect. My mind is racing at all the possible uses of such technology in the hands of Al-Quds. None of them make me feel secure."

"Let's get collection emphasized over the area. Do we want Karl to brief this to the front office?" Sheryl said as she madly scribbled notes in her journal.

"I think you can handle briefing your superiors. I want to return to the KFFC and talk to Virginia Tech's hover specialist. I had an unsettling opinion of him when we talked last week. He gave off markers that he was lying to me but I'm not sure why. The similarities of the swarms are too much of a coincidence for me."

Milo looked at his analysts. Heads nodded in agreement. "We've got work to do. Karl, we will want to conduct a community briefing on this material. Are you willing to brief your work?"

"I guess so," Karl replied but was unsure he wanted to present the untested theories in front of a large audience.

CHAPTER THIRTY-TWO

SEPTEMBER 16, (Saturday)

KFFC

Responding to Karl's request from the previous night, Dan and Zak were at KFFC's hangar.

"What does your dad want to talk about today?" Zak enquired with some trepidation. His thoughts over the past few days continued to make him uncomfortable. *Mr. Mattingly wanted to talk to him. Had he somehow learned of the activities with the Radford Ammunition Plant? Did he know about Project Atomize? I really must confide in someone. I can't carry the weight of my guilt any more."*

"Dad didn't say. He just wanted to speak to both of us about a sensitive matter." Dan replied feeling a bit confused himself.

Seeing that Zak was anxious, Dan tried to shift his attention to another task. "Zak, do we still need to clean and test the drones after our last performance?"

Jumping at the chance to take his mind off the upcoming meeting, Zak moved to the workbench and remarked over his shoulder, "Yah. We've got about 50 drones to rehab. A few of them hit the ceiling and might need some repairs."

Both men busied themselves at the workbench and didn't hear Karl enter the building.

Seeing the young men engrossed in work, Karl tried his best not to startle them. "Hi, boys."

"Hi, Dad."

"Hello, Mr. Mattingly."

"Zak, please call me Karl. Dan, you're welcome to continue calling me Dad," said Karl as he tried to make the boys relax.

"What can we do for you?" asked Zak.

"For starters, why don't you show me what you're doing"?

Inviting Karl to join them at the workbench, Zak described the process for rehabbing the small hover drones. "The first step is to look them over for any missing parts, cracks or deformities. Second, we pull the battery pack and replace it with a new one. Many times that fixes any issue. Third, we pull the circuit board and run diagnostic checks. Later we will run tests on the battery and repair it if necessary or practical."

Holding one of the small spherical drones in his hand, Karl asked, "How much abuse can one these things take?"

Dan moved to the end of the workbench, bent over and scooped a couple of old drones from a box. The drones' outer shells were missing parts and pieces off of the propellers. "These look bad but they are still flyable. It takes someone with Zak's skills to get them airborne," offered Dan.

"Who wants to run me through the steps required to fly a swarm?" asked Karl as he looked for reactions from the boys.

Zak hesitated, looking over at Dan, hoping he would handle the discussion. Dan picked up on the visual signal and began, "Dad, let's walk into the office so I can sketch things on the whiteboard. Zak, you okay with finishing up here?"

"Sure, go right ahead. Thanks."

Dan and Karl walked into the office and Karl shut the door. Looking at his son, he said, "I wish I could share with you the reason for my interest but I can't. I do ask that you not become too curious or jump to conclusions. Is that agreeable?"

"Sure, dad. You make it sound so serious."

"It could be."

"Where do you want to start?"

"Help me understand how you get the individual drones to perform that awesome display of fireworks."

Dan walked to the whiteboard and started writing what looked like algebraic formulas. "Whoa there, son. All your math skills come from your mom's side of the family. Anything after Algebra I was wasted on me."

"That's okay dad. These are just memory joggers for me."

For the next 45-minutes, Dan filled the board with diagrams and formulas as he explained how swarm technology worked. His head still spinning from the magnitude of the problem, Karl sat back on his stool not sure how to ask the next question.

"For that series of light 'explosions' you guys did where the balls explode outward and form a circle with all the drones lighted at the same time, how does that work? I'm not sure if I asked that clearly enough," Karl said, hoping his son understood.

"I think I grasp what you're asking," Dan replied, much to his father's relief.

"It's a function of time and space. The time it takes the drones to form into the circle and confirm that they are in a circle – that's the space. Each drone discerns its spatial relationship to those around it and an algorithm is developed to assure or confirm the desired pattern."

"That accounts for the shape but how do you get the lights to illuminate at the same time?"

"That's the easy part. We make one drone the command module and all the rest are slaved to it. Once it gets the confirmation signal that the circle is complete, it sends a signal to all the others to light up with a nanosecond delay allotted for the signal time."

"Another question," said Karl as his eyes drifted toward the door to make sure it was still closed. "How much extra weight could one of the small drones carry and still be able to perform the maneuvers we've discussed?"

"Maybe two or three ounces. Keep in mind that the extra weight would draw down on the battery and shorten the travel distance." Curiosity started to creep into Dan's mind, '*What is my father up to?*'

"Let's go join Zak," Karl said moving toward the door.

Zak was still at the workbench processing the drones as Dan and Karl approached. "Hey, Zak. I've got one more question for you and then I'll leave you boys alone."

Biting his cheek and almost drawing blood, Zak feared the next question.

"Does anyone else, that you know of, do the same thing or similar activity with swarms?"

"Several other universities in the States and in Europe have worked on the mechanics but I don't think anyone does it as good as we do," Zak replied with great relief. Feeling better he added, "To the best of my knowledge, no one has approached the complexity of our displays."

"Thanks, gents. You've been very helpful."

HALFWAY BACK TO the Fredericksburg area, Karl continued mulling over the data dump from his son and Zak's last statements. *If no one else has mastered the complexities attained by Zak and Dan, how did the IRGC learn to do it?* Karl was now convinced the circle shapes he saw at Seidir were explosions intended to breech through various barriers.

CHAPTER THIRTY-THREE

SEPTEMBER 16, (Saturday)

Ann Arbor, Michigan

DaQuin Anderson, or Hussein al-Brighton as he preferred to be called, completed the last touches on the box-bodied truck. He stepped back to admire his work. *"Not bad, dude. Not bad,"* he thought. Working in the prison maintenance shop had given him a useful skill – auto detailing. *"Too bad it wasn't what the system expected of him as rehabilitation."*

The truck, painted to look just like a UPS delivery vehicle, took up most of the little garage. "In two days we'll make history," Hussein remarked as patted the truck. "Yes, we'll be remembered by the infidels."

Hussein converted to a form of Islam at Southern Michigan Correctional Facility while serving a ten-year sentence for armed robbery. He became a member of a radical group that had been suppressed by the State's prison authorities at the turn of the century. It regained momentum and membership after the explosive riots around the nation regarding "Black Lives Matter" in 2015. Hussein joined the Melanic Islamic Palace of the Rising Sun, a gang with a history of violence and militaristic attitudes. Islam drove the focus for the group, determined to free black men from the 'white slavery'. The Melanics, as they were called, tried to contact Al Qa'ida and pledge its allegiance. Al Qa'ida never responded. They even tried to affiliate with the remnants of Islamic State in Iraq and Syria (ISIS), also to no avail.

Hussein read most of the current Al Qa'ida literature on the Internet, focusing on the calls for individual acts. While still incarcerated, a plan began to form in his mind. He would build a mortar and launch an attack against the Michigan National Guard. He selected Selfridge airbase because it supported the A-10C Thunderbolt close-air support squadrons. Many congressional leaders wanted to retire the A-10C but its usefulness against ISIS forces in 2016, saved the airplane from the bone yard. Congress supplied money to develop either a follow-on version or a remotely controlled airborne weapon with the firepower of the Thunderbolt. Hussein developed a plan to launch a barrage of mortars onto the base, mixing shrapnel laden rounds with chlorine gas canisters. Since his release from prison, this mission became his only passion. He found details on the Internet that helped him manufacture the mortar tubes and shells. Further research provided step-by-step directions to make the chlorine gas. He planned to attack the airbase in November, just before the 107th Red Devils unit was due to deploy to Jordan.

After discussing his plans with a few members of the 'Melanics', Hussein figured he could get into the base disguised as a UPS truck driver making deliveries. It took him a year to find an old UPS truck in a junkyard north of Detroit. It needed repairs and bodywork to fix the damage caused by a head-on collision. As he completed the repairs and modifications his plan changed.

It started as a rumor, later confirmed, that President Wolton and his wife, along with two former presidents, would come to Ann Arbor for a big event in September. Hussein decided this event presented him the opportunity to become famous, maybe even a martyr.

The last touch-ups to the paint job were done. He replaced the roof panel with a sliding fiberglass section permitting the two mounted mortars to fire unhindered. He planned launching at least six mortars before someone discovered him and started shooting at the truck. He practiced loading and firing the mortars in the remote areas of Dead Stream Swamp near Cadillac Michigan.

CHAPTER THIRTY-FOUR

September 16, (Saturday)

CIA HQ

As much as Maddie avoided working on Saturdays, the file box containing old records related to Mughniyah inexplicitly called for her attention.

So far, she found little that she didn't already know. She added a couple of possible links to unknown people on her whiteboard. She called it her Osprey nest; a multitude of unrelated sticks at odd angles trying to serve a function.

Maddie pulled the last file from the box, sat down in her chair and started to page through the documents. A small slip of paper fell to the floor and almost went unnoticed. Maddie found it later when she reached down for her purse. The only thing written on the scrap was 'SGBoxer/1.'

The digraph SG and crypt represented an Iraqi agent. Other than that, she knew nothing about the person. Opening the asset search function on her computer, she typed the crypt into the blank space and clicked the search button. Seconds later a warning notice appeared. Access restricted to authorized personnel only. '*Well, that isn't helpful,'* thought Maddie. Just to check her memory, she reviewed the various people and places scattered on the whiteboard. *'Nope, nothing on the board matches. Maybe there's a connection in this last file.'*

Twenty-minutes later she had no new information about SGBoxer/1 or Mughniyah. She started to call Phillip until she remembered that on Saturday mornings he played rugby in the park. *'Crazy man. Why did he risk injury playing that stupid sport?'* His phone went to voice mail. "Flip, it's me," she said trying to hide the disappointment in her voice. "I'm still at work but flummoxed. I'm headed to my apartment soon. Call me."

She no sooner hung up than a thought flitted across her conscious, *'I can call Ken and ask if he has access to SGBoxer's file.'*

Ken was one of several mid-level managers who had a much sought after secure cell phone. Maddie wasn't sure if it was originally developed by NSA and later available on the open market, but a limited number of phones were available to agency employees. Far East Division's counter-terrorism chief granted Ken the use of a phone.

Looking through her contacts list, she found the number and dialed it from the secure phone on her desk.

"This is Ken," came the calm response.

"Hi, Ken. This is Maddie. Sorry to bother you on a Saturday but I've got to run something by you. Are you in a location where you can talk securely?"

"I'm sitting in my boat feeding the fish."

"Are you alone?"

"Mia is with me but she's got her headphones permanently imbedded in her ears."

Maddie had a mental picture of Ken decked out in shorts, a fishing vest with a large brimmed hat and enough suntan lotion on to cause a significant oil spill on the Chesapeake if he fell overboard. His 12-year-old daughter Mia, avoiding all interaction with her dad, sat in the bow of the boat. A year ago, Mia would beg him to take her fishing. Now he had to plead with her to go ... hormones are crazy things.

"I need your help getting access to a restricted asset file. I found a small slip of paper in Mughniyah's records. It just said SGBoxer/1. It might be a dry hole. It could have fallen in the box from someplace else but I have to track it down."

"SG is Iraq right?"

"That's correct."

"What happened when you searched the system?"

"I got a warning notice that said Access Restricted to Authorized Personnel Only."

"No contact information or phone number?"

"Nothing. Just the statement."

"H-m-m," Ken muttered as he searched his brain. "That might be a hurdle we can't get over. I've got a buddy in the Near East Division that may be of help. I don't have his secure number on me."

"Give me the name and I'll look it up," offered Maddie.

"Adam Sullivan."

Typing the name into the agency's directory, Maddie found the number and passed it to Ken. He said he would get back to her in ten minutes with an update.

True to his word, Ken called in ten minutes. "You live a charmed life, Maddie. Sully remembers you from Jordan. You impressed him with your dedication during language school and the extra help you gave Amman Station during that tour. He is calling the Watch Office."

"What do I need to do?" asked Maddie trying to contain her excitement.

"You need to hoof it up to the 7th floor and ask for the duty officer. If Sully is successful, the duty officer will give you temporary access to the file. You'll have to remain in the watch center to read the file."

"Thanks, Ken. I hope you catch something other than sunburn."

"If you run into any problems, give me a call."

"Bye," Maddie said as she hung up the phone and left her cubicle.

Avoiding the bank of elevators, Maddie took the three flights of stairs to the 7th floor. The Watch Office handled all breaking issues that surfaced after a filtering system targeted the vast number of messages passing through the Agency's worldwide communication network. The 24/7 nature of the center required access to everything in the Company's databases. Watch officers were held to a stricter level of background checks and polygraph sessions than regular employees.

Pushing the doorbell, Maddie waited for the telltale buzz before pushing on the door. A SPO sat at a desk and requested that Maddie sign in. She asked her for identification. Maddie thought this odd since her ID photo, hanging from the VATech lanyard was in full view of the SPO. Not wanting to question inane procedures, she accommodated the guard.

"I'm here to see the duty officer," she said.

"I'll call him and let him know you are here, Ms. Mattingly."

"Thank you."

Maddie looked around the area and down the short ramp. Photographs from far off lands hung on the wall to the left of the ramp. Full glass panels on the right permitted a view into the Watch Office. At least 20 desks with two monitors on each were scattered around the room. Some were tuned to 24-hour news services while others cycled through blog sites and YouTube. Several large flat-screens were mounted along one wall. Maddie tried to imagine how the watch officers kept from being overwhelmed when the SPO caught her attention and motioned her to go through the door.

"You're Miss Amanda Mattingly?" asked the duty officer, giving her a once over look but lingering just a bit too long at her chest.

"Yes, I am. Amanda is my given name but everyone calls me Maddie."

"I understand you want to review an asset file?" Looking at a sheet of scrap paper in his hand, he continued, "SGBoxer/1?"

"That's correct."

Leading her toward an empty desk, he activated the monitor and entered several passwords into the system. "Please enter your mainframe User ID and password, please." Maddie complied.

After a few keystrokes and mouse clicks the file for SGBoxer/1 displayed on the screen. "You may not copy anything from this file. That includes making any notes. You are not to discuss anything you read in this file with unauthorized personnel. Do you understand?" asked the watch officer with a tone in his voice like someone pumped up with a misunderstanding of power.

"I understand," replied Maddie.

For the next hour Maddie paged through SGBoxer/1's file.

Maddie tried to keep the facts straight in her head; *'Jammal Hussein Dhardi, an Iraqi citizen who fled to Morocco just before Desert Storm ... recruited on December 17, 1989, by COS Rabat while conducting a false-flag approach to illegal arms merchants. Dhardi agreed to provide information on shipments of lethal weapons to warring parties in the Levant. He was jointly run with [redacted] (also false-flagged) when it became difficult to handle assets inside Lebanon. Dhardi used a one-time pad and secret writing to communicate with his handler. Last contact was June 2013.*

Digging deeper into the record, Maddie found the history and evaluation of reports attributed to Jammal. *Impressive to say the least,* thought Maddie. Several were included in the President's Daily Brief and the majority had high ratings. He had unique access. To Maddie's surprise, both Mughniyah's and al-Bayruti's names appeared in the reports. *'I have to get unfettered access to this file,'* she thought. *'How else can we complete the picture and show that al-Bayruti took over Mughniyah's position as Operations Commander for Hezbollah?'*

An even bigger surprise turned up several pages later. A report précis revealed ... *'In 2002, SGBoxer/1 was contacted by an Iranian wanting to acquire several Russian naval rocket mines. Iranian believed part of IRGC-Navy. [redacted] controls report.'*

Annoyed that information wasn't available and stymied by the redactions, Maddie wondered how to proceed. The last few entries in the file did nothing to shed light on any future contact with the Iranians.

Finished with the review, Maddie waited for the watch officer to clear her from the system and walk her to the door.

CHAPTER THIRTY-FIVE

SEPTEMBER 1 7, (Sunday)

Karl's home

The oppressive summer humidity finally succumbed to a beautiful autumn day. Liz, Karl, Maddie and Phillip sat on the ground level deck overlooking the lake. A slight breeze danced on the surface. The next-door neighbor's dogs cavorted in the water, having a great time chasing a Frisbee. Further down the lake several fisherman tried to coax large-mouth bass out from under docks and low hanging branches.

"Look," Karl said, pointing down the lake, "the fleet has arrived." Two muted swans, four Canada geese and at least eight mallards came into sight around the cove entrance. "Looks like two battleships escorted by a bunch of destroyers and frigates," explained Karl.

"You have a wild imagination," Liz added, giving her husband a nudge as they sat together on the wicker rocker. "Shug, Flip, it's so nice of you to join us for the rest of the weekend. Did things finally slow down at the office?"

"Hardly." answered Phillip; "At least it doesn't seem so for Maddie."

Karl looked at his daughter trying to see her reaction. Not seeing anything specific, he asked, "How did you get free?"

"I ran into what I hope will only be a bureaucratic hurdle." Maddie answered her father with disappointment in her voice.

"Those can be tough. Anything I might be able to help resolve?"

"I don't think so, Dad, but thanks. By the way, I heard you stirred up NGA again," Maddie smiled at her dad.

"I'm not sure I stirred them, but may have brought a couple of things to their attention that need closer monitoring."

"What is that, dear?" asked Liz.

Karl took a bite from a gyro sandwich that Maddie and Phillip brought with them from Reston. Karl claimed the best gyros, outside of Tunis or Rabat, came from Reston Kebab, now called Grill Kebab in Herndon. When Karl worked in the Northern Virginia area it was his 'go-to' place. Many times Liz would call in a take-out order for Karl to pick up on the way home. After swallowing he said, "It's that boat I found covered with the camouflage netting and the odd activity at Seidir airbase in Iran."

"Dad, you shouldn't be talking about that here," cautioned Maddie.

"Caution is in order, I agree," replied Karl, adding, "but everything is discoverable on commercial unclassified imagery. Your mother and I have already talked about my concerns. She knows when something is bothering me and proceeds to squeeze it out for discussion." Shifting in his seat to pick up Liz's hand, "You are the best sounding board around. Your logical style helps ground my buckshot approach to examining and solving problems," he said with a smile expressed in his eyes.

"Thanks, Hon. What did NGA say? That is if you can share."

"NGA agreed the boat, really a tramp steamer, is of concern. The crescent shapes and circular marks on the ground near Seidir initiated more discussion. I think they all accepted my theory that drones, small drones, are used as a breeching tool."

Phillip, normally quiet during these exchanges, asked, "What do you mean by breeching tool? When I think of breeching tools, it's anything from a crowbar to explosive tape or even a tank."

"Explosives is the thought here," Karl remarked. "I believe that the Iranians, more specifically the al-Quds Force, developed a process that uses small drones loaded with explosives. They fly them in a circular formation to a target and instantaneously trigger them to explode. The result is a circular hole cut into a wall, ceiling, roof or other structure."

"Then ... then this would make our facilities like embassies and military buildings very vulnerable to attack," Liz said as her hand went to her mouth. "Karl, what can be done to stop this threat?"

"I have the same concerns, but extend the threat to domestic targets as well. We know these groups like to share information. I'm at a loss about how to alleviate the threat."

"Dad, this is frightening," Maddie said as she started to look a little pale.

"Karl," interrupted Phillip, his hands tightened on the wine glass, "do you mind if I share this information with my colleagues in DS&T? I think we need to start looking at defensive measures."

"Feel free to share with anyone you think can help."

"Does this revelation have anything to do with your trip to Virginia Tech yesterday?" asked Liz uneasily.

"It does. I wanted to talk with Dan about the drone 'fireworks' display at the Pep rally. I needed to understand how groups of drones could fly in a circular formation and illuminate simultaneously."

Three heads looked at Karl and said in unison, "And?"

"Dan says it took Zak and him about a week to program the drones for show. What I asked wasn't difficult. As long as you had someone with Zak's flying skills to populate the flight path memory.

"What still bothers me is the timing. I saw a drone swarm at KFFC and then observed the same thing at Seidir. Almost like Al-Quds copied Dan's and Zak's work," Karl said with a puzzled look on his face.

"Could some Iranians be stealing those programs?" asked Liz.

"Maybe we should change the subject before we all get too depressed," Maddie pleaded. "Mom, I think Flip and I have settled on a date. Let's go compare calendars and create a 'save-the-date' note. We can print them when we go into town for a movie."

"That's wonderful news. You cheer a mother's heart."

CHAPTER THIRTY-SIX

SEPTEMBER 18, (Monday)

Ann Arbor, Michigan

Rivulets of sweat ran down Hussein al-Brighton's armpits. The thought of stains showing on his shirt made him even more anxious. He couldn't let the authorities see his nervousness.

'I've got to calm down' Hussein said to himself as he tried to ease his nerves. *'I've got a good plan. The truck looks real. I'm dressed like a UPS driver. The mortars work ... let's get this done.'*

His research on the president's visit gave him two possible locations, the country club where President Wolton and President Bush would play a round of golf or the University of Michigan stadium, the venue for the Red Cross Gala. He settled on the Gala for two reasons. First, the presidents and their wives, plus hundreds of important people, would be present. Second, a small strip mall to the southeast of the stadium offered great cover. Last week he scouted various routes and monitored activity in the neighborhoods around the time the Gala would be in full swing

Hussein didn't mind becoming a martyr but preferred to escape during the melee that would follow his attack and make it to Canada.

The Melanics covert training facility north of Winnipeg offered a safe place to hide while plans to get out of North America solidified. *'Remain calm and get into position,'* he told himself.

Hussein reached for the phone he purchased yesterday and dialed his friend Hakeem. Hakeem was a cellmate for one year and a fellow Melanic. Hussein kept in touch and even told Hakeem of his plans to attack the military base. He needed to talk with him now to help calm his nerves. Dialing the number had a soothing effect.

"Wrong number," Hakeem said gruffly as he answered the phone when he saw the caller ID indicate unknown.

"Wait, Hakeem. Don't hang up. It's me, dude. Hussein."

"Hussein, you getta new phone?"

"Yeah. Don't want the man tracing my calls."

"What's doing?"

"Gettin' ready to finish my plan."

"You still gon'a hit dem planes?"

"Nope. Got a better idea ... gon'a blowup the man himself."

"You crazy, dude. Downright crazy."

"Just you wait. Gon'a be famous by the end of the day. In case I don't make it out, I left a message for you at the office."

"Don't talk like that man. You talking crazy."

"I'm finally feeling like I'm worth something," Hussein said as he disconnected the call and threw the phone into a nearby trashcan.

CHAPTER THIRTY-SEVEN

SEPTEMBER 18, (Monday)

Washington, D.C.

ISIS attacked the United States in 2015 and 2016, causing hundreds of deaths throughout the Nation. The attacks caused such a popular outcry that the small number of liberals calling for protecting privacy were shouted down. Congress reinstated the Patriot Act with even broader search capabilities than in the past. That reinstatement paid off on many an occasion in the last two years; helping to thwart several plans by homegrown terrorists intent on doing great damage.

NSA's massive signal sweeps picked up Hussein's telephone exchange with Hakeem as part of an increased effort in the Ann Arbor area because of the president's visit. *Blowup, hit and plane* were just some of the keywords the computers at NSA highlighted for further analysis. Included in that list of keywords was *kashteen*. As each threat went through a filtering process, it was sent to the most logical desk responsible for the area in question. Hussein's call was immediately passed to the Joint Terrorism Task Force, Domestic

Terrorism Division. From there it was sent to a special team monitoring threats in the Michigan area.

"I think these guys are planning to attack the president," Marty said, glancing around the quad making up the other team members.

"Let's not take any chances and get an alert out to DHS, FBI and Secret Service. What is this, number 20 for the day?" asked Suzanne as she began to fill in the report template with the available information.

"I think it's higher than that," chimed in Special Agent Bob Coffee. "A bunch came in overnight. They're keeping those guys busy in Ann Arbor."

"Okay. Alert sent," Suzanne added as she pressed send on her computer. "It's going to be a long day, I think."

CHAPTER THIRTY-EIGHT

SEPTEMBER 18, (Monday)
CIA HQ
'Why hasn't he called? Ken said Sully would call her first thing in the morning.' Maddie continued to pace back and forth in the tight corridor between the cubicles.

"Maddie, you trying to overload your Fitbit?" inquired a colleague.

"No. Just anticipating a phone call," Maddie said without missing a step and knowing Fitbits weren't allowed in the building. *'I sure hope Sully isn't one of those guys that shows up for work at 9 AM?'* At the farthest point away from her desk, her phone rang. Almost spilling the mug of coffee in her hand, she turned and raced back to the cubicle, grabbing at the phone like she was a drowning swimmer reaching for a life jacket. "This is Maddie," she answered, taking a deep breath that started her coughing.

"Uh, are you alright? This is Sully."

"Sully, thank you for getting back to me and for arranging permission to review SGBoxer's file."

"Well. Good morning to you too. How was your weekend?"

"I need to get in touch with Boxer's handler," Maddie said ignoring Sully's sarcasm.

"Okay. Okay. I forgot how driven you are. Getting the file wasn't an impossible task but contacting the case officer or handler might be more difficult."

"The file indicated we ran him jointly with another service. Unfortunately that service's name is redacted in the file."

"That's not good," Sully said as he tried to come to terms in his mind with how much he could share with Maddie. *I need to tread carefully here,* he thought.

Arriving at a rationalization and remembering his wife's favorite saying, *It's okay to rationalize as long as you know that's what your doing,* he spoke into the phone, "Maddie, come over to my office. We need to talk."

"Where's your office?"

"I'm in 6E00."

"I'll be there in less than five minutes."

"HAVE A SEAT, MADDIE," Sully offered pointing to several comfy chairs and a couch. Selecting one of the armchairs, Maddie slowly lowered herself into the chair.

"I've asked Oscar to join us. He's the last officer to handle Boxer. He should be here shortly. May I ask why the urgency?"

As Maddie pushed farther back into the chair, her feet came off the ground making her feel like a little girl. She hated that but, at only 5'2", you just have to accept some circumstances. Regaining her composure, Maddie noticed it drew no reaction from Sully. "We, well I, think he might be a critical link in understanding a current threat to either POTUS or some of our Navy's aircraft carriers. The information we have to date is nebulous. Based on my review of his file, it appears B/1 had significant contact with al-Bayruti. I think al-Bayruti replaced Imad Mughniyah as Hezbollah's chief operations planner. I want to question B/1 about this relationship and do it quickly," she rattled off hardly taking a breath.

A knock at the door stopped Maddie from going any further. Oscar entered and Sully introduced him to Maddie. After a few minutes spent talking about her dad and Oscar's career overlaps, they got down to business.

Maddie repeated for Oscar what she just told Sully, adding, "NSA intercepted a message between al-Bayruti and a Qatari merchant who helps out al-Qa'ida in the Peninsula. An NSA analyst is doing an in-depth search of the archives. Some preliminary analysis suggests al-Bayruti was involved in the USS Cole bombing. Hezbollah played the surrogate roll for Iran in several attacks on US interests. We also know that it is odd for Hezbollah to work with al-Qa'ida since religious backgrounds and political goals differ. You might recall the battles fought between Syrian Sunni groups and the Shia fighters from Hezbollah. Hezbollah, a proxy for IRGC and the al-Quds Force soundly defeated the Sunnis at Kobane, Iraq along with help from the Kurds. The Sunnis were getting help from ISIS."

"What a mess. Was that another one of those, 'an enemy of my enemy is my friend,' scenarios," asked Sully.

"Most certainly," replied Maddie. "A source reported that Hezbollah demanded compensation from Iran in the form of more sophisticated weaponry. I think B/1 was the most logical link since he had a history of serving as an arms merchant for these guys."

"Still doesn't help me understand how B/1 is so important." Oscar stated.

In a conspiratorial voice, Sully said, "Something I learned during my long career was this Agency has secrets."

Maddie chuckled but then realized Sully was being very serious. "Secrets?"

"Some sources are off the books, at least to us peons. Anytime I got that restricted access warning without any contact information, the source usually involved someone on the 7th floor."

"Why's that?" Maddie asked with increasing interest.

"Sometimes it's at the sources request - a security blanket effect. The source doesn't want to get passed from handler to handler. It exposes them to security breeches.

"Other times the exclusive nature of the information and/or the official position of the individual, a senior General or even a presidential aide, requires someone from the Agency who would have reason to be in the same room."

"Do you think that's the case with B/1?" Maddie asked Oscar.

Before he could answer, Sully interjected, "No. I think Boxer's case lies in the joint relationship with a foreign service. Those relationships can be very dicey and political bombshells if the relationship was leaked."

"Are you telling me I'm heading down a dark alley without a flashlight?"

"Not yet. Let me talk to the Deputy Director first. I may need you to attend the meeting to explain the urgency of this request. Are you going to be around all day?"

"I'll be here. From 10 – 11:00 am I've got a community meeting to review progress on the threat notice. Otherwise I'm free."

"I'll track you down if needed."

"Oscar, you know the joint service, don't you?" Maddie declared, her eyes trying to penetrate the wall of silence surrounding Oscar.

"I'm not at liberty to say. Sorry."

Maddie struggled to gain release from the chair. Seeing her predicament, Sully offered his hand. Accepting the offer, she broke free and exited the office as gracefully as possible.

CHAPTER THIRTY-NINE

Sᴇᴘᴛᴇᴍʙᴇʀ 18, (Monday)
CIA HQ

" ... and we continue to pressure the Chief of Staff to convince the president to cancel ..." Alexander halted mid-sentence as Maddie entered the back door of the conference room. "As I was saying," continued Alexander while glaring at Maddie, "the Chief of Staff has yet to get the president to cancel his trip to Norfolk for the change-of-command ceremony. Questions?"

"Alexander, am I to understand that you still hold to the assessment that the threat is directed at POTUS and former presidents? Even though NSA and CIA believe the threat is against our Navy?" asked one of Maddie's colleagues.

"POTUS and FPOTUS are still at risk. NSA and CIA are relying on the differences in translation of a Farsi word."

"We've documented the unique use of that word," Sam stated as he rose from his chair. Walking toward the front of the room he continued, "In the last few days I've reviewed thousands of transcripts. Only a limited number of occurrences have that intonation of the word *kashteen* exactly as it's recorded in the intercept from almost two weeks ago.

"Imad Mughniyah, al-Bayruti, Abyar Abu Sami, a Syrian Intelligence Officer, and four unidentified Iranian males are the only people using the Shibboleth."

With disgust in his voice, Alexander replied, "Mughniyah is dead."

"True. However, Mughniyah used the word several times in discussions as early as 1998 when talking about the Nairobi and Dar-es-Salam bombings. He's suspected of reporting those successes to an unknown person in Iran after the USS Cole bombing."

At this point Maddie stepped forward, "Our research continues but we have ample evidence at this point to declare al-Bayruti claimed Mughniyah's role as the operational planner for Hezbollah. He is as dangerous as his predecessor. We are attempting to contact a sensitive source that may have access to al-Bayruti.

"We take threats against the president as very serious matters and would not wish to downplay their importance. At the same time we believe manpower should be shifted to scrutinize our theory."

"I disagree," Alexander said, almost shouting. "Focus should be on the president and his safety. Homeland and Secret Service will continue to expand all efforts toward thwarting an attack."

"Mr. Mumford," Maddie said as gently as she could, shocked by Alex's outburst. "I can appreciate your concern but putting blinders on when an open mind is necessary won't help the president."

"Ms. Mattingly, I am not wearing blinders," Alexander said as he reached down, grabbed his briefcase and started for the door.

"Mr. Mumford, do you have a moment to talk in private?" implored Maddie hoping to calm the situation.

"I do not have nor do I care to make time.," replied Alex as he left the room in a huff.

"Folks," Maddie called out to the room. "Let's take a 15-minute break. NSA has more information to share."

Sliding past several individuals and trying not to be too disruptive, Maddie left the conference room and began searching for Alex. She spotted him heading for the Green elevators. Increasing her speed, she briskly walked down the corridor but reached the bank of elevators just as the door was closing. "Darn!" she said aloud. *'Why does he act that way? Is he always so rude or is it just to women?'* Those and other less lady-like thoughts flitted through her mind.

After a quick restroom stop and fresh lipstick, Maddie picked up a bottle of water from the refrigerator and headed back to the conference room.

Sam was bent over the back of a technician sitting at the computer terminal explaining which files he needed for his briefing, when Alex burst back into the conference room. "I have more proof," he yelled, causing a hush over the attendees. "Yes, more proof that the attack is against the president. NSA just intercepted a phone call in Ann Arbor. A plan is in effect! For Today! To kill the president!"

"Please share what information you have on the source and the extent of this threat," stated Maddie.

"I received a phone call just as I stepped out of the elevator," said Alex to a somewhat surprised audience. "It's okay. This is an approved secure cell phone. I have authorization to carry and use it in classified spaces.

"A member of the JTTF called and then sent me an email copy of the alert message. Seems a man named Hussein al-Brighton called a man named Hakeem, last name unknown at the moment, to brag about a plan to kill *'the man'*. Seems he had a previous plan to attack some planes but switched to a new target."

"Still doesn't mean he's going to attack the president," piped up a member in the audience. "He could be planning to kill a coworker or boss."

"Please read the full text of the call if you have it," asked Maddie.

Alexander fumbled with his phone. His excitement took him three tries to get his numeric password correct. He finally got to the email folder and read to the now-crowded conference room. Composing himself, Alexander said, "Wrong number," interjecting that the NSA analyst thought the recipient, Hakeem, was gruff with his response as if surprised or just distracted by something else. *"Wait, Hakeem. Don't hang up. It's me dude, Hussein,"* Alexander continued reading.

"Hussein, you getta new phone?"

"Yeah. Don't want the man tracing my calls."

"What's doing?"

"Gettin' ready to finish my plan."

"You still gon'a hit dem planes?"

"Nope. Got a better idea ... gon'a blowup the man himself."

"You crazy, dude. Downright crazy."

"Just you wait. Gon'a be famous by the end of the day. In case I don't make it out, I left a message for you at the office."

"Don't talk like that man. You talking crazy."

"I'm finally feeling like I'm worth something,"

"That's the extent of the call." finished Alexander.

"Certainly bears due consideration," another member of the audience said.

From the back of the conference room came a soft but penetrating voice, "Isn't President Wolton, his wife and both Bush presidents and their wives at the Red Cross Gala in Ann Arbor today?"

"That's correct," offered Alexander as he shifted his balance and leaned on the conference table with both hands, looking at the whole room in a wide glance. "I think we've got our threat confirmation. Now we need to make sure it doesn't happen," he smiled as he looked directly at Maddie.

Sam arose from his chair, cleared his throat and looked at Alex, "Not so fast, Alexander. The original threat came from overseas. There's no indication in that telephone conversation of a link with the original threat, or are you withholding information?"

"I'm withholding nothing," Alexander angrily replied. "Everything I received I read to you."

"At the moment, it appears to be a homegrown terrorist rather than an al-Qa'ida, ISIS or another international terrorist group's plan," responded Sam.

"I'm convinced this is a threat against the president and former presidents. Case closed," Alexander growled as he picked up his briefcase and left the room.

CHAPTER FORTY

SEPTEMBER 18, (Monday)
CIA HQ
Sully's office was on the 6th floor, high enough to see over most of
the trees. The only significant view was the A-12 Oxcart on the edge
of the north parking lot. Maddie remembered her dad taking her to
see the plane on her first day as a summer intern. He told her the
plane flew so fast and so high that it traversed three states just to turn
180 degrees. Her dad interpreted imagery from many missions flown
by the Blackbird, or SR-71, a follow-on version of the A-12.
  "Come on in, Maddie," said Sully with a grin on his face. "You
are a lucky lady. I didn't expect the DDO to grant you further access
to SGBoxer/1 but he is greasing the skids for a teleconference with
the DGED officer handling the case."
  "DGED?" she questioned, sucking air through the space between
her two front teeth.
  "Yes, the Directorate for Studies and Documentation. Sounds
better in French. The relationship has a very convoluted and tortuous
path that you can read later. We should hear something early this
afternoon. Can you make yourself available at a moment's notice?"

"I won't leave my desk." Maddie replied and, as an after thought said, "If I have to leave for any reason, I'll have someone monitor my phone and come get me."

"Good. Attendees will be the DDO, his deputy, myself and you."

"Any chance Ken can attend? It would make it easier for me to discuss this issue without needing to involve you," she asked cautiously.

"I'll broach it with the DDO."

"May I discuss questions I intend to ask and tasking I have in mind with Ken? I would feel more comfortable having him review my plans."

"Good idea." Picking up the secure phone, Sully called the DDO and requested Ken be added to the bigot list. He passed along Maddie's concerns. Returning the handset to its cradle he said, "DDO agrees. Feel free to include me in those discussions you have with Ken."

"I will and I appreciate your assistance."

Maddie got up from the chair without assistance this time. She planned ahead and sat only partially back in the chair, keeping her feet on the floor. She gazed out the window, marveling at the sleekness of the A-12, imagining it piercing the atmosphere and crossing the United States in just over an hour. Impressive.

BEFORE HEADING to Ken's office, Maddie picked up the folder that contained her notes, questions and ideas related to the threat.

Knocking on the partially open door, Maddie said, "Got a minute, boss?"

"Sure, Maddie. Come on in."

"Did Sully just call you?"

"He did. I guess we've got some work to do before this teleconference."

"How cooperative do you think Morocco will be regarding B/1?"

Maddie asked as she sat down at the small conference table in Ken's office.

"Probably like pulling teeth out of a chicken."

"I'm hoping to find out his current status, access to al-Bayruti, any dealings he had with Mughniyah, connections with Iran…"

"You're not asking for much, are you?"

"Ken, this is the only lead we have that could help us understand where al-Bayruti fits in overall and who he contacts."

"I wish you the best. Our history with the DEGD is littered with false hopes. We give far more than we get."

"Any idea who might be on the other end of the line?" Maddie asked trying to prepare for disappointment. She so hoped to get answers that would put life onto her whiteboard.

"Since the DDO will be attending, I expect at least a brief appearance by Bidawi. After some niceties, he'll probably turn things over to a lackey who's been told not to sell the stand with the shawarmah."

"I hope that's not the…" Ken's desk phone rang and interrupted Maddie, "case," she concluded.

Ken picked up the phone, "Ken here." He looked directly at Maddie with a surprised look on his face. "Sure we can be there in less than five," imploring Maddie for confirmation which he got as she nodded her head. "Okay, we'll take what we can get," Ken added as he took the handset from his ear and placed it back in the cradle.

"Seems Bidawi is available now. We're due in the National Clandestine Service conference room in five minutes."

NCS was the new name for the former Directorate of Operations. It was responsible for all Human collection assets – known in the business as HUMINT. The NCS was the traditional agent/spy organization that Hollywood liked to portray in the movies. Nowadays the lines between Directorates were hard to define, most notably with the creation of new centers for Counter-proliferation, Counter-Terrorism, etc. Holding the teleconference in NCS's conference room instead of the normal liaison conference center was unusual.

As the technician brought up the secure connection with DGED, Maddie looked around the room. Besides herself and Ken, the DCI, DDO and Sully occupied seats around the table. She started to feel nervous in this very senior group. Although she briefed the DCI several times, she knew she was just a worker-bee.

"Director, the connection is green," the technician said as she walked toward the door.

"Thanks, Wanda. Just close the door as you leave."

Mark Baker moved the touch screen closer to him and activated the speakerphone button. "CIA is on the line."

A hollow sound like an echo came back over the speakers as the flat-screen sprang to life and displayed a conference room halfway across the world. "Allam here."

"Thanks for granting us this short notice call. Sitting with me are my Director of Operations, Deputy Director of Intelligence, and two analysts." The DCI touched the controls that moved the small camera in a quick pan across the assembled group, then moved the screen out enough to capture all those in attendance."

"Mark, Ken, good to see you. Have you changed Sully's bio and made him an analyst?" DGED's Director Allam M. El Bidawi joked.

"Allam, you are good. It was our poor attempt at disinformation. Sully remains operational."

"And the lovely lady in attendance ... is that Miss Mattingly?" Allam asked with a wide grin on his face.

"Show off," Mark replied with a hint of concern. *'How does Allam know Maddie?'* he thought.

"Don't be upset, Mark. Miss Mattingly, Maddie, was especially helpful to us during her time spent in Jordan. How's your father, Maddie?"

Blown away by the biographical data about her from the Director DGED left Maddie speechless. Not sure what to do, she looked to Ken for guidance. Ken's blank look and slightly open mouth offered no help. Maddie could only stare at the screen. After what seemed like minutes, she said, "Director, I don't believe we've ever met."

"If I might take a moment down memory lane ..." Allam asked, conscious that he wouldn't be refused.

"You have us all intrigued, Allam." Mark replied, wondering where this was going.

"I worked with your father for several years during information sharing programs. Morocco's army is small so we try to be trained in multiple facets. As a mid-level officer trying to learn the intricacies of imagery analysis, your dad was extremely patient and very gifted. He taught my staff and me the tradecraft behind extracting truths from satellite imagery.

"About 10 years ago, he got permission to remain in Morocco for a short vacation after a conference. You and your mother joined him and toured our country. He wanted to visit the ancient Roman city of Volubilis. I own a small cottage nearby. You might remember a midnight hike through a village and along the ancient Roman road to my olive orchard?"

"Director El Bidawi, I do," Maddie exclaimed with memories filling her head. "We thought that your neighbors would shoot us, thinking POLISARIO troops were sneaking through the area. My dad laughs every time it comes up in family discussions."

"Please tell your dad we miss him at the exchanges. Maybe you are taking his place?"

"He didn't pass along the genes for the imagination it takes to do his business."

"I disagree. Your imagination uncovered that Syrian spy network, posing as Moroccans, in the Jordanian government. We were able to leverage that for vital information on Hezbollah and Iranian plans for an expansion in Morocco. I'm in your debt."

The DCI interrupted, "It appears I don't need to establish Ms. Mattingly's bona fides. Allam, I'll go back to pushing papers unless you think I'm needed to bless any tasking?"

"My staff and I are comfortable with continuing discussions with Maddie and Ken. Sully too if he wants to stay."

"Thank you, Allam. Guess I'll have to look for a good case of

Napa Valley wine before my next visit. I'm sure I will get an update after this meeting. Assalamualaikum."

"Wa alaikum asalaam, Mark."

The DCI turned his chair toward the rest of the group, "Just keep me informed, Ken," he said as he got up and left the room.

"Maddie, due to the sensitivity of our upcoming discussion, I will have only my deputy with me in the room. Please, call me Allam. So, how can we help with Malakimu?"

Maddie chuckled. Malakimu was Arabic for boxer, also translated as Gladiator. Her notes indicated Gladiator was the DGED's preferred translation for this agent.

Over the next 40-minutes, Maddie learned about Gladiator's life as an arms merchant in the volatile Levant. Allam said he personally ran the asset for five years, always in disguise. His rising status within DGED brought more public appearances and the case was transferred to his deputy. A year ago, the arms merchant dropped out of contact. This wasn't unusual. Over the lifetime of the contact, Gladiator had gone dark for as long as two years. The last time he broke contact was during the Iraqi Army's fighting to take back Mosul from ISIS in 2017. Allam wasn't sure why he was silent now.

Maddie asked if emergency contact instructions were in place. She explained to Allam what information she needed to learn from Gladiator and that it was urgent. Allam promised a quick transfer of files related to the asset and would initiate the emergency contact as soon as the call was complete. He cautioned that a response from Gladiator could take several days to several weeks.

"Let's pray for hours instead of several days," said Maddie.

"Such an optimist. This is the Middle East. The only thing that happens quickly here are tempers."

"Thank you for the open exchange, Allam. I will pass along your comments to my dad. I'm sure he won't mind my speaking for him by saying he calls you a friend and prays for peace."

"Assalamualaikum, Maddie, Ken. I'll have those files sent immediately to our liaison officer in Washington. You should have them by tomorrow morning."

The monitor went blank. "I would never ever in a million years believe that the Director of DGED knew you or about your work in Jordan," Ken said in awe. "I've never known the Moroccan's to be so open. Bidawi didn't even ask for anything in return."

"Let's hope I don't mess this up."

CHAPTER FORTY-ONE

SEPTEMBER 18, (Monday Afternoon)
Ann Arbor, Michigan
As Hussein turned the corner by the strip mall, he noticed a roadblock established halfway down the block. He almost crapped in his pants. *'What do I do now?'* he thought. *'Keep calm, keep calm,'* he told himself. *'You're a UPS driver delivering packages to the businesses in the strip mall.'*

Hussein slowly pulled ahead and got in a line of four other vehicles waiting at the roadblock. He sighed, knowing that a cursory glance into his truck would pass inspection. The two mortar tubes were covered with large boxes with UPS shipping labels. He just hoped these guys didn't have a bomb-sniffing dog. If so, he was going back to jail for a long time.

Intently watching the activity ahead of him, Hussein did not see any dogs, just local police. He gave another sigh of relief as he ran his fingers through his beard.

He was next in line, took a deep breath to help calm himself and drove forward.

"Good afternoon, sir. May I see your license and registration?" asked the officer

"Good afternoon to you, officer. Let me get them from the glove compartment," Hussein said as he got up from his seat and got the documents out of the box. Handing them to the officer, he conjured up enough nerve to ask, "What's going on? Looking for someone?"

"Nope. Just additional perimeter security for the president's visit."

"I've got deliveries to make to the mall. Will you let me through?"

"Your documents look in order. Mind if I look in the truck?"

"Jump right up here," Hussein managed to say without gagging from fear.

After a quick glance around the cargo bay and cab, the officer jumped to the ground and conferred with his partner. "You're good to go. How long will you be?"

"I've got ten deliveries and will probably have to wait for DSW to finish packing up some shoes. They're always holding me up. I say about 30 minutes."

"Alright, just don't stay too long."

Hussein couldn't believe it. He hadn't planned on a roadblock and couldn't believe his luck at being able to get by the officers without them noticing his nervousness. *'Allah be praised,'* he intoned silently. Now he needed to get into position to fire his mortars. He hoped the attack would cause the police at the roadblock to abandon that post and head to the stadium. If not, he had a pistol hidden under his seat and would use it to shoot his way out.

A FEELING of dread sweep over Patrolman Dennis Lehman shortly after the UPS truck left the roadblock. A line of cars backed up, some honking their horns, which didn't help with his feeling of unease. *'What was it? What was bugging him? Something was out of place but he couldn't pin it down.'* He strolled back to his partner and asked, "Joey, did you notice anything odd about the UPS driver or truck?"

"Nothing. Guy just looked like he wanted to get his deliveries done."

"Has he come back out? Seems like he's been in there a long time." said Lehman as he glanced at his watch.

The blast of a horn startled Dennis as he tried to sort through the interaction with the UPS driver. He started to walk down the line of cars looking for the culprit who thought his time was more important than anyone else's. He'd gotten down to the fourth car in line when it all fell into place.

Running back down the line of cars to his partner, he reached for his radio. "Officers request backup for suspicious vehicle at station 57. Repeat, officers request backup for suspicious vehicle at station 57."

"What's going on, Dennis?" asked Joey.

"That UPS driver; he had a beard."

"He had a what?"

"He had a beard. UPS doesn't allow beards and he had on white socks."

"You've got to help me out here, Dennis. What are you talking about?"

"My brother-in-law used to drive for UPS. He would complain about all the rules the drivers had to follow. He said it was like Big Brother looking at them all day long. They had strict uniform regulations. If you wore the shorts, you had to wear the proper socks; brown with the UPS logo on them. That driver was wearing white socks, a definite no-no. The company fires drivers for such a transgression. Beards weren't allowed either, another big infraction of the rules."

"So, you want to pull him over for breaking UPS rules?"

Exasperated, Dennis continued, "He's a fake. We have to consider him a suspicious individual and check him out. We'll just turn people around without explanation until backup arrives. Then we'll cautiously approach the van, unless he leaves the area before hand. Either way, I want to talk to him."

HUSSEIN DROVE the UPS truck to the parking spot he'd previously surveyed that gave him the best distance to the stadium. "I can do this, I can do this," he chanted out loud. Moving around the back of the truck, he lifted the two cardboard boxes hiding the mortar tubes and set them aside. He repositioned the two wooden boxes filled with mortar rounds. One box had high explosive (HE) shells and the other held the chlorine gas warheads. His plan was to launch two HE shells to start a riot inside the stadium where a huge tent had been erected to protect all the attendees from inclement weather. The stadium acted as a controlled facility where the Secret Service and other authorities could regulate ingress and egress of all personnel and materials. Hussein read all about it in the local newspaper. He looked at the compass and level attached to the side of each tube and confirmed the preset azimuths and elevations that would put the explosives on the tent.

Looking at his watch, Hussein knew he had three minutes to go. The President and First Lady were due to arrive at 3:00 PM. He planned for a slight delay and figured they would be inside the tent by 3:20. At 3:18, Hussein reached up for the cord attached to the fiberglass accordion screen he had installed in place of the truck's roof. He pulled it back and felt cool air pour into the truck. At almost the same moment, he heard sirens and screeching tires.

Patrolman Lehman and three other police cruisers sped into the nearly empty parking lot.

"Station 57 to command," Dennis almost yelled into the microphone at what seemed like an octave above his normal voice.

"Go ahead 57,' responded the command center communications operator.

Getting control of his nerves while assessing the situation,

Dennis continued, "Suspect vehicle is parked at an isolated area of the parking lot. No activity observed. Responding units will block any escape routes. Station 57 will attempt to make contact with the driver."

"Copy, 57. Update as necessary."

Dennis enabled the camera on his vehicle and on his bulletproof vest. He grabbed the microphone for the PA system, cleared his voice with a cough and said, "This is the police. Everyone in the UPS truck come out with your hands behind your head. You have 10 seconds to comply."

The loud voice over the PA startled Hussein. The only thing that registered in his brain was the 10 seconds. During his practice sessions in the swamp, he could launch 4-5 mortars in 30 seconds. He only had this chance before the police charged the truck. Seeming to shift out of his body, Hussein reached down for an HE round, lifted it and dropped it into the tube. The reassuring 'whoosh' caused a rush of euphoria throughout his body. He was going to be famous.

Dennis and the other patrolmen were outside of their vehicles, using them as shields against the UPS truck when he heard the 'whoosh' immediately recognizing it as an outgoing mortar. Two tours in Afghanistan taught Dennis to respect that sound.

Relying on training and quickly assessing the threat he told the team to fire at the truck's cargo bay. Five guns started a fuselage of lead that penetrated the thin metal side of the truck.

Reaching for a second HE round, Hussein positioned it above the second tube just as three rounds hit him in the chest. The mortar dropped into the tube. Hussein collapsed atop the tube just as the round fired. The force of the launched mortar lifted his body above the top of the van just as the round exploded. All that followed was silence, interrupted by a muffled explosion in the distance.

CHAPTER FORTY-TWO

SEPTEMBER 19, (Tuesday)

White House – Oval Office

"Please remind the president he has a photo op with Iowa's 4H'ers at 10:00," Marcie told Paul Albrecht as he entered the Oval Office.

"I won't be long, Marcie, and I'll do my best to remind him."

President Wolton was on the phone staring out the nearly opaque window as Paul entered. As he walked toward the couches near the center of the room, the president spun around and motioned for Paul to take a seat. He continued toward the couches but changed his mind and sat instead on one of the winged-back chairs near the president's desk.

"I'll be with you in just a moment," the president said returning to his conversation. "Yes, Mom, we're both fine. God continues to watch over me. No one was hurt because the round landed in the second tier of seats in the stadium. Yes, Mom I'm grateful that you are praying for us and I'm so very appreciative of your prayers. I can't promise I'll be able to attend your art show ... Yes, I am the President of the United States but that doesn't mean I'm in charge of my schedule ... Mom, if I came, it would only pull attention away from your artwork ... You've worked very hard for this show," Chester said with a look of exasperation on his face.

Ever since his dad died, Chester's mom looked for something to keep her busy. She was a great help during his campaign, volunteering to speak at senior centers and colleges. She loved telling people about her son, *The Admiral*, which helped to emphasize his background as a normal kid. He wished there was a way he could break free without all the security issues. He was proud of his mom's accomplishments too. She was being presented with Charleston's 'Artist of the Year' award. Chester had to agree, she had talent. Two of her paintings were displayed in the White House. One of the paintings hung in the Oval Office, depicting a stormy winter scene on the Chesapeake. The watercolor had soft greens, browns, and grays highlighting the reeds, sand, and surf. What caught people's eye most was the plastic Walmart grocery bag floating in the sea foam. She had titled it 'Flotsmart'. His favorite hung in the study in the private quarters. It was another watercolor but the subject was a 'jack-in-the-pulpit' plant, *Arisaema triphyllum*. Chester remembered finding them in the woods when he was a youngster. His dad used it as a learning experience, telling him that even if something looked beautiful, it didn't mean it was good.

"Ok, Mom. I'll talk to you later in the week. I love you. Bye."

"I think she's concerned about her son's safety," Paul said with a grin.

"I wish I had half the power and influence my mother thinks I have as president."

"Let's see if we can get you to use that power on your schedule."

"Before we do, that article in the PDB this morning about another Chinese aircraft carrier in the works ... "

"I've already got Langley looking for additional reporting and any satellite confirmation."

"Good. Now what's the problem with the schedule?"

"Next week, Thursday, is Roger's chain-of-command ceremony.

Homeland and Secret Service are adamant that the threat against you and the other presidents is still valid. They want you to cancel. The mortar attack yesterday didn't help ease the tension."

"I can't, Paul. Roger and I were roommates at the Academy, served together on three different ships and almost married sisters. I want to be at the ceremony and pin on his second star."

"Mr. President, I canvassed the NSC members this morning. Other than the CIA, the others think the threat is still focused on you and your 'brotherhood'. Homeland says they have reports of suspicious activity in the Norfolk Naval Base area but didn't pass along any specifics."

"Could that just be the 'nuts' coming out to play? We did alert the Press awhile back of my intention to attend, right?"

"We did. Most of the reporting is coming through the local FBI office and NCIS. The wildest report was from Virginia's Department of Game and Inland Fisheries."

"The Game Wardens?" asked the president in puzzlement. "Someone threatening to sink the USS Bush with a Bass boat?"

"Odder. Some fisherman was in Hampton Roads at the entrance of the Elizabeth River and swore small drones attacked him."

"Drones?"

Shuffling papers on his lap, Paul tried to locate the report. "Here it is," and passed it to the president.

'...*buzzing sound, like hornets ... could only hear them ...* 3:00 *am. A little early to be drinking, but then he could have been drinking.*' Chester thought as he read through the report. "Says here there was early morning fog."

"I saw that too. Probably got him confused."

"Fog is a mysterious thing. Not how fog is created but what it does to sound," replied Chester as he came out from behind the desk and sat on the couch. "I spent some time on small-boys, frigates and old destroyers early in my career. You're close to the water in those ships. Standing watch in the fog is no fun because the sounds play tricks on you when you don't have a landmark. This guy may have heard someone's weed-whacker."

"At 3:00 am?"

"Not all communities have HOA's, Paul."

"Nevertheless, Homeland's Threat Task Force is pushing for cancellation."

"What about the CIA?"

"CIA continues to work on the notion that the threat is against the Navy's carriers." It's one of their analysts and an NSA Petty Officer?"

"Ms. Mattingly and CTI2 Ives," interrupted the president.

Paul marveled at the president's ability to remember names out of the hundreds of people he interacted with, many for only a brief moment each day. "That's correct, Sir. They are continuing to research old files. The DCI told me this morning that a sensitive source was being contacted to help fill in some gaps."

"What do you think, Paul? Give both theories a few more days?"

"I would like to pull some staff together and look at alternative venues for the Chain-of-Command, Sir. We will have to commit a large protection force at Norfolk; Marines, Coast Guard, Naval personnel, not to mention Secret Service, FBI, etc."

"Let me think on that," Chester said as he settled into the couch and crossed his legs.

Paul got up to leave, gathering his notes and slipping them into a leather bond folder. He got to the door, turned and said, "Sir, Marcie wanted me to remind you that you had Iowa 4H'ers coming in for photos."

"Thanks, Paul," he said, uncoiling from the couch but not before thinking he'd never had a nap on this couch. It felt soft and probably would accommodate his body. '*Maybe I should pencil some time to give it a test run.*' As an after thought, '*like that will ever happen.*'

CHAPTER FORTY-THREE

SEPTEMBER 19, (Tuesday)
    CIA HQ
    The smell of fresh coffee and a toasted cinnamon-raisin bagel with lite cream cheese spread did little to lift Maddie's spirits. Sitting in front of the whiteboard, staring at the names and notes only made her feel less productive. She turned toward the adjacent cubicle and asked, "Martin, has all the stuff from Mughniyah's file been inputted?"

"Yes. It's in the group access file under Mughniyah."

"Thanks, Marty."

A couple of mouse clicks later Maddie's screen came to life with the link analysis program. The small monitor wasn't giving her an overall scope so she closed the program and moved to the conference room. After a few minutes and a thousand passwords later, the large 60" flat-screen monitor showed the relational links for Mughniyah. Displayed on a smaller monitor was Maddie's whiteboard scribbling.

Two hours later, Maddie was still clicking on each link and rereading the supporting documents. She then shifted to al-Bayruti and any of the links shared by both men. Multiple links internal to

Hezbollah's organization appeared, but only two links shared external connections and both of those were with Iranians. *'That's understandable,'* thought Maddie, *'since IRGC is a significant support point for Hezbollah. Yet,'* Maddie continued to think, *'these are only the phone and Internet links we've identified. There's got to be more interaction.'*

Another hour passed. "Maddie, we're going to get lunch. Want to join us?" Marty asked as he ducked his head into the conference room.

"No thanks. I brought a bowl of soup. I'll get to it later."

By noon, Maddie didn't seem any closer to an answer than when she started at 6:00 am. For that matter, she wasn't any closer to formulating some questions that would produce useful answers. As an afterthought, she shifted the emphasis on the link analysis filters to geographic locations, overlaying both al-Bayruti's and Mughniyah's travel information.

On a hunch, she added the known cargo flights between Iran and Syria, highlighting those identified to carry weapons for Hezbollah. "There it is," she said out loud. "It's a start."

Looking at it for a while longer, she got up and closed the blinds on the door to the conference room. She took the 'Classified Meeting in Progress' sign off the credenza and hung it on the hook before locking the door from the inside. Now she could add data that DGED had shared on SGBoxer.

It was almost 3:00 pm when she finally finished manually entering El Bidawi's data. No direct links appeared between or among the three key individuals; however, multiple secondary and tertiary links with Boxer applied. *'Probably how he got his tasking and set up deliveries,'* thought Maddie as she rubbed her eyes and tried to focus her brain. *'It was obvious cutouts were being used to protect not only Boxer but also al-Bayruti. Additionally, the timelines confirmed Mughniyah's functions were subsumed by al-Bayruti.'*

Another surprise came when she ran the geographical filter. SGBoxer was reported in Syria and sometimes Tehran at the same time as al-Bayruti. B/1 was a key player and she needed to get in contact with him.

Maddie pulled up the last reported location for Boxer from the DGED file – Frankfurt, Germany. She reached for her secure phone and called Ken.

BY 4:30 pm Maddie was racing for Dulles airport to catch the 5:30 Lufthansa flight to Frankfurt. The packed 3-day bag she kept under her desk was her dad's idea. When he was at the Company, he traveled at a moment's notice and passed on that 'be prepared' psyche to Maddie.

When Maddie called Ken, he simply asked if she thought a meeting with Boxer/Gladiator was critical to the threat. Maddie explained how she thought Gladiator's interaction with al-Bayruti could be the key to understanding the focus of the threat. Ken moved into high gear and called the DCI who called Allam, catching him just as he headed to bed. Allam, as promised, initiated the emergency meeting protocol with Gladiator. His officer in Germany confirmed receipt from Gladiator and was putting together a meeting. El Bidawi was planning on calling in the morning when he had contact instructions.

"I'll have my officer meet Maddie at the Domplatz in Old Town Frankfurt at 10:00 am on Wednesday," El Bidawi offered.

Lufthansa Flight #419 was just off the west coast of Ireland when Maddie received a text from Ken – *Meeting confirmed. Paroles to follow.*

CHAPTER FORTY-FOUR

SEPTEMBER 20, (Wednesday)

USS Nimitz – CVN-68

Approaching East China Sea

Commander Benjamin Buehl, senior navigator, stood next to the digital plotter located toward the back of the Captain's Bridge onboard the USS Nimitz. The ship was 20 miles outside of Sasebo, Japan, passing Darlly Island as they dropped off the harbor pilot. "Course setting to 210 degrees. We will be in position to recover the air wing in 30 minutes," said Ben.

"Aye, aye, sir. Course 210." replied the officer of the deck.

The USS Nimitz just completed a two-week stay in Sasebo after almost three weeks of conducting operations in the Sea of Japan. The next duty would probably be the last one for the old girl. She was going to relieve the USS George Washington in the Gulf of Oman. This final tour would last five months, providing the area remained calm. After the Gulf, the Nimitz would probably spend her remaining days as a training platform for the new F-35 Lightning pilots on the West coast. The USS Nimitz, in service since 1976, only had two major overhauls during those 40 plus years. Now her aging systems would cost almost as much to refurbish as building a new ship.

Ben looked over the plotter at the route he had worked up for the deployment to the Arabian Sea. The rendezvous with a Military Sealift Command replenishment ship would take place tomorrow. Weather conditions were predicted as favorable in the East China Sea, a difficult place to give more than a six-hour prediction. If the weather remained as planned, they should reach Singapore in a week, after a couple of days of flight operations in the South China Sea to maintain the illusion it was still international waters and the Freedom of Navigation laws were being upheld. Ben would send a message to the Malacca Strait coordinator tomorrow after completing the underway replenishment and block out a two-hour arrival time to pick up a harbor pilot on 26 September. Ben was looking forward to a two-day stay in Singapore. The two previously scheduled stops were interrupted by flare-ups in the Middle East and North Korea. Singapore was tantalizing when seen from the water but Ben wanted to walk the streets. After the port visit, it would still take the Nimitz another six days to cover the 3,600 miles to the Gulf of Oman.

Ben must have gotten lost in his thoughts about Singapore because the Air Boss was calling for wind over the deck. A quick calculation and Ben replied, "We can stay on course. Increase to 28 knots."

"Aye, aye, sir. Course 210, 28 knots," repeated the officer of the deck.

CHAPTER FORTY-FIVE

SEPTEMBER 20, (Wednesday)

Frankfurt, Germany

Omar Youssef Nassiri occupied a window seat at the Metropol Kaffeehaus am Dom which gave him a clear view of the Domplatz and the eastern exit of the Kunsthalle. He assumed his American contact would take the U-Bahn from the airport to the Dom/Romer station. Rabat sent him a photo of Ms. Mattingly. He was early. Sipping an espresso, he looked out over the plaza, hoping to catch a glimpse of the pretty American.

Her plane arrived 45 minutes early, thanks to a favorable jet stream. Maddie requested a day room at the Hilton Garden Inn and took a quick shower. She had about 2 hours before her initial meeting with the DGED officer. Even though her stay would be very short, she was booked on United Flight #933 leaving at 5:10 that same evening. She wanted to visit the Kleinemarket for old times sake. The plethora of food odors assaulting her nose was always a delight. The small stalls and the diverse selections of sausage, cheese and breads were overwhelming.

She exited the Willy-Brandt Platz U-Bahn station and headed

north on Neue Mainzer Strasse. She walked along the street at a good pace for four blocks before stopping to consult her small map. The map was part of her cover. Maddie was blessed with great spatial relationship skills. Consulting the map allowed her to look like a tourist and make abrupt changes in her planned route. She reversed course and turned right at Taunusstrasse, then left into the small park that ringed Old Frankfurt until she stood in front of the Frankfurt Opera House. Skirting the building to the right, she headed for the Untermainbrucke, crossing over the Main River and taking the stairs down to the path along the river. She paused at several locations to take pictures with her phone as cover for action. Maddie wanted to make sure she was clean of any surveillance before her meeting. As she walked east along the river, she looked for parallel activity across the river and for any possible stationary spotter on the pedestrian bridge – Eiserner Steg.

She stopped at the center of the bridge, taking photos of the Dom and the old town. She reversed course once more and headed back toward Sachsenhausen. She finally crossed the river at Alte Brucke, turned left on Mainkai Strasse and right on Zum Pfarrturm to the first intersection before taking another right. She walked through the small parking lot for Evangel school to the backdoor of Metropol Kaffeehaus am Dom. She was an hour early for the meeting, allowing her the luxury of a quiet breakfast and time to savor a Jacobs cup of coffee or two. She sat as far back in the coffeehouse as possible that still afforded a view of the main entrance and most of the café.

Maddie saw him enter the café and order an espresso before sitting at the window overlooking the plaza; just the place she would consider if she was making a meeting with someone she didn't know. She watched him for 10 minutes. He didn't glance away from the window, even when the barista dropped a tray of mugs making a huge crash. At 9:55 am he got up and exited the café. Maddie followed him out.

She turned to the right after the officer turned to the left. She walked east on Weckmarkt Street for half a block before turning to take a picture of the cathedral. She watched him disappear around the corner of the building and looked for any indications he might have a tail. Maddie then briskly walked around the east and north sides of the Dom before catching a glimpse of him standing in front of the Cucina delle Grazie.

Omar saw her at the same time she looked at him and crossed the street. In broken German he asked, "Excuse me, miss. Is the Europaturm nearby?"

"The Spargelturm is about 3 kilometers to the north, near the Duetches Bank headquarters," answered Maddie.

"The Spargelturm?"

"A nickname for the Europaturm. It means Asparagus Tower," Maddie said to finish the contact instructions.

Switching to English, Omar said, "Hi, I'm Omar Youssef Nassiri. You are Ms. Mattingly?"

"Maddie, please."

"Welcome to Frankfurt."

"Thank you. How was your espresso?" Maddie asked, trying not to show off, but letting Omar understand she wasn't just a desk jockey analyst.

"I'm sorry, what?" he sputtered, trying to remain calm.

"You looked intense as you sipped your coffee by the window up there," she said pointing to the coffeehouse.

"I'm impressed. How long were you spying on me?"

"I got there about 30 minutes before you did. Did you hear the commotion behind the bar?"

Omar looked at Maddie, trying to figure out how he had missed seeing someone as pretty as her in the café. "I heard something but didn't want to get distracted."

"Seems your office prepared you better than mine did. Obviously they sent you my photo?"

"Yes, though it doesn't do you justice."

"I hope that was a compliment?" she laughed.

"It looked like a passport photo."

"Oh my! Must be the photo from last summer. I think that was the hottest and most humid day ever in D.C. The weather did me no favors except wilt my hair and streak my makeup."

"Frankfurt's weather appeals to you."

They were walking now toward the river, chatting like a young couple. Nassiri informed Maddie that he had never met Gladiator but had all the paroles for the emergency meeting at noon. He recommended meeting the asset first for a very brief consultation. He would arrange a second meeting at the Palmengarten's Rock Garden at 12:30 pm. Maddie would provide counter-surveillance when they left the Entrance Hall before proceeding to a DGED safe-house at 22 Schubertstrasse Apartment 5, less than two blocks from the garden. Omar would introduce Maddie as 'Mariam'. Special care was required to avoid letting the asset realize that the Americans and the Moroccans were running him. He was under the impression he was acting on behalf of the Bundesnachrichtendienst or BND – the Federal Intelligence Service.

"I sure am glad my German skills are current." Maddie said in German.

The DGED safe house had never been used before. It was reserved for a one-time use. The protection of the source and the owners was paramount. The neighbors were aware the owners would be absent for several days. A team of interior designers was scheduled to arrive and spend several hours drawing up plans for upgrades. At 1:00 pm Maddie rang the buzzer for Apartment 5. The door buzzed and she heard the distinctive snap of the heavy metal latch spring open. She walked up two flights of stairs in a well-kept building. Small tables with expensive looking vases, overflowing with cut flowers, were located on each landing. She lightly knocked on the door. Nassiri opened it seconds later and directed her to a small living room. The curtains were drawn and the smell of fresh coffee hung in the room.

"Najib," said Omar, "this is my colleague Mariam. She is one of our senior analysts assigned to incorporate and plan appropriate action to the information you provide. She has some questions that demand immediate responses. We are beholden to your schedule but hope that you can give us time to walk through the issues."

"It is my desire to assist in any way that I can," Najib said in broken German.

"Najib, are you more comfortable speaking in German, Arabic or English?" asked Maddie.

"Arabic is my mother tongue, but my English is better than German."

"Let's try English and use Arabic to reduce any confusing points."

"Naam. Uh, sure," replied Najib.

CHAPTER FORTY-SIX

SEPTEMBER 20, (Wednesday)
USS Nimitz
Petty Officer Third-class Sinclair Evans sat at his duty station in the cold confines of the computer server room. He was an Information Specialist detailed to troubleshoot any problems that surfaced. In his ten months onboard the Nimitz, only one occasion called for his attention. It was boring duty; made even more so since the chief caught him watching pornographic movies on his personal laptop while on watch. No personal electronics were allowed. The chief threatened to write him up and send him to Captains Mast if it happened again. Now the duty days became unbearable. To make matters even worse, his thoughts drifted to his good fortune. For ten days in Sasebo he enjoyed the company of a young and vivacious hooker who turned his world around several times. He especially liked how she teased him into near ecstasy. As a parting gift she gave him a thumb drive saying, "This will keep you excited until we meet again." He had to confess, he was addicted to porn. The thumb drive was in his right front pocket. Its presence seemed to burn a hole in his

leg and mind. He doubted he could wait until getting off duty to see what special viewings it contained.

CHAPTER FORTY-SEVEN

SEPTEMBER 20, (Wednesday)

White House – Office of National Security Advisor

"Paul, the CIA and that NSA Petty Officer are taking away the focus of the threat against POTUS," said Alexander trying to gauge where the National Security Advisor stood. Paul and Alexander attended an offsite retreat three months ago. A kind of meet and greet event the president requested so his staff could be seen as ordinary people. Too many times presidential staffers felt they were in some rarified atmosphere, far above the common worker they dealt with on the phone. Paul and Alexander hit it off, finding they had several things in common, one being home-brewed beer. Alexander tended to capitalize on the budding friendship by requesting face-to-face meetings when a videoconference would suffice. "I think, that is DHS thinks, the latest reports from Norfolk substantiate the threat is against the president."

"How do you figure that, Alexander?"

"Norfolk, Hampton Roads and Portsmouth police departments have all reported suspicious activity in the last week."

"Reports?" Paul asked and wondered if the CIA had intentionally downplayed additional reports to keep their theory on the front page of the PDB.

"Both Hampton Roads and Portsmouth reported sightings of box-bodied vans in the parks adjacent to the James River and with direct line of sight to the Norfolk Naval Base's piers. These sightings were during the very early morning hours."

"Were they investigated?"

"The police just drove by looking for suspicious activity."

"And?"

"The van at Portsmouth was empty but a K-9 Unit was called to the scene and reacted to possible explosives," Alexander added, thinking he had the smoking gun.

"What happened next?"

"We are still waiting news from the police. They were checking the registration."

"Not enough to cancel the president's visit, Alexander."

He looked away, not wanting Paul to see the disappointment on his face. He had to convince Paul of the threat and keep the Secret Service in the spotlight. "Paul, the Hampton Roads police responded to a small park directly across the river from the base to a report someone was flying a drone at 3:00 am."

"Probably some pervert peeking into windows or a criminal checking activity in the neighborhood," Paul said offhandedly. "Ever since the FCC allowed private drones to fly at less than 500-feet, those guys have been bending and breaking the laws."

"Paul, please listen to me," pleaded Alexander. "This could have been a practice session. An assassin could penetrate the base's protection with a drone carrying just enough explosive to kill the president and those near him during the ceremony."

"I agree that is a possibility, but not enough to cancel the event. Isn't the Secret Service prepared for something like that?"

Feeling he had lost the momentum gained by mentioning the drone, Alexander softly said, "Yes. The Secret Service trains for just such an event, now that drones are so prevalent. As you know, several intrusions here at the White House, all unsuccessful, kept them busy."

"Alexander, POTUS and I discussed the drones earlier today and he doesn't think there's much to the Hampton Roads report. He continues to press for attending the Change-of-Command. Get back to me when you have a substantiated threat."

"NSA has reported an increase in chatter among operatives of Al-Quds and Hezbollah in the Middle East."

"I saw those reports too. Chatter in the Middle East doesn't necessarily corroborate a threat in the US," Paul said as he turned to his computer, typing in his password as an indication the meeting was over.

Alexander picked up on the hint, collected his notes and stuffed them into the lock bag. As he turned the key for the outer bag and stood up, he looked at Paul with a face pleading to be heard.

"Alexander, call me when you have something of substance. Alert Secret Service to the drone report and make sure staffing can cover that threat. Thanks for stopping over."

CHAPTER FORTY-EIGHT

SEPTEMBER 2 1, (Thursday)
CIA HQ
Maddie was able to catch the United Airlines flight from Frankfurt at 5:10 pm that put her back in Washington about 8:00 PM. Business Class was just what Maddie needed. In just over 24 hours, she had crossed the Atlantic, spent four hours debriefing Boxer and was now on her way home. She tried to sleep but too much was crashing in her brain.

She wanted to take out her notes and start working on formulating a report but the Agency frowned on conducting classified work in non-secure areas. Maddie's cover story didn't permit a stop at Frankfurt base to write up her notes, nor did she have the time. She would have to let her memory of the meeting guide her thoughts as she tried to make sense of the information she'd extracted from Boxer. Maddie knew she had other tidbits in her notes but the wear and tear of the trip finally got to her and she closed her eyes.

"Miss. Miss. Would you care for dinner?" asked the flight attendant.

In that stupor zone before being fully awake, Maddie realized she hadn't put up a do not disturb sign. Still a bit groggy after two hours of sleep she adjusted her seat position and told the attendant a cup of coffee was needed before she made any other decisions.

The lavatory 'in use' light was dark so Maddie made a move to freshen up while waiting for the coffee. Every time she used an airplane bathroom, Maddie was glad for her small size.

Back in her seat and sipping her coffee, Maddie knew the next few days would be hectic. She pulled out her phone and sent a quick email to Phillip, giving him a heads up and hoping that they could carve out a little time for themselves over the weekend. She then sent a short email to Ken, *good meeting, exciting stuff and a lot of work ahead.*

Flight 933 landed on time at 8:03 pm. It was approaching 9 pm before Maddie reached her car and exited the airport. She hesitated for just a moment when she saw the directional signs for the Dulles Toll Road and Route 28. She desperately wanted to go straight home but regulations forced her to stop at Langley and deposit her classified notes in the office. Too keyed up to sleep, she ran a few searches against the names provided by Boxer/Gladiator before heading home. Four hours of sleep was all she managed to squeeze out of the night before heading back to the office.

Ken leaned back in his chair and rubbed his chin. "So, Boxer confirms al-Bayruti is Mughniyah's replacement and that he is even more ruthless?"

"That's his opinion," said Maddie, "but he told me a couple of anecdotes that characterized al-Bayruti as a Mafia boss."

"That's not good."

"The last three items on my list are the most unsettling to me. The request for advanced naval mines, the threat against America and the new C4++ or 'Super C' as Boxer said the Iranians called it."

"Do we have any other reporting on those items?" Ken asked, with a look of impending doom.

"I ran some searches as soon as I got back. Nothing additional or any specifics to the threat against the 'Great Satan' other than the normal rhetoric stood out. I sent Sam the apparent code names, 'The Shadow and The Light', for two Iranians, to see if NSA has anything that might match. If not, he's going to put them on the watch list with a focus on the IRGC-Navy. Boxer said something I found interesting about the advanced naval mines. Apparently the Iranians only wanted 12-24 mines."

"They might just want a few to test and then try to reverse engineer the mines using the rest for design."

"That sounds logical but Boxer had the feeling this was a special request. He overheard several one-sided telephone conversations between the naval representative and the Shadow and Light characters. Boxer thinks the IRGC-Navy is planning something special."

They looked at each other, neither wanting to think about the potential scenarios that could take place based on that tidbit. "We'll have to be careful in our reporting to highlight that this is source opinion rather than hard facts." Ken replied, still rubbing his chin.

"The 'Super C' bothers me the most," Maddie added. "Do you mind if I ask Phillip to investigate if there is such a thing as C4++?"

"I think the DS&T is a good place to start. They are the techy guys."

"I'll stop and see him as soon as we're done."

"I think we're done. As soon as you finish talking to Phillip, please finish your report on B/1's information and send it to me. I'll forward it to the DCI. I'm sure he will want to have a face-to-face later this morning."

Maddie stopped at her desk before heading for Phillip's office. She rummaged under her desk for a pair of flats and changed out of her heels. The floors were hard and the New Building was a bit of a hike.

"This is a pleasant surprise," said Phillip as he gave Maddie a hug and quick kiss. "I didn't expect to see you until tomorrow, if then. You sounded like your day would be filled trying to catch up after the whirlwind trip to Frankfurt."

"I thought so too, but I've got a question that you might be able help me understand."

Phillip grabbed a chair from the adjacent empty cubicle and invited Maddie to sit. "Just don't change the position of the chair," he said with a grin.

"Why not?" Maddie asked, wondering why Phillip was grinning.

"Samantha is TDY and left specific instructions not to touch her chair or change it's height. Seems she has it adjusted to the optimal position for her."

"Why don't I just stand? This won't take long."

"What? Deny me some quality time with my fiancé?"

"Funny fellow. I don't have the time. I need to understand if you've ever heard of something called C4++ or Super C? Or some other new untraceable explosive material."

"Not right off hand. From the names, it sounds like an improved C4 plastic explosive. I can touch base with some of our explosives experts. How soon do you need to know?"

"Sooner rather than later," Maddie said as she started for the door, but turned back toward Phillip.

"It's been nice chatting with you too. You could have just called."

"What? And deny me this opportunity to get a hug," she said coyly as she gave Flip another hug before heading back to her office.

CHAPTER FORTY-NINE

SEPTEMBER 2 1, (Thursday)

White House Situation Room

DCI Mark Baker just completed giving the NSC members a summary of the information provided by SGBoxer/1, referring to him simply as a well-placed sensitive source. Even though this group had all the necessary clearances, they didn't need-to-know the source's true name, occupation or nature of the contact. He completed his summary by emphasizing the information was still under review but could be significant when viewed in conjunction with the threat.

"Tell us again what's the significance of this, what did you call it, 'Super C or C4++' explosives?" asked Paul Albrecht.

" Super C. Based on limited information uncovered by the DS&T, it's an enhanced form of C4 plastic explosives. The enhancement gives 'Super C' five to seven times more explosive power than the equivalent amount of C4."

"Didn't you say it was undetectable?" asked Angela Kohlstead, Director of Homeland Security.

"I did. Again, based on limited information available to our technicians, 'Super C' is believed to be an experimental explosive. As such, none of the trace chemicals have been added. Production plants don't do that until after extensive testing. It appears 'Super C' is in that early stage of development."

Shifting in his chair, Lt. General Nelson, Director of NSA, asked, "Is this stuff being manufactured by Iran?"

"Unfortunately and fortunately it's not."

"You'll need to expand on that for us," said Paul.

"To the best of our knowledge, it's only being developed at Radford Army Ammunition Plant in Virginia. That's the fortunate part because we've determined Iran isn't making the stuff. The unfortunate part is that someone is smuggling the stuff out of the US and into the hands of the Iranians."

"What are we doing about that?"

"As soon as we made the connection to the Radford Plant, we notified Homeland and FBI."

Looking a bit sheepish, Angela said, "My staff hasn't alerted me yet."

"We just got the information. DS&T called me while I was enroute to this meeting," mentioned Mark, "and I told them to make those calls immediately. I knew I would see you at this meeting and could tell you personally. I had no intention of keeping you in the dark."

"What's CIA's assessment now?" Paul asked as he looked at the rest of the Council members.

"There's no definitive connection for the various pieces of information provided by the source to our current threat. We still place emphasis on the possibility of an attack against our aircraft carriers, specifically those named after presidents."

"Thank you, Mark," Paul said as he gathered up his notebook. "Everyone, please protect the information discussed here. We don't need the media blowing it out of proportion and scaring the public. Let's get together again on an ad hoc basis as new or supporting information develops."

CHAPTER FIFTY

SEPTEMBER 22, (Friday)

Norfolk Naval Base – USS Bush

Three FBI and Secret Service teams arrived at the gangplank of the USS Bush on Friday morning at 8:00 am. They constituted the bulk of the forward security and liaison teams scheduled to review procedures related to the presidents' visit for the Change-of-Command ceremony.

The USS Bush is the last ship in the Nimitz-class aircraft carrier design. Her flight deck is almost 1,100 feet long covering more than four acres. From waterline to highest point, she is at least 200 feet high. CVN-77 is an imposing structure that's been compared to the Empire State Building lying on its side.

Special Agent Lonnie Lincoln stood on the pier awed by the great ship. He spent four years in the Navy riding Kitty Hawk-class carriers – USS America and USS Kitty Hawk – while attached to the Air Wing. He thought those ships were big. They were but this ship was massive.

For two months, Lonnie and his team of FBI agents mulled over detailed blueprints of the carrier. They plotted out the routes each president would take from the pier to the Change-of-Command ceremony. They had a 3D digital model, courtesy of the Navy, to plan those areas of the ship needing extensive security reviews. The task seemed overwhelming. This ship has 1,600 miles of wiring, 246 miles of piping and over 5,000 personnel. Thankfully, the normal complement of 80 combat aircraft would be positioned at Oceania Naval Air Station.

"Okay folks, let's get going. We've got the weekend to conduct our searches and establish secure boundaries," Lonnie said over his shoulder as they started to walk up the boarding platform. Reaching the main deck he turned aft to acknowledge the national ensign and then to the Officer Of the Deck requesting permission to come aboard. He stepped onto the Quarterdeck and showed the OOD his credentials.

Lonnie talked with the Combat Direction Center duty officer to determine what plans were in place for the president. President Wolton requested a tour to see first hand the Navy's latest air, surface and subsurface threat assessment tools and weapons. CVN-77 just installed the newest Laser Weapon System, dubbed the LaWS.

The first deployments of LaWS took place in 2014, with great success. This laser weapon is designed to destroy small boats, drones and helicopters. Unlike Hollywood, there isn't a visible light beam. The system finds a target and the next thing that's observed is the target burning up. The Navy loves the system for various reasons – no ammunition to carry which reduces the possibility of accidents, plus a considerable savings in cost per 'bullet'.

Lonnie's cellphone vibrated in his pocket. The Navy, while standing on tradition, slowly progressed into the 21st Century. The USS Bush is one of several Navy ships outfitted with Pico-cells that give sailors access to cell connections in almost every area of the ship. "Lonnie. How can I help?"

"Lonnie, we need you to come to the second deck, right side uh, sorry, starboard," said Special Agent Wilson.

"Wilson, what's the frame and compartment number? The starboard side is a big area."

"Just a second. Let me look for one of those plaques." It took Wilson a few seconds to find the numbers and pass them to Lonnie.

"Ok. I'll be over in about 15 minutes. I'm just finishing up in CDC. Can this wait?"

"We'll wait for you."

THE OBJECT, slightly larger than a softball, looked like a Whiffleball with larger holes. Inside the ball structure were four small propellers and several smaller black objects.

"Looks like a toy drone to me," said Lonnie with a puzzled look on his face.

"We thought so too, at first. But we found it attached to one of the power cables in an overhead wire tray."

"Attached to a wire?"

"Yeah. The thing has a small clamp and wire. Probably allows it to siphon a trickle charge off the wire without compromising the cable's integrity."

"What do you think it's doing here?"

"We'll have to take it back to our lab and evaluate its functions."

"Excuse me, sir." interrupted a sailor who was an escort for the group, "That's probably one of Reggie's drones."

"Reggie who?" asked Lonnie as he took out his small notebook.

"Petty Officer 3rd Class Reggie Patterson."

"Where can we find Mr. Patterson?"

"He's an ET. Sorry, that's an Electronic Technician. Those guys are usually in the lab on the 02 level."

"Wilson," Lonnie said as he motioned to Wilson, "go to the Quarterdeck and ask the OOD to locate ET3 Patterson. Bring him to the Chief's Mess and then text me."

Lonnie talked to Petty Officer Patterson for almost an hour before releasing him. Patterson denied the drone was one of his but marveled at its sophistication. He said it wasn't any kit drone he'd ever seen. It had to be a custom build.

The petty officer mentioned this was the second such drone he had seen. The Captain threatened him with a Court Marshal if he continued to harass people onboard the ship with his drones. Reggie swore the drone wasn't his and he restricted his flying sessions to the ET Lab and sometimes in the hangar bay on weekends.

Lonnie sent the drone with a team member back to the lab at Quantico, asking for a rush evaluation. Something didn't seem right. To his remaining team members Lonnie said, "We'll need to thoroughly search all the cable trays and pipe runs within our established security zones. Let me know ASAP if you find any more of these drones."

CHAPTER FIFTY-ONE

SEPTEMBER 23, (Saturday)

Suak Seumaseh, Sumatra

The courier spent an entire day getting to Mohammed's base in West Ache. He handed an envelope to Mohammed who handed it to Junaedi. As the courier walked off to a nearby hut, Junaedi opened the envelope and slowly read the message.

Trying to hide his enthusiasm, Junaedi calmly summarized the letter. "Good news from our contact in Singapore. He sends confirmation that the American aircraft carrier Nimitz is scheduled to make a port visit at Singapore on 26 and 27 September before completing it's transit of the Malacca Strait on the 28th."

"That means we must leave no later than the evening on the 25th to be in position," added Mohammed. "Let's get the crew together tomorrow and give the ship a complete check-out. We can also get our supplies loaded."

Looking at the courier's note, Junaedi paused for a second before deciding to confront Mohammed. "Why are you preparing to leave?"

"We will watch the Great Satan die a horrible death," Mohammed replied with eyes wide with excitement.

"The Iranians fixed the mines to activate on their own. We will only draw attention to us and the mines," Junaedi said with frustration building. He could understand Mohammed's desire to watch the Americans die but the success of the mission was more important. "You will see the destruction over and over again on television."

"With my own eyes I wish to see them humiliated, Inshallah."

"What are we going to do with the camp?" asked a crewman.

"Send the women and children back home. Tell them we will join them in a week's time, Inshallah." Mohammed said.

"What about the courier?"

"Send him back to Jakarta in the morning but don't let him arrive," indicated Mohammed.

"Why should we kill him? He has been very helpful to us. How can he hurt us?"

"He knows too much. He saw the ship, the containers and probably what they hold. He realizes who we are and probably where we are going."

"We should just kill him now and throw his body in the sea."

"His family will come looking for him. Make it look like an accident. That will stop any investigation leading to us."

"Alright, Mohammed, I will make the arrangements."

CHAPTER FIFTY-TWO

SEPTEMBER 24, (Sunday)

Kentland Farms Flight Center

It was quiet at the KFFC as the sun started to sink behind the nearby ridge. Zak was standing outside the hangar, trying to get some fresh air to settle his mind and stomach. He hadn't slept well since his last meeting with the lawyers. It didn't seem like any progress was made toward getting his father out of prison. Zak spent some time praying for guidance. He felt a peace finally, knowing he had to do the right thing. He was glad Agent Baxter asked for a visit. When the time was right, he would explain his predicament. He would tell him the whole story about what the lawyers were making him do and hope that Agent Baxter could get him some leniency, at the same time getting the US government to pressure the Iranians to release his dad. Zak convinced himself that, if going to prison got his dad out of prison, it would be worth it. American prisons were much better than Iranian.

NCIS Agent Baxter drove along the narrow road leading to Kentland. He notified Zak he was coming to pickup one of Zak's hover drones to show the CNO. He bumped along the road and kept an eye peeled for any deer. It might be a little early for the annual rut but, at dusk, it was always good to stay alert. As he pulled up to the hangar, Baxter saw Zak's Honda CRZ, the only vehicle in the small lot. Zak was standing next to his car.

"Hi, Zak," said Baxter.

"Hello, Agent Baxter," replied Zak, holding back an urge to vomit. The tension was too much. He couldn't continue with the lawyer's demands.

In the dark, Agent Baxter couldn't tell that Zak just wiped a tear from his eye. "I'm glad you agreed to meet me on such short notice. I just got the request from the CNO's office this morning. He wants a demonstration of one of your larger toys. I hope this didn't inconvenience you?"

Zak took a deep breath, slowly let it out and replied, "No problem. I was going to be here anyway getting the drones, or toys as you call them, ready for my next attempt at gaining access to the control room."

Agent Baxter and Zak walked into the hangar and entered the hallway to the workshop, passing by drones of various sizes and shapes stacked on shelves and some in boxes. Zak tripped on a power cord laying on the ground and let out a curse. Baxter was taken by surprise. He had never heard Zak swear. "I'm okay," said Zak as he recovered. "Those freshman were in here all day and forgot to pick up. They can't seem to get things back in their proper place either."

"When are you planning your next attempt?"

"I don't have any classes on Monday so I thought I would go down to Virginia Beach this afternoon."

"Are you close to obtaining access to the control room?"

"This next attempt should get me inside or, at the very least, to the main hatch."

"Will you have the full scenario mapped and loaded in the drones for autonomous flight?" asked Baxter, trying to hide the excitement in his voice.

"Once I run the flight paths, I will review them on Tuesday and update the programs. If I can get into the control room, then you will have the complete package to present to the CNO. I hope you don't mind the extra expense of a hotel room? I'm just worn out and don't think I could leave here real early on Monday to conduct the test. I'd like to get the drones up and into the ship by 4:30 AM."

"I don't think it will be a problem. Any chance you can get the updated programming completed Monday afternoon or early evening and get it on the file in the MacBook Pro?"

"I could but I wouldn't have time to conduct a full review. I need a day off to just get my mind clear," sighed Zak.

"You look spent, Zak. Is everything alright?"

"Not really," sighed Zak again.

"Girl problems or exams?" questioned Baxter

"Neither. I don't know where to begin. It's all just terrible and I don't want to go to prison." Zak said with a tear welling up in his eye.

"Whoa there, young man. We told you that we would get you out of trouble if anything happened while you were doing this project. Have you been contacted by any authorities?"

Zak turned in his chair, placed his head in his hands and started to cry. "It's, it's not your project," he sobbed. "I've done something terrible."

"Do you want to tell me what's going on?"

"I think I might be helping some terrorists," Zak blurted out between breaths. At once, he felt a little better. That cleansing feeling after confession settled over him. He slowly sat straight up in the chair, turned toward Agent Baxter and said, "I've been coerced into stealing something from the Radford Ammunition Plant for the Iranian government."

Zak divulged to Agent Baxter how his father was imprisoned in Tehran and how two Iranian lawyers forced him into picking up packages from the ammunition plant at night. The floodgates opened and Zak felt better after each declaration.

"Let me get this right," interjected Baxter. "You picked up items with your hover-drones that someone placed behind a dumpster at the ammunition plant and took them to a storage locker in Christiansburg?"

"That's correct, sir."

"What's in the packages?" asked Baxter.

"I don't know. They told me not to open the packets and that they could tell if I did. I'm assuming that, because they are from the ammunition plant, that they must be explosives."

"This is serious, Zak. I need to get back to my office and start contacting the appropriate authorities."

"What will happen to my father? I realize what I did was wrong. I'm ready to accept the consequences. Can you help save my father's life?" pleaded Zak.

"At this point I don't know, Zak. I'll get my partner to contact the Department of State and we'll try to move fast to get the lawyers arrested. If they have Diplomatic immunity, then our only option is to kick them out of the country."

"Are you going to arrest me?"

"Not at this moment. Do I have your promise that you won't leave the area?"

"Yes," said Zak haltingly.

"I suggest you delay your plans for the next test. Keep your cell phone charged and I'll be in contact. Don't talk to anyone else. Right now I've got to get back to the office."

Agent Baxter plugged numbers into his phone as he walked toward the exit. "Reynolds. We've got a problem."

Agent Baxter filled Reynolds in on what Zak had confessed to him.

"You want me to make arrangements for an emergency meeting with the lawyers or send a message to our contact?" asked Reynolds.

"Let's meet with the lawyers and decide what we will do about Zak. We can't have him confessing his activities to anyone else."

CHAPTER FIFTY-THREE

SEPTEMBER 25, (Monday)
    Fredericksburg, VA
    Tallyho sounded in Agent Filmore's earpiece that alerted him to an incoming computer message. He was sitting in the FBI's Alexandria, Virginia Field Office command center. For the last hour, he had been monitoring the progress of a counter-surveillance training exercise taking place near the intersection of Possum Point Road and Highway 1 in Dumfries. Three new students were on their first night exercise. He opened the notice and read, "*Automatic License Plate Detection System reports Jubilant 1 approaching the southern limits of the 50-mile exclusion zone. Last identified location was at 2:15 AM passing the Route 243 exit on I-95. Movement is outside of normal patterns.*'

    When the FBI was briefed by Britain's MI-5 about ALPADS capabilities, they lobbied for budget money to get the system installed in all the US cities where embassies or consulates resided. After a couple of years, they discovered a huge cost savings in the physical surveillance budget. The system could automatically scan a car's license plate, take a picture of the driver and process the information instantly against a database of targeted numbers and facial recognition. The data was kept for one week and only information on targeted plates or personnel was retained indefinitely. The FBI could use the records to develop travel patterns on suspected intelligence operatives and assign surveillance teams only when activity was outside of the norms.

Agent Filmore selected a file that contained the code words for FBI persons of interest, entered another password and typed *Jubilant* into the search function. The computer opened to a file that gave the names assigned to Jubilant 1 plus the make, model and license number of all the vehicles used in the past. He returned to the home page and selected a link to the Fredericksburg Resident Agency (FRA) and sent the following text. *'Jubilant 1 passed exit 143 at 0215 heading south. Records indicate target has never been out this late at night or farther south than Woodbridge. Target has remained on I-95 since leaving DC. The Diplomatic plate number is DM 0418. The automobile is a Silver Mercedes C300. Request Fredericksburg availability to intercept.'*

FRA surprised Alexandria Field Office by responding almost immediately. *Agent Schofield is available in Falmouth. Will preposition at rest stop just south of the Rappahannock Bridge. Awaiting updates.*

Filmore clicked on his computer mouse several times, selected the file on Schofield and entered his phone number into the official cell phone.

"Schofield. Filmore here."

"Hello, sir. Do you have an update for me?"

"I do. You can call me Dan. I sure hope this doesn't turn into a wild goose chase. A lot of times these guys just forget to request permission to travel outside the zone. I'm guessing they are headed to Richmond for a little fun outside the prying eyes of the embassy."

"That could be. I'm Peter by the way."

"You took me by surprise with your quick response. What are you doing out and about at 0220?"

"I just got home from two-weeks of night shift baby-sitting an informant in that multiple murder case in Richmond."

"Well, Peter, I hope you don't mind a little drive. We'll continue to monitor ALPADS and give you updates. Do you think you can be in position at the rest area in under five minutes?"

"No problem, Dan. I live just west of the Highway 17 exit. I should be in position in three minutes."

Dan looked at the ALPADS screen showing the last captured image. "Peter, looks like we have a driver and passenger. I'm guessing the passenger is Jubilant 2. I'll run a facial recognition search to confirm."

"I understand, two targets. Send the photos to my phone please and I'll try to corroborate the information."

Filmore went back to the ALPADS and quickly calculated, *if the Iranians continued at their current speed, Peter should be in place 5 minutes before they passed his location.*

"Peter. I'm going to notify Richmond's Resident Agents of the activity so they can back you up. You can either contact me by phone or radio."

It was seven minutes before the silver Mercedes passed Peter's position. No sooner did Peter enter the interstate and get in position a quarter mile behind the Mercedes, than it moved to the right lane and indicated it was exiting.

"Peter, subject vehicle just exited onto Route 3 West. Confirm license plate DM-0418," Agent Filmore asked.

"Confirmed. DM-0418 exiting onto Route 3 West."

Peter stayed back about ten car lengths and watched the Mercedes make a right hand turn onto Carl D. Silver Parkway. Peter knew the area well. It was the Central Park Shopping Center and was filled with many small shops, restaurants and the big guys – Lowes, Best Buy, Walmart and Peter's favorite, Krispy Kreme.

Caught by a yellow light he couldn't risk trying to beat, Peter was unable to maintain contact. Within seconds though he let out a sigh of relief. He could see the Mercedes, stopped at the next light. Once the light turned green, Peter moved to the center lane until he saw the Mercedes turn left into the Walmart parking lot. The green turn arrow changed to red before Peter got to the intersection. He could still see the Iranians as they pulled into the small lot near the gas pumps.

"Alexandria, Jubilant 1 is parked at Walmart lot in Central Park. Taking up position to observe."

"Roger."

AGENTS BAXTER and Reynolds pulled up to the Mercedes as it parked in the small lot near the Walmart gas station. Baxter and Reynolds exited their car, scanned the parking lot and then climbed into the back seat of the lawyer's vehicle.

Turning toward the agents, the driver said, "Asr bekheir."

"English, please. We don't want to draw attention if someone walks by," demanded Baxter.

"Four guys sitting in a car at 3:00 AM in a Walmart parking lot isn't going to look odd?" commented one of he lawyers.

"We need to do this quickly. What did your contact suggest we do about the drone kid?" asked Agent Reynolds.

"Our contact says the kid has to be removed. He knows too much. We can't take the chance that he will tell someone else."

"Did the contact have any suggestions on how to terminate the kid?"

"Use some of the explosives you've gotten from the ammunition plant. Only a small amount is needed because it has an explosive power four times that of plain C-4," said the lawyer in the front passenger seat. "The explosive material is in research and doesn't have any of the chemical tags added to help law enforcement detect or track it. Your task will be completed before the forensic people can find a link to the Radford plant or us."

"The kid was planning on traveling to Norfolk to conduct what he believes is a final attempt to access the reactor control room. Do we want to wait until we get that data?" asked Baxter.

"No. Your orders are to eliminate him swiftly. Can you complete your task with the flight processes and equipment you already have?"

"We just finished producing the last of the drones on the 3D printer. We have enough UAVs to accomplish the job. Both Reynolds and I uploaded all the data and conducted simulated flights. The final data from the kid would increase the likelihood of success but we think we have sufficient explosives and delivery vehicles to create enough damage to satisfy the planners in Iran."

"We must get going before we draw attention," said the driver uneasily. "We'll be leaving for Frankfurt today. It would be nice to see something on the news about a Virginia Tech student's accidental death before we leave."

"Don't get too anxious. It will take some time to develop a plan."

"Why not use one of the kid's drones? Put the explosives in it and tell him it doesn't work. When he plugs it into a power source, it will blow him to pieces."

"That's a good idea. We still have to get back to our facility in Hampton Roads, install the explosives and deliver it to Blacksburg. That's going to take at least nine hours."

Agent Reynolds interrupted, "Wait. The kid wanted to be in the Hampton area early this morning. Why don't we let him know he has clearance to continue?"

"That's right. He's running his final attempt at the control center."

"Do you think he can get there in time to be productive?"

"We can tell him the CNO is eager to have the final results. He'll just have to adjust his previous schedule."

"Good. We'll contact him and pass off a defective drone for him to fix when he gets back to Blacksburg."

One of the lawyers sat shaking his head. "That will not work. The planners want the kid dead sooner than later."

"But that means going to Hampton, configuring the drone and driving all the way to Roanoke?"

"It must be done," said the lawyer in a tone that closed off any discussion.

Agent Baxter smacked the palm of his hand against his forehead, "Of course!" he shouted startling everyone else in the car.

"I've got a drone and some of the explosives in the trunk of our car. I just visited the kid to get one of the larger drones that the brothers wanted after I stopped in Christiansburg. I can replace the battery guts with some of the material and then tell the kid it's not working."

"That should work and save time."

"Well, we are done here? Time to get moving. Everything set for Thursday?"

"Yes, Inshallah," said Reynolds as he climbed out the car.

"Inshallah. Shab bekheir."

AGENT SCHOFIELD'S position near the Garden Center's entrance afforded him a clear view of the Mercedes C300 just as a blue Dodge Charger parked adjacent to the Iranians. As he reached for his radio, he noticed his hand was shaking from the excitement. He saw two men getting out of the Charger and get into the Mercedes. Less than five minutes later, they exited the Mercedes and both vehicles left the lot in different directions. Schofield was able to record the license number for the Charger --WKU-119, Virginia plates.

Peter kept the Mercedes under surveillance until he determined it was heading back towards Washington and north of Stafford.

"Our cameras will follow the vehicle from here, Schofield. Thanks for your assistance," said Dan.

"Do you want me try to find the Charger?"

"Negative. We've submitted the license plate number into the system for collection and a general BOLO for the car."

"Acknowledged. Returning to Falmouth."

"That's a negative. Please return to Walmart and obtain the parking lot surveillance video that covers where the meeting took place. Have the store's security person forward a digital copy to the Center. I'll need an incident report from you before noon."

"Roger."

Dan opened the Jubilant file and entered what had taken place, adding the license plate number of the Charger in the 'affiliated' section.

CHAPTER FIFTY-FOUR

SEPTEMBER 25, (Monday)

Kentland Farms Flight Center

Zak had been in a funk all day. He thought he would feel better now that he told the NCIS agent about his getting packages from the ammunition plant. Instead, he had dreadful thoughts that his actions put his father in grave danger. He prayed that the agents would be successful in getting his father released. He didn't care if he had to go to prison. Sadness flowed over him that was so enveloping he almost didn't hear his phone ringing in his jacket pocket.

"Zak, this is Agent Baxter. We're having problems with the hover-drone you gave us for the CNO briefing. We aren't getting a signal to the flight controls." After meeting with the lawyers, the NCIS agents decided to make the drive to Roanoke instead of having Zak come to Hampton. The loose end at the ammunition plant played into their decision. Better to eliminate the plant steward now rather than later.

"Have you run any diagnostics?" asked Zak.

"We had a glitch with our computer but the same problem persists even after a reset. We're almost to Roanoke. Can we meet at

TOPS' parking lot and give you the drone? We've got some other business in the area. We'd like to get it fixed quickly and get back to Washington to prepare before the briefing tomorrow morning."

"I can meet you at TOPS. I'm only 20 minutes away."

"Meet you there. Thanks, Zak."

"IT JUST STOPPED WORKING about ten feet off the floor and dropped," Agent Reynolds told Zak as he handed him the drone. "After that, we couldn't get it to accept any commands. Diagnostics didn't point to any particular problem. We're under a tight schedule and hope you can get it working as soon as possible."

The hover-drone, one of the larger ones Zak had provided the NCIS agents, didn't have any outward damage but he couldn't rule out issues with the wiring. "I'll have to take it back to the workshop and run some tests."

"We're going to be in the area until 8:00 PM. Can you get this fixed by then?"

"It's six o'clock now. If I can't fix it, I'll replace it with one I have on the shelf."

"That will work. By the way, we reported your information on the explosives to the CNO. We can't go through our normal channels because it would expose you and the project. It's going to take a few days to get things moving. By then we should have the State Department onboard. They will draft a démarche to the Iranians to release your dad."

"Oh. That sounds like great news to me," Zak replied feeling his heart thumping against his chest.

WITH THE NON-FUNCTIONING drone sitting on the passenger seat, Zak started back to his workshop. As the sun settled behind the tree line, he removed his sunglasses and fumbled for his prescription glasses. As he brought his eyes back to the road, he caught a glimpse of movement to the right. A deer bolted out of the cornfield and Zak slammed on the brakes. The drone slid off the seat crashing against the dashboard and careened around the foot well. Zak's chin struck the steering wheel hard enough to rupture the skin. Blood was dripping from the wound. Zak pulled a napkin from the center console storage to staunch the flow of blood. "Crap," he yelled as his hand pounded on the steering wheel.

Picking up the drone, Zak noticed the power cell had broken free of its mount and was lying on the floorboard. He picked it up, spotting loose wires ripped from the connectors. That would need to be repaired. He slipped the power cell into his shirt pocket. Three minutes later he was at the Flight Center.

Zak put the broken drone on the worktable and considered calling Agent Baxter to tell him to just come by and pick up a replacement. Instead, he decided the challenge of detecting the problem would take his mind off his father. It would probably require a quick fix and a rapid test. He gave the drone an overall visual look. The structural integrity looked fine except for a scratch or two. Those could have occurred when it was in the hands of NCIS. Moving to the diagnostics bench, Zak removed the power cell from his pocket and reached for a replacement from the bins on the shelf.

'That was odd,' he thought. 'The power cells feel different. The one from my pocket is heavier than the one from the shelf.' He shifted them from hand-to-hand and remained convinced the old one was heavier. He reached for a screwdriver and undid the screws. The interior didn't look right.

"Hi, Zak," called Dan as he entered the workshop.

Zak dropped the power cell onto the table and turned around, startled by Dan's appearance in the building. Instinctively he tried to conceal the power cell.

"What are you working on?"

Something told Zak he had to show Dan what he had found. Zak held out the power cell. "Something's wrong. This thing is filled with what looks like silly putty." Dan moved toward the table, took the object from Zak and stared at the interior of the cell. Zak was right. Where a specialized rechargeable battery should be connected was a 2 by 2 by 1-inch void filled with silly putty. Dan picked at it with his finger and the putty fell into his outstretched hand. Wires protruded from the putty. "What do you think it is, Zak?"

"I don't know." Zak was in a perplexing situation. He couldn't tell Dan who gave him the drone because of the secrecy of his support for NCIS.

"Let's see where these wires go," Dan said as he picked up an *Exacto* knife and begin separating the wires from the putty. A minute later Dan and Zak stood staring at a blasting cap. Shocked, they stepped away from the table. His voice cracking, Dan asked, "Zak, where did you get this power cell?"

Zak trying hard to hold his composure said, "I think I'm in terrible trouble."

"I think this is a bomb and that putty material is plastic explosives. Where did you get this?" demanded Dan.

Still trying hard to remain calm, Zak clutched a nearby stool to lean against. His head was spinning. Nothing was making sense. *Was NCIS using his drones as lethal weapons? Was it possible he was the target? From the looks of it, had he done his normal testing and powered up the drone, the blasting cap would have ignited the plastic explosives, killing him.*

His pulse raced. His breathing was shallow and quick. Trying to regain control of both, Zak just stared at the bomb for what seemed like a lifetime. Finally gaining a little composure, he looked at Dan. "I need to talk to someone I can trust. I'm involved in something I don't understand. I think someone wants to kill me." Slowly sitting back on the stool he explained to Dan what he did for the lawyers and now his suspicions about the NCIS agents. Looking forlorn and grasping for any possible help he said, "Dan, didn't you tell me that your dad was with the CIA?"

"My dad retired from the CIA but I think it's a good idea we call him," replied Dan as he pulled his cell phone from its holster and began dialing. A few moments later a connection was made. Dan put the phone on speaker. "Hi, Dad."

"Dan, what a pleasure," Karl said.

"Dad. I've got a problem. Actually, Zak has a problem that we hope you'll know who to contact. I've got you on speaker so Zak can hear too."

"I'll see what I can do. What's the issue?"

Dan hesitated and looked over at Zak who was pale and leaning against the stool for support. "Dad, someone tried to kill Zak tonight."

"What? Where? How?"

Trying to remain calm but unsuccessful, Dan blurted out, "NCIS tried to blow him up with a bomb. He's been stealing stuff from the Radford Army Ammunition Plant. The Iranians have his dad."

"Whoa. Slow down. You'll need to fill in a lot of blanks here."

Zak motioned to Dan that he would talk. "Mr. Mattingly. I would like to tell you the whole story, or at least as much as I understand, but I'm afraid our conversation might be overheard. I don't want to put you or Dan in danger because of something stupid I've done. Is there someone I can talk to that you trust explicitly?"

"Do you feel safe where you are right now?" questioned Karl.

"I'm not sure. I think, if the NCIS guys don't hear an explosion or hear about one, they might still come after me," Zak responded as the realization of his words started to sink in.

"In that case, don't go to your room. Leave your car. Dan, can you drive Zak here?"

"Sure, Dad. I don't have any classes until Thursday. I was just going to work with Zak on our drones."

"Leave now and drive straight here. I want you to text or call me every 30 minutes and give me a status on your location. Make sure you aren't driving and texting though."

"Alright. Zak will text and I'll drive."

"Don't get excited and exceed the posted speeds. Use caution and keep your eyes open for anything that looks suspicious. Do you remember what I taught you about picking out surveillance?"

"I do, Dad. We'll try our best," sighed Dan.

"Good. It's about three and a half hours with light traffic. I'll contact your sister and see what we need to do next." Sounding just a little perplexed, Karl continued, "Help me out though. How does he know it was NCIS that tried to kill him?"

As Dan and Zak were getting into the car, Zak held the phone and said, "I was working on a secret project for them related to the vulnerabilities of aircraft carriers to a massive hover-drone attack. They wanted me to access the reactor control room."

"Crap," was all that came out of Karl's mouth. "Be very careful. I'll have things lined up by the time you get here. Remember, every 30 minutes I want a location update."

"We understand, Mr. Mattingly."

"Zak, shut your phone off and remove the battery. I don't want to give anyone the possibility of tracking your movements. Only use Dan's phone."

"I'll do that right now, Sir."

As an afterthought, Karl said, "Do you feel safe bringing the drone and power pack? If you think it's unstable, don't."

"We removed what we think is the blasting cap. We can bring everything."

"Quickly take some pictures of the cap but only bring the explosive material and the drone," cautioned Karl.

CHAPTER FIFTY-FIVE

September 25, (Monday)

Mattingly Home

Karl slowly placed his phone on the counter as Liz entered the room.

"Who was that on the phone?" she asked.

"It was Dan. He and Zak are on their way here."

"You don't look good. Honey, what's wrong? Are they okay?"

"I've got to get in touch with Maddie. Zak is in some terrible trouble and it sounds like someone tried to kill him tonight."

Liz reached for the counter to steady herself. For just a moment she remained speechless. "Oh! Is he hurt?"

"They are both a little shaken."

"Both?" Liz interrupted grabbing the stool and sitting down, unsure if her legs would keep her upright.

"Yes. Zak and Dan were together." Karl saw his wife's face grow ashen. Coming around the counter he took her in his arms, holding her for a few seconds before continuing, "I told them to come straight here and call me every 30 minutes with a location. Maddie's in town, isn't she?"

"Yes, she's here. I think next week is when she has a trip."

"Here's my phone. If I don't get a text or call every 30 minutes from the boys, come get me. I'm going to my office and call Maddie on the land line."

"Oh no you don't, buster. You don't drop this on me without telling me more," demanded Liz.

"Fine. Come with me downstairs and you can listen as I fill Maddie in on what few details I have at this point."

Karl turned and poured himself a cup of decaffeinated coffee, all the time thinking he should make a pot of regular. This night would probably be a long one.

MADDIE HAD JUST PICKED up her purse and was about three steps away from her cubicle when the phone rang. She hesitated, trying to balance the thought of having dinner with Phillip or getting stuck with some additional project. Her dedication won out and she turned to pick up the phone, noticing that it was her parent's number on the caller ID. "Hi. I was going to call you tomorrow."

"Maddie. Sorry to interrupt whatever plans you may have had but we have a possible crisis," blurted Karl.

"Dad, are you okay? Is something wrong with mom?"

"Your mom and I are fine, it's Dan's friend Zak."

"I'm so sorry but I don't know how I can help," Maddie said with a little irritation creeping into her voice.

"Shug, bear with me. I've got the phone on speaker so your mom can hear all of this too."

"Hi, mom."

"Hi, Shug."

"Dan called me about ten minutes ago all in a fright, saying his friend Zak was in trouble. They gave me just a few details, enough to concern me, but wouldn't speak any more on the phone. Zak was afraid someone might be listening. I told them to come here right away."

"You have me intrigued but unsure how I can help."

"According to the boys, someone tried to kill Zak tonight with a bomb. He thinks its NCIS. He also said he's been stealing stuff from the Radford Army Ammunition Plant, something about his dad being held by the Iranians. I'm not sure how the Iranians play into all of this. Zak said that NCIS asked him to test the vulnerabilities of an aircraft carrier using his drones."

"Unbelievable!" exclaimed Maddie.

Karl leaned toward the phone and spoke with some anxiousness, "I think we need you here to talk to the boys and plan the next steps."

"I was just leaving to have dinner with Phillip. Can this wait until later tonight?"

"It's going to take the boys three hours or so to get here. You could come down right after dinner."

"Dad, our dinner reservation isn't until 8 PM."

"That's too late, Shug. I need you here before they get here so we can talk through a strategy. Bring Phillip along unless he has to be at work early in the morning. We can have dinner for everyone here."

"I'll call Phillip now and see if he wants to postpone dinner. We'll drive together."

Liz waved her hand to catch Karl's attention and asked, "Karl, if Zak's life is in danger, what about his family?"

Karl said, "Maddie, your mom just brought up a good point. Zak's family could be in danger. I recall that his mom and at least one sister live in Countryside, not too far from your apartment. If needed, could you pick them up on your way here?"

"I guess so. What does Zak think?"

"I'll call him right now and ask. I'll text you with an answer and address, if needed, shortly."

Fifteen minutes later Karl texted Maddie and asked her to pick up Zak's mom and little sister. *'Zak's mom is expecting you and*

Phillip.' They all decided that he could use his mom's comfort and support right now.

CHAPTER FIFTY-SIX

SEPTEMBER 25, (Monday)

Mattingly home

It was Liz's idea that they all sit down for dinner. Zak protested but his mom told him it would be beneficial to get some good food into his system before talking with Karl and Maddie.

Sitting around the table were eight people: Liz, Maddie, Mrs. Hashemi, Houda (Zak's little sister), Zak, Dan, Phillip and Karl. With heads bowed, Karl asked for God's blessing upon the food, safety for all those around the table, Zak's dad and for guidance and strength to confront what was before them.

Mrs. Hashemi was asked to explain the circumstances of her husband's incarceration in Tehran and the subsequent actions by the lawyers. In all, it sounded like a typical blackmail operation with Zak as the victim. Mrs. Hashemi couldn't provide too many more details since Zak was the family's sole representative at the meetings.

After dinner, Karl explained to Mrs. Hashemi, Dan and Houda that he and the others needed to speak with Zak in private. He would share as much as he could when the time was right. He explained that it was in their best interests, in the event that legal actions were required. Maddie, Phillip, Karl and Zak headed to the basement office.

Liz pulled at Karl's arm as he passed the central hallway, "Karl, don't you have to notify the FBI or police? Someone tried to kill that young man."

"At some point soon we will have to turn Zak over to the FBI. At the moment we need to find out what he's been doing and then take the appropriate steps."

Liz stood still, folded her arms across her chest and asked, "If he's involved in something illegal, are we harboring a fugitive?"

Placing his hand on Liz's, Karl smiled and responded, "You are correct. We could be sheltering a criminal. At the moment we don't have enough information to make an informed decision. Do you want to join us?"

"No," she replied, taking his hand in hers. "I know you will keep me up-to-date."

"MADDIE, grab my chair from the office and pull it around here to the den. You and Phillip can sit on the couch. Zak, please take the Lazy-y-Boy," Karl said as he lowered himself into his office chair. He preferred it over the other options for the extra support it gave his back.

"Zak," began Karl, "just so nothing was misconstrued during earlier introductions, I want to make clear to you who we are and what's going to happen." Pointing to his daughter, Karl continued, "Maddie is my daughter and an official with the CIA. Sitting next to her is my future son-in-law Phillip. He also works for the CIA. I trust both of them with any information you care to share with us. We are going to take copious notes and produce a report on what you tell us. Later this morning Maddie will brief her superiors and we will take whatever action is required at that time. Is that okay with you?"

"Mr. Mattingly, I will do what ever you want. I just want this nightmare to be over and hug my dad."

"I must also warn you that anything you tell us could be used to prosecute you in criminal court."

Karl thought that Zak would sink to oblivion in his chair. The young man held his head in shame, shoulders hunched so low they almost disappeared. "Mr. Mattingly, I acknowledge that I will have to suffer the consequences of my actions. God has given me a peace about all of this and I'm ready to help, no matter what happens to me."

"Okay, young man, let's start," said Karl.

Over the next two hours Zak poured out what had happened ever since his father was arrested in Tehran. He told them how the lawyers made him get packages from the ammunition plant – eight in total and all weighing about three pounds. He also walked though the request from the NCIS agents and everything he had accomplished.

"Do you have any documentation for any of this?" asked Maddie.

"It's all on the laptop they gave me. I kept a journal of everything I was doing and all my research related to the drones," said Zak excitedly as he rocked back and forth on the Lazy-y-Boy.

"Where's that laptop now?" asked Phillip.

"It's upstairs in my backpack. I grabbed it as we left the flight center."

Karl rose from his chair, considered hollering up the stairs but stopped when he remembered Zak's mom and sister were probably asleep in the room just off the landing. He walked over to his office, grabbed his phone and texted Dan, *"Look in Zak's bag for his laptop and bring it down here please."*

A few minutes later Dan poked his head into the den and handed the laptop to Maddie. "Thanks, Dan." Turning back toward Zak she asked, "How long has it been since you discovered the bomb in the drone?"

"That was about 6:30 PM, and its after 1 AM now, so almost 7 hours. Why?"

"From what you said, this laptop was given to you by the NCIS agents and they accessed your files remotely." Thinking out loud Maddie continued, "They may have already wiped the hard drive remotely."

Maddie passed the laptop to Phillip, "This is your area of expertise, techy." Looking at her dad, she asked, "Do you have an external hard drive or thumb drive around."

"I've got a Terabyte external but it's loaded with imagery. How about a 32 Gig thumb drive?"

Looking up from the laptop to Zak, Phillip asked, "How big are the files, Zak?"

"Total shouldn't be more than 15 Gigs."

"Fine." A quick check revealed no remote entry attempt and Phillip immediately started copying all the files.

Maddie was looking over her notes, paging through a bunch of yellow legal pad sheets. "Zak, tell me again what Agents Reynolds and Baxter told you at the first meeting."

"They said the CNO initiated several war games and determined that US ships were vulnerable to an attack by small drones. They wanted me to prove that I could get access into the depths of an aircraft carrier to include entry into the reactor control room. I really thought I was helping my country."

"Rest assured, Zak, that we will make sure the authorities are aware of all the facts as we have them," interjected Karl.

"Phillip and Maddie, do you need anything more at this time?"

"I'm fine, but I want to start making contact with Langley and get an alert out quickly. From the sounds of it, this could be the planned attack against the president we've been working for the last two weeks," Maddie said while holding her breath. "I've got to wake Ken and get the ball rolling."

"I just checked the files. Everything from the laptop is here," said Phillip as he held up the thumb drive. "I want to get this laptop to the office and set up a monitoring program to trace any remote access activity. That might give us a clue to the whereabouts of the NCIS agents. I'll take the drone and other materials for our lab to inspect," Phillip added.

"Dad, Phillip and I will leave now to get to Langley's secure phones and systems. I suggest Zak try to get a good night's sleep." Turning to Zak, she took one of his hands in hers and looked into his eyes. "These people took advantage of you. What you did at the ammunition plant was wrong but I think people will understand. I will try my best to convince them. I need your promise that you will not leave this house unless accompanied by my father."

His head hung in disgrace. Zak took a moment but then raised his head to look at Maddie. "I promise I will do what you ask. I owe my life to you."

"We are all governed by God's plan. I suggest you spend a little time in prayer, thanking Him for surrounding you with people that care about you and love you."

"I will."

CHAPTER FIFTY-SEVEN

SEPTEMBER 26, (Tuesday)

CIA Headquarters Langley, VA.

Her head held at a slight angle to the right and fingers attacking the keyboard, Maddie didn't hear her boss call her name.

"Maddie," Ken said a little louder. "Where do we stand?"

Startled for a second, Maddie turned her chair and faced Ken. "I've put out a Directors' Only message alerting them to the probable threat against the USS Bush. I've contacted the Watch Office, DNI, NSOC and the White House Situation Room with the current information. Homeland and FBI are expanding the task force to include looking for the lawyers and the probable false flag NCIS agents."

"Good. The DCI will be here in about 30 minutes and wants you to bring him up to speed. Walk with me to Division. Yasha is already here and wants to get briefed on the situation."

"Ken, I don't have time for all of that. Can't you do it?" pleaded Maddie.

"Wish I could. Powers-that-be want it from you, even though I told them you were working the research for links."

"Can't they just read my memo? I covered every aspect of what we know, what we are doing, who's been notified and what our immediate next steps entail."

"You know the 7th floor motto – Why read when you can listen. Besides, it doesn't leave a paper trail," smirked Ken.

By the time Maddie finished talking with Yasha, it was time to brief the DCI. It was almost an hour and a half before Maddie got back to her desk. Upon refreshing her computer, she saw 75 new emails marked Urgent and it wasn't even 6:00 AM. She needed caffeine.

CHAPTER FIFTY-EIGHT

SEPTEMBER 26, (Tuesday)

DHS Headquarters

"Look at this!" said Alexander holding up the CIA alert cable. "Why didn't anyone call me?" He was almost screaming as he looked around the conference room. Zeroing in on Molly, Alexander took out his frustration on her. "We've been saying all along that the intercepted message was a threat against the presidents. This proves it. The target was the USS Bush and, based on the Virginia Tech kid, it would probably happen soon. Well, that soon is this Saturday, 28 September, when POTUS and FPOTUS plan to attend the Change-of-Command ceremony."

"We don't know that for sure," came a very tentative response from across the table.

"Bull hockey. It's all right here in the memo from CIA: explosives stolen from the Radford plant by Iranian lawyers and fake NCIS agents planning on attacking the carrier with drones. What's not sure?" demanded Alexander.

Fearing Alexander's wrath but still trying to make her point, Molly responded, "We don't know if the two parties are linked.

There's nothing that links the lawyers and NCIS agents. We don't even know if the agents are imposters. Granted, we can make those assumptions but we don't have proof."

"Then let's find those connections. Molly, work with the FBI and track down the whereabouts of both parties. Contact me as soon as you learn anything. It's 6:30 AM. I want answers before 8:00 AM. Wake your contacts up if you have too."

Alexander left the conference room in huff. How come they couldn't see the connections? This was it. This was what the threat message was all about. Kill the presidents when they are all aboard the USS Bush. Maybe they thought they could make it look like an accident by striking the reactor room.

Alexander returned to his office and sat at his computer. He sent a quick email to Lt. Davis at NSA. The two of them had become fast friends over the past two weeks as they worked toward resolving the threat message. *"Ed, hope you saw the CIA memo outlining the threat against the USS Bush. I'm sure you agree that the Change-of-Command ceremony is the target. You got anything else off the wires?"* He would have to wait until 8:30 to get a response from Ed. *"Just arrived in the office. Looking over the night's traffic now. Will let you know."*

CHAPTER FIFTY-NINE

SEPTEMBER 26, (Tuesday)

Oval Office

"Let me get this straight," said the president as he glanced at the small group sitting around the coffee table. "The Iranians are trying to kill me and the former presidents?"

The National Security Advisor uncrossed his legs, shifted position on the couch and placed his coffee mug on the table. "Based on the information provided by the CIA, it appears a valid plan exists to blow up the USS Bush. DHS believes that your planned attendance at the ceremony on Saturday is the impetus for the attack."

"Do the intelligence agencies and DHS think the terrorists will get the word that we've cancelled my appearance on the USS Bush?"

"No one wants to confirm that the threat is over or that the carrier is safe from attack."

"Typical. They might as well be weathermen," uttered the president.

"I've convened a meeting for later today to discuss our options. We want to locate the perpetrators before they can do any harm."

President Wolton settled back into the armchair as his right hand unconsciously groped for a pack of cigarettes in his left sock. He was a heavy smoker during his early days in the Navy. To keep his shirt pockets clean and neatly creased, he, like most of his fellow sailors, kept a pack of cigarettes tucked in a sock. Smoking had become such a habit then. Even now, after quitting 20 years ago, he still felt the urge to pull out an unfiltered Pall Mall, tamp it on his wristwatch to pack down the tobacco and then flick his Zippo lighter. He had used that activity over and over again to give him time to think, especially when he was angry. It was the equivalent of counting to ten.

CHAPTER SIXTY

SEPTEMBER 26, (Tuesday)

FBI Field Office - Norfolk

Special Agent-in-Charge Richard Vitalli looked out his office window at the blazing street lamps that illuminated the perimeter of the FBI's Field Office – Norfolk. Technically it was located in Chesapeake, Virginia on the edge of a swamp. His domain covered almost nine acres; surrounded by 2,500 feet of chain-link fence, microwave motion sensors and those powerful street lamps. They were so bright it was difficult to see into the darkness beyond the perimeter. He shrugged his shoulders and thought, '*Not much to see anyway. An edge of the swamp, a farmers field that rotated corn and soybean crops and traffic on Highway 168 – known to locals as the Great Bridge Bypass.*'

Vitalli just got off the phone with his wife, explaining to her why he was going to be late and why he didn't know when he would be home. He blamed it on FBI Headquarters. After all, they told him to keep all assigned agents in the building, cancel leaves and order anyone on leave within the immediate area to return to work. HQ was sending a team to brief everyone at 8:00 pm.

What they didn't tell Vitalli was how large a team they were sending. For twenty minutes he watched unmarked Suburban tactical vehicles and special communication vans enter the vehicle gate and proceed to the covered parking area. The main gate parking was packed with local law enforcement vehicles from all of the greater Hampton Roads districts. Vehicles were parked at nearby office lots and the occupants were walking along Resource Road to the Field Office.

Special Agent Vitalli was happy that the architect for this building anticipated an event such as this by adjoining two large conference rooms with a temporary wall. Vitalli's deputy informed him at 7:30 pm that the conference room was near, if not at, fire code capacity. He wasn't going to take a head count to make sure.

Sitting on Vitalli's couch with a phone jack from his Blackberry plugged into his ear was Special Agent Tinsley, Chief of the FBI's Counterterrorism Division. Tinsley gave Vitalli a very brief overview of the developments surrounding the threat against the president and the debriefing of a Virginia Tech student involved in stealing explosives. Tinsley was here to brief and manage a task force committed to finding those personnel intent on assassinating the president.

"That's the latest?" Tinsley said as he got up off the couch and motioned to Vitalli to follow him. "What if we have more questions? Yes, I will send them as they occur. Thanks."

Tinsley reached out and touched Vitalli's arm, bringing him to a halt. "I intend to be as brief as possible so we can get these guys on the street. I will be here as long as needed and we can discuss best management practices with the local law enforcement. How many liaison officers do you have available?"

"Just two," said Vitalli but even he knew that sounded insufficient for the tasks ahead.

The loud din of multiple conversations could be heard 30 feet from the conference room door. As soon as Vitalli and Tinsley entered the room, the sound nearly vaporized. You could have heard a cockroach scurrying for cover.

Both men headed for the lectern set up just to the right of a large movie screen. Vitalli was a bit taken back as he saw himself on the big screen and then realized the entire session was being recorded for review or for new personnel brought into the Task Force. Vitalli stepped to the lectern and leaned into the microphone. He tapped it twice and received the reassuring 'tac-tac' that it was working. "Ladies, gentlemen, guests, I'm Special Agent Vitalli, Agent-in-Charge of the FBI's Norfolk Field Office. I thank you all for braving the swamp (a short chorus of laughter could be heard) and joining us. I'm going to turn this over to Special Agent Tony Tinsley, Chief of the Counterterrorism Division." Glancing back at Tony, he stepped to the side and down the short step to a seat left open for him in the front row.

After a quick survey of the room, Tony stepped up to the microphone. "I too extend my thanks to all of you for responding on such short notice. I appreciate your concerns that spouses, children, family members and significant others will require appeasement over the next few days as you work long hours. I'm here to convince you that those hours will be worth it and that your families will thank you for your dedication.

"Almost three weeks ago, NSA intercepted a message that threatened to kill the presidents. Two theories were offered – 1. An attack against POTUS and all the living former presidents. 2. An attack against US Navy aircraft carriers or buildings named after presidents. Two days ago, a student at Virginia Tech turned himself over to the CIA and confessed he had used his drones to remove packages from the Radford Army Ammunition Plant. Although he never opened the packages, we are under the assumption the packages contained explosives. A task force is at Radford right now beginning an investigation. The CIA and the FBI are currently continuing to interrogate the student. Here are the highlights," said Tinsley as a list of items appeared on the screen.

Elaborating on the bullets, Tinsley said, "The Virginia Tech student was completing a Master's degree in Aerospace Engineering

– focusing on hover-drones. He's known throughout the country as one of the best, if not the best, hover-drone pilot in the United States. He was being blackmailed by the Iranian government, forced to pickup the pre-positioned packages from the Radford plant in hopes of obtaining his father's release from an Iranian prison. The kid's story checks out so far. He picked up at least eight packages, each weighing about three pounds. Possibly related to this activity is chatter in the Middle East about a new Super C explosive that CIA's DS&T analysts think is C4 on steroids. Of specific concern to us are two, possibly more, personnel intent on attacking the USS Bush during the Change-of-Command ceremony scheduled for this Saturday. Individuals posing as NCIS agents approached this kid and convinced him to work on a special task from the CNO. They said the CNO was trying to determine the vulnerability of aircraft carriers to drones while in port. Over the course of a year, the kid was able to penetrate the interior of the USS Bush. His drones got all the way to a passageway outside the reactor control room. DHS is convinced one or more explosions were to occur in this vicinity while the presidents were touring the control room spaces. The CIA thinks an attack was planned to significantly damage or even destroy the carrier.

Looking over the room, Tinsley saw he had the attention of every officer. "We will let the intelligence analysts work out that issue on their own. We have the task of finding and neutralizing the threat against the USS Bush no matter what is planned for a finale.

"We have detailed plans from the kid, including proposed launch points for swarms of drones. These were all made available to the fake NCIS agents. Last Friday, the 22nd, an FBI and Secret Service forward security team began preliminary searches on the USS Bush. During those searches, a small, sophisticated hover-drone was discovered in some overhead wires. The Virginia Tech student identified it as one of his. A thorough search of the ship is ongoing.

"A BOLO is out for the two NCIS impersonators based on information provided by the student. In your packets you will find photos, license plate numbers, vehicle information and proposed launch sites. I've taken the liberty of assigning initial tasks to local law enforcement and have assigned a special agent to each team as liaison to this command center.

"Please work through your normal chain-of-commands. I believe this will facilitate the movement of information and orders."

The screen flickered for a second and a map of the area was displayed. "The plan is to work outward from the USS Bush. FBI and NCIS-Norfolk, along with Norfolk Base Security, will handle all searches on the Naval Base. Local jurisdictions will handle all areas under their control." Tinsley paused for 20 seconds, scanned the room until he felt he had regained everyone's attention. "While finding the NCIS imposters is important, we can't be sure they are working alone. Locating the drones is paramount. Thank you all for your dedication to this task. Are there any questions?"

A police officer, about midway down the conference table, stood up and asked, "If the carriers are the targets, why doesn't the Navy just send them to sea?"

"Very good question, officer. The CNO, in conjunction with the White House, does not wish to unduly increase the public anxiety nor disrupt plans for the Change-of-Command ceremony."

"As a follow up comment, sir," continued the officer, "am I to understand that 5,000 plus men and women and an eight billion dollar aircraft carrier are being placed in jeopardy because the CNO fears raising the anxiety level of the public?"

"Officer, your pay grade and mine were not consulted when the decisions were made. We are simply to follow orders. Any other questions?"

Fifteen minutes later the conference room was empty except for the police chiefs of each local area, the assigned special agent for each, Vitalli and Tinsley. For the next hour they discussed procedural issues for orders, reporting and de-confliction. By the time the meeting broke up, the first field reports were received in the Command Center. No trace of drones was found at the two launch points provided by the student.

CHAPTER SIXTY-ONE

September 27, (Wednesday)

Pulau Jemur, Malacca Straits

The only movement Junaedi could feel on the tramp steamer was caused by the wakes of passing ships. Sometimes, when two large ships would pass in opposite directions, a riotous collision of waves would toss the little ship about like a cork.

Standing next to him at the rail of the flying bridge, watching night befall the Strait was Mohammed. As leader of the operation, Mohammed could hardly contain his excitement, conscious of the fact that less than 10 km away lay his destiny – twelve naval rocket mines resting on the bottom of the Malacca Strait, awaiting the Great Satan's pride and joy.

"Tell me again, brother, why do we have to be here? Those mines will explode by themselves. We shouldn't be here!" insisted Junaedi.

"They will explode by themselves. From here we will witness the lethality."

"We risk being discovered and boarded if we remain here," Junaedi said, clearly upset with Mohammed.

"My brother, please know that I wish us no harm. Do you not

want to savor watching the destruction of the Great Satan's symbol of power? Is not the observation, in person, more compelling than seeing it on a television newscast?"

"I am only concerned about the Americans catching us."

"How can they? They do not even know the mines are already lying in wait for them. We are a simple vessel, stopped at anchor trying to repair an aged engine."

CHAPTER SIXTY-TWO

September 27, (Wednesday)
Willoughby Split, Virginia
The Norfolk Police Department cruiser pulled into the Willoughby Harbor Marina parking lot at 4:30 am. Officers Staves and Inaton slowly emerged from the vehicle. It had been a long night of searching all parts of Willoughby Split.

A morning marine layer of fog was just developing and promised to hang around for several hours. Visibility would drop to a couple hundred feet. Both officers knew that spelled trouble for the morning commuters. Crazy fog. It could be crystal clear and sunny on one section of Interstate 64 and almost immediately plunge a car into dense fog. The commuters still thought they could travel at 70 miles per hour through the stuff and be worry free. Both officers had investigated deadly accidents in the past because drivers wouldn't slow down.

Looking over at the Sunset Grill slowly enveloped in fog, Officer Staves verbalized what Inaton was thinking, "Wish the Grill was open. I'm getting hungry."

"I am too but we've got to search these properties for drones and those NCIS phonies."

Willoughby Marina was located on the south side of Willoughby Split. The marina provided protected berthing for many sailing vessels that used the normally calm waters in the adjacent bay. In a few hours, the place would be packed with day sailors. Getting here early would allow the officers to search unimpeded by gawkers.

"Are we going to break this up and get done faster or search together?" Inaton asked his partner.

"Let's split up. I'll take the marina," Staves said as he started walking toward the dock.

"Not fair!" shouted Inaton to Stave's back as he disappeared around the Marina building. "I'm not digging in any smelly dumpsters again."

The marina had five main piers, some with additional finger-like projections to accommodate specific vessels. Overall, the berths were filled mostly with sailboats and the occasional large motor craft. Several small day-fishing charter boats were also present. Officer Staves made his way down each dock, stopping sporadically to chat with a boat owner awakened by the sound of footsteps. The questions were always the same: have you observed any unusual activity, seen anyone that looks like this, as he showed them the composite sketches of the NCIS guys. He left his business card with each person encountered and asked them to call if they saw anything suspicious.

"What's your status, Staves?" crackled over his radio.

"I'm just about done. Got to hike around to the point and look at that barge moored to the dredger. Probably take me another 20 minutes. Why?"

"I've checked everything here. I'll wait for you in the car unless you want help?"

"Go sit on your duff, partner. I've got this."

It took longer than expected to hike around to the point. *'Man, I'm getting out of shape,'* he thought as he tried to catch his breath. He finally reached the quay where the barge was moored. In the middle of the barge was a large canvas covering measuring 10 by 14 feet estimated Staves. On the farthest end of the barge was a metal shipping container. Staves thought it was 20 x 6 x 8 feet. He'd have to look over both items to feel confident nothing was left unchecked.

He had a slight problem. The barge was loosely moored and about three feet from shore. *It's probably stuck on the bottom since it's low tide,* thought Staves as he pulled on a rope without success. Staves looked around for an old plank or anything else he could use to span the distance from shore to barge. He remembered seeing an aluminum ramp back near the boathouse but going back for it seemed like too much work.

'I can just jump,' he reasoned. '*Its only three feet to the barge and a drop of maybe two feet. I can stretch that far to get back. Might be a plank under the tarp,*' Staves continued to process in his mind. '*Not a long jump. I used to compete in the long jump in high school at much greater distances.*'

Officer Staves approached the seawall edge, balanced himself and squatted into a long jump takeoff position. He swung his arms a couple of times to build up his courage and momentum. With one more full swing behind him, he began to lean forward and at the same time he started to straighten up. As his arms went past his centerline and moved forward, he felt his feet leave the seawall. He had failed to calculate two important items: the fog had left a heavy dew on the seawall making it slippery and he was carrying 20 pounds of police equipment around his waist. Instead of going forward, his feet went up making his head fall backward. He felt his head strike the seawall for a nano-second before blacking out and hitting the water. His clothes soaked up the water and he sank beneath the brackish waters leaving just a trace of bubbles.

Ten minutes later, "Are you done yet, Staves?" asked Inaton over his radio. "Come on, Staves. Don't make me come down there."

After trying several more times, Inaton moved over to the drivers seat and drove the patrol car around the marina building and down the access road along the small peninsula. The road was very bumpy and rutted making travel slow. The fog was denser here and contributed to the caution Inaton was taking. He could barely make out the A-frame structure of the dredge when he stopped the car.

"Staves. Timothy. Where are you?" he yelled at the emptiness. Walking along the seawall, he shined his flashlight over the water until he caught a glimpse of the barge. He tried to illuminate the barge but the fog was too thick. His powerful flashlight just provided a cone of bright fog.

He called out again for his partner but got no response. He noticed a splotch of blood on the seawall as he turned to go back to the cruiser. In a smooth, natural reaction, he pulled his service revolver and grabbed his mike. "Injured officer, Willoughby Harbor Marina at the peninsula."

CHAPTER SIXTY-THREE

September 27, (Wednesday)

USS Nimitz – Singapore

"Cdr. Buehl, the skipper would like to talk with you," said the Marine Corporal.

"Thank you, Corporal. Is he in his quarters?"

"Yes, sir."

"Good. I'll walk back with you," the ship's navigator said as he grabbed his Toughbook. "It's rough having duty when we're in such a nice port."

"I'm heading for shore as soon as my watch is over, sir."

"Going any place in particular, Corporal?"

"A few of us are going to Gardens by the Bay. I'm told it's a fantastic botanical garden with some really cool sculptures."

"Good choice. I went yesterday and it was amazing. If you have time, try the cable car ride to Mt. Faber. Fabulous view and a nice place to have a Monster Green Lager."

"Thank you, sir. I'll mention it to the guys."

Both men were quiet as they climbed several ladders and ducked through the 'knee-knockers'. "Enjoy your day, Corporal."

'You too, sir."

Cdr. Buehl knocked on the skipper's stateroom door. "Enter," said a gruff voice behind the door.

The Skipper, or Commanding Officer of the Nimitz, has the rank of Captain. Compared to other accommodations on the ship, his were palatial. As Cdr. Buehl was walking toward the Skipper's desk, he was waved to take a seat on one of the couches. "Thanks for coming on such sort notice, Ben."

"Your command, Skipper. Not good to ignore it," laughed Ben as he settled into the soft couch under the three portholes.

"I want to discuss our route options based on the threat message from Washington," said the Skipper as he moved from behind his desk and sat down next to Ben. "Seems the Secretary of Defense is covering his butt. Much of the message lays out support for a threat against the president. That last paragraph concerns me. The CIA's objection holds considerable support for the theory that all aircraft carriers named after presidents are the target."

"That's ten carriers. That would entail a massive planning effort, certainly something state-supported. Especially if the plan is to strike simultaneously."

"True. We've got ships spread out around the world. How's someone going to destroy us?" the Skipper said with a look of indifference.

"Are you considering a change of route to the Persian Gulf?"

"What do you think? I really don't want to delay our arrival. The Washington has been on station for a long time and is eager to get home."

"Well, we could run back down the coast of Sumatra and take the Sumatra Strait instead of going through the Malacca Strait. We would have less exposure to nearby land but add two days onto the trip."

"That won't work. Is there anything we can do to speed up our trip as planned?"

Ben looked at the charts on his Toughbook before answering.

"Regulations restrict us to no more than 12 knots in the Straits. Once we get out we can run at 30 knots."

"I'm uncomfortable with how close we have to steam by Indonesia and Malaysia while we're in the channel. I chatted with the Air Boss earlier and he thinks we can coordinate with the rest of the Carrier Group and keep two helos aloft during the transit."

"Any chance we can launch a couple of E-2D Hawkeyes? Fly one up to Phuket and switch them out during the transit? That would give us an additional platform to watch small craft," asked Ben as he worked the distances on his computer.

"The Air Boss suggested the same thing. I like it. I'm going to put the ship on a modified General Quarters and post marines on outboard watch stations. I wish we had those new Laser guns but they wouldn't give them to me. They said we were too old of a ship," the Skipper said with a sour taste in his mouth.

"I'll set up a track that includes a launch window shortly after we leave anchorage tomorrow. We can also try to open up the space between the Carrier Group and us during transit. That should give us a better view and earlier warning if some small boat or boats try to swarm us."

"Thanks, Ben."

CHAPTER SIXTY-FOUR

September 27, (Wednesday)

Norfolk Area

Even after the fog lifted, the police couldn't find any trace of Officer Staves. They put police tape all around the marina area and brought in a K-9 crew. Nothing was found until high tide. A Navy diver finally got under the barge and located Stave's body pinned against the bottom of the barge.

It was now 6:00 PM and twilight was beginning to affect the scene. Most of the patrol vehicles had left the marina. Two officers remained on site awaiting orders from the chief to stand-down.

Several wooden planks now spanned the distance between shore and the barge. Officer Calhoun was perched on a bollard, his thoughts focused on an imaginary fishing pole in his hands. He was just about to cast when he heard a hushed curse from his partner.

"Calhoun, do you hear that buzzing?" Officer Samantha 'Sammy' Sartorius said with a note of apprehension in her voice.

"I don't hear a thing, Sammy."

"I hear buzzing coming from that shipping container."

Officer Calhoun dropped down from his perch and started to walk alongside the container. "Ok. I hear it now."

"I'm getting out of here," Sammy said as she turned for the makeshift bridge. "I'm allergic to bee stings and my Epi-pen is in the car." As she neared the squad car, she turned and saw several globe-shaped objects slightly larger than a softball exit the top of the container. Quickly grabbing the squad's radio she yelled into the mike, "Chief, this is Officer Sartorius at the marina. We've got some of those drones flying out of the shipping container on the barge."

"10-4, Sammy. Can you contain them?" asked the chief as he motioned to his deputy to call the FBI Task Force.

"We can try," she replied as Calhoun removed his service pistol and took aim. The sound of gunshots could be heard through the open mike.

"What the hell is going on, Sammy?" the chief asked in bewilderment.

"Calhoun is shooting them out of the sky. I don't think that will be of much use. I've seen at least 25 leave the container."

"Do something to stop them! We've notified the FBI."

"Calhoun," she yelled over the gunfire as she ran back to the barge. "Help me get on top of the container."

"Why do you want to do that?"

"Chief wants us to stop those things from getting out. I'm smaller and lighter than you. All I need is a boost to grab the top. I can pull myself up then. Hurry!"

Calhoun placed his back against the container and put his hands together as a foothold. Sammy placed her foot in his hands and her hands on the side of the container to steady her balance.

"On three, Calhoun."

It was a smooth move as Calhoun hoisted her up. He almost tossed her completely to the top. Scrambling along the surface, she saw the gaping hole at one end of the container. More and more drones were flying out each second. "Calhoun, grab something to cover a 3 by 3 foot hole. I'll try to block as many as I can while you get something."

Sammy crouched near the opening and shifted her body so her legs hung down in the hole and started swatting at the drones with her baton. She felt like she was playing 'Whack-a-Mole' at Busch Gardens. "Come on, Calhoun, I need something fast!"

Officer Calhoun glanced around the barge for anything that might cover the hole. He quickly cut the ropes that secured the tarp and dragged it to the corner of the shipping container. He pushed a corner of it toward Sammy with his nightstick. It was just enough height so Sammy could grasp the corner. She pulled the tarp over the hole. The buzzing continued, a sound that still unnerved her.

Reaching up to her lapel mike, Sammy called the Chief. "Container secured, Chief."

"Good work. How many drones were released?"

"'I'm guessing about 50-60, Chief."

"An FBI Team headed to you now. Keep those things contained."

"10-4, Chief."

"Calhoun, I'd feel a lot better if we had something a bit sturdier to cover this hole. Can you drag those planks over here?"

"GENERAL QUARTERS, General Quarters. All-hands man your battle stations. This is not a drill. Repeat, this is not a drill," blasted from the 1MC aboard the USS Bush.

Sailors on the mess deck had momentary 'deer-in-the-headlights' looks but immediately headed for their assigned battle stations. One petty officer was overheard muttering as he ran down the passageway, "We're in port, at Norfolk for Pete's sake. Who's attacking us?"

"Now hear this. Now hear this," hissed the public address system – known as the 1MC or less lovingly as the 'Bitch box'. "All Marine personnel onboard, report to the armory for weapons issue and immediately take posts to repel boarders."

A flurry of activity was interrupted by the Skipper's voice, "This is the Captain speaking. We have received word that an unknown number of drones have been launched from a small barge at Willoughby Marina. The FBI believes we are the target of a planned attack. All cautions to protect life must be maintained. Standard General Quarters reporting procedures are in effect. That is all."

"Where are they? I can't see anything beyond the lights."

"Just keep looking, Private. The drones have to enter the lighted area to get to us."

APPROXIMATELY 75 DRONES converged on a rendezvous point halfway across Willoughby Bay awaiting the next sequence of commands from the relay drone hovering at 10,000 feet above the Veteran's Hospital in Hampton. Agent Reynolds stood on the roof of his apartment building at Litchfield Close in Hampton, Virginia. As the bird flies, he was only 6.5 miles from Carrier Pier on Norfolk Naval Base. The relay drone positioned over the Veteran's Hospital allowed him to direct commands to the drones without any interference.

Reynolds and Baxter weren't supposed to launch the drones until early tomorrow morning; however, an emergency text message told them to move the operation forward to tonight. Baxter was positioned at the truck weigh station off I-664, south of the Monitor-Merrimac Memorial Tunnel and adjacent to the Nansemond Treatment Plant. Baxter had a large trash hauler semi trailer in the parking lot of the weigh station. If anyone asked, he was having engine overheating problems and waiting for a company tow truck.

Baxter was seven miles from Carrier Pier but line of sight to the relay drone allowed him to utilize it for commands too. In the back of his truck were over 150 drones. Only 50 were armed with the Super C4++ explosives. The rest were tasked with keeping the USS Bush's defenses engaged, if needed, while the 50 armed drones maneuvered toward the Reactor Control Room.

HIGH ABOVE NORFOLK HARBOR were four Autonomous Real-time Ground Ubiquitous Surveillance Imaging System (ARGUS) reconnaissance drones, launched and controlled by the CIA but authorized by the Secretary of Defense. Each of these highly specialized drones could image a small to mid-size city in a single frame with continuous video coverage, day and night. Tonight, the four drones were looking at Hampton, Portsmouth, Virginia Beach and Norfolk. Downlinks served operation centers at the Pentagon, FBI HQ, FBI Field Office Norfolk and the CIA.

After Zak's story was reviewed, the NSC authorized a full court press to negate the threat against the USS Bush. Not knowing when or even if the drone would be used against the carrier, Phillip had suggested using the new technology offered with ARGUS. CIA's DS&T had worked with the contractor to enhance the special drones capabilities. ARGUS was quickly deployed to Norfolk.

Sitting in CIA's Ops Center were Ken, Maddie, Karl and Zak. The area immediately around this small group was partitioned from the rest of the Ops area by temporary panels. Two security officers were also present to maintain watch over Zak. "What should we look for, Zak?" asked Maddie.

"My last foray used one relay drone at approximately 10,000 feet altitude. I was able to control all the drones from 10 miles away. Most of the approaches to the USS Bush were already mapped and loaded into the command drones. I tried to find routes that helped cover the drones approach with cluttered backgrounds but also isolated areas that wouldn't alert people on the ground."

"You didn't make this easy, Zak," Ken said as he surveyed the image on the large interactive screen.

"We have word from the FBI that your selected launch points

were empty but they just reported activity at Willoughby Marina," Karl said as he activated an enlargement of the marina on the computer screen. "I'm not aware of all the bells-n-whistles for this system so bear with me. Here's the marina and the barge in real-time. I'm going to back it up one hour and quickly look at the activity. We can only go as far back in time to 1600 hours when the ARGUS drones were launched."

"My drones are only eight inches in diameter. The relay is 20 inches in diameter and is an Octo-copter," added Zak.

"We may need to lower the ARGUS to increase our resolution. I don't want to do that yet until we have a better fix on the activity." Karl switched back to a real time view and let the impressive ARGUS software do its job.

The first version of ARGUS, developed in 2013, could monitor an area about 3.5 miles in diameter. The 'autonomous' part was the Ground Exploitation System that could monitor upwards of 70 moving targets. Those targets could be cars, trucks, planes, people and even birds. Analysts could display up to 65 different video windows from the overall image. The data could be shared with several intelligence services at the same time to assign analytical work and corroborate on observed activity. Today's version of ARGUS was several magnitudes better and CIA was keeping the full capabilities classified. What could be shared was the unique ability of the ARGUS software to mosaic the feeds from the four units into one seamless image over the Greater Hampton Roads area.

Glancing at the 'Tasks' selection on the menu bar, Ken reviewed the assignments. He displayed the overlays on the screen and said, "FBI Norfolk is reviewing activity at Willoughby and those areas outside of the Norfolk Naval Base. The Navy is searching all of the area under its command at the Atlantic Intelligence Command's Fusion Center. The 48oth Intelligence Surveillance and Reconnaissance Wing at Langley is concentrating on Hampton and Newport News neighborhoods. We've been assigned Portsmouth north of Highway 164 from the Elizabeth River to the Highway 17 Bridge for starters. Once we've cleared that area, we are to start looking south of Highway 164."

"That's a huge area," groaned Karl. "The immediacy of our issue suggests we need more eyes on the targets. I think Milo's team at NGA could help."

Ken took a moment to reflect on the tasks ahead and then said, "Karl, you get started and I'll make arrangements with NGA. What areas should they concentrate on that will help you?"

"Get someone to look at all waterborne craft along the Elizabeth River and then along the James. Another person can concentrate on rooftops and industrial parks for suspicious activity. I'm going to review the roads and then help with the public areas like parks, schools, etc.

'I'll have Zak and Maddie start working on Zak's planned paths of approach to the carrier. Maybe by working backwards we can detect a launch point."

CHAPTER SIXTY-FIVE

SEPTEMBER 28, (Thursday)

Malacca Strait

Commander Ben Buehl was up long before dawn, taking his place on the bridge as the USS Nimitz prepared to maneuver through the congested waters around Singapore.

"Now hear this, now hear this. All hands, man the sea and anchor detail," was the message broadcast over the ship's 1MC. It was 0500 hours.

At 0600 hours they picked up the Strait's pilot who would navigate the ship through the Malacca Strait over the next twelve hours.

"Pilot on the bridge," said the officer-of-the-deck.

Turning to his computer, Ben released STRAITREP 9 to the Malacca Strait Control Center. The Strait Repot was required by all vessels over a certain tonnage to identify their call sign, speed, heading, time and pilot's name at each of nine reporting sections of the straits.

Ben kept that all in mind, thankful that the Strait pilot calmly navigated this route daily. In the background, he heard the Air Boss grant permission to launch the Search-and-Rescue helicopter.

The SAR helo's task would be more difficult today. The weather forecast was for steady winds of 5 knots from the west. That meant the smoke coming from the forest clearing operations on Sumatra, a result of illegal lumbering, would blanket the Strait, reducing visibility to less than a kilometer at times. All hands on deck were apprised of this and told to report any suspicious activity to the bridge immediately. Ben looked over yesterday's satellite image of the area and noticed three 4-5 kilometer wide bands of smoke. If the southwest monsoon winds increased today, they might have to slow down to fewer than 10 knots. The next images weren't due until about 1000 hours local.

Two seamen flushed the final chain links on the starboard anchor with fresh water as it was retrieved and secured. The normal hustle and bustle of getting underway on the USS Nimitz was interrupted by the piercing sound of the bosun's pipe that preceded an announcement over the 1MC. "Secure from sea an anchor detail. Secure from sea and anchor detail. Now, set the special sea and anchor detail. Set the special sea and anchor detail."

"Bravo Zulu, Mister Combs," the skipper said as he settled into his swivel chair on the bridge. "You got us underway in record time. Commander Buehl, what's our course?"

The navigator quickly glanced at the plot table and replied, "180 true, sir. In thirty minutes we can launch the Hummers. Air Boss is standing by."

"Carry on, Commander.

"Aye, Aye, Skipper."

'ACTIVITY on the flight deck always looked like a traffic jam trying to sort itself out,' thought the skipper as he peered out the bridge windows. He knew, of course, that it was a highly scripted and rehearsed scene, intended to keep personnel safe and government property intact.

Two E-2D Hawkeye Early Warning aircraft from VAW-123, branded as the 'Screwtops', were positioned on catapults ready for launch as soon as the Air Boss gave the order. The distinctive hum of the turboprops gave the airplane its common nickname – Hummer. One Hummer would fly directly to Phuket, Thailand and be prepared to replace the other Hummer after four hours.

Each aircraft had a black and white design on top of the radar dome. When the dome turns, the pattern gives the appearance of a screw being turned. The radar can search for enemy aircraft, ships and missiles at ranges greater than 400 miles and simultaneously track over 2,000 targets.

Launching these surveillance aircraft to provide cover while transiting the Malacca Strait is an unusual move for a Carrier Group. The confined space of the Strait and the overlapping air space restrictions for Singapore, Malaysia, Indonesia and Myanmar makes coordination difficult, but not impossible. The skipper spent much of the night discussing his options with the CNO and Defense Ministers of the various countries. All except Myanmar were understanding and supportive.

The skipper watched the first Hawkeye catapult off his ship. Just after launch, the aircraft sank below the bow and struggled to gain altitude. Slowly, ever so slowly, it reappeared and turned to starboard; the eight-bladed propellers digging into the warm moist air like a drowning man grasping for a log to keep himself afloat. Three minutes later the second Hawkeye went through the same routine.

THE MALACCA STRAIT comprises a 435-mile long narrow and busy waterway. A Traffic Separation Scheme is in place for the 250-miles covering the most difficult stretches for navigation. Shipmasters and experienced pilots face many challenges. These seasoned seamen all report that cross-traffic, involving small local craft unfamiliar with internationally agreed upon regulations and practices, is the greatest threat to a safe transit. At 12 knots, trying to stop a 90,000-plus ton mass before it collides with a small dhow, sailing or fishing vessel is a challenge no carrier captain wants to experience.

Shortly after welcoming the assigned Strait's pilot onboard, a MH-60R Sikorsky Romeo helicopter lifted off the Nimitz's deck and began search operations ahead of the carrier and the battle group.

Lt. Patricia 'Bosco' Gibson and Lt. Walter 'Battleship' Sims finished the checklists and began what they hoped would be three hours of uneventful flight. Lt. Gibson's nickname from childhood followed her into the Navy. She loved Bosco Chocolate Syrup, to the extent she poured it on scrambled eggs, in her coffee and even on saltines. At 6'6" and 240 pounds, Lt. Sims' broad shoulders and huge biceps made him look like a battleship. He was the Airborne Tactical Officer and co-pilot. Chief Jorge served as crew chief and systems operator.

"Hyper-vigilance is today's mission," Patricia said over the internal mike. "I want constant video streamed back to CIC. The Weather-Guesser said we can expect some periods of dense smoke so I want FLIR and LIDAR on standby." Forward Looking Infrared and Laser Illuminated Detection and Ranging were two tools onboard the Sikorsky that helped with visual identification.

"Copy that," came the reply from Jorge.

The MH-60 Romeo helicopter reached an altitude of 1,000 feet and turned northwest. Bosco planned to run parallel to the starboard side of the battle group, watching for movement from the small surface vessels that were in close proximity to the Nimitz. She and the rest of her crew would look for surface objects in the ship's path and attempt to classify them as benign or dangerous. Her Romeo was armed with several Hellfire missiles and a door-mounted 7.62 mm machine-gun. She would use the bullhorn to persuade any errant vessels to turn away from the Nimitz. Firing her machine-gun as a warning was a last resort. Lt. Gibson figured that her greatest challenge was the slower vessels that the Nimitz would pass in the narrow passages and choke points of the Strait.

THE MORNING MARINE layer slowly burned away as the sun rose above the horizon. Commander Buehl checked the radar for the disposition of surface contacts around the Nimitz. With a little surprise in his voice, he asked the Quartermaster, "Where did that ship come from?" pointing to a large blip on the scope directly astern of the Nimitz.

"It was in the lineup as we entered the westbound lane, sir."

"Looks awfully close. What's the range?"

"Range is six thousand yards, sir."

"Have we identified her?"

The quartermaster highlighted the blip on her scope and read the information displayed, "She is *The Star* and belongs to the China Ocean Shipping Company. She's one of China's newest container ships; one of the largest in the world at almost 400 meters long. Bigger than us, sir."

"Keep and eye on her and let me know if she gets within five thousand yards."

"Aye, aye. sir."

CHAPTER SIXTY-SIX

September 27, (Wednesday)
DHS HQ

Alexander was alone in his office trying to wrap his head around the recent activity. The CIA and FBI debriefing/interrogation notes from Zakari Hashemi seemed to support CIA's claim that the threat was against the aircraft carriers. No smoking gun clearly connected the Iranian lawyers and the false NCIS agents with the threat message. Alexander still wasn't convinced. The recent nearly successful attack against POTUS in Michigan weighed heavily in favor of more attempts on the president's life. He had to convince the director.

He knew it was an uphill battle. The ongoing search for the drones at Norfolk had the attention of all the NSC members. His director was sitting in the Situation Room right now watching some of the live feeds. He believed this might be a diversion intended to make all the security details relax their guard after negating the current threat. Alexander knew that the Secret Service would recommend the White House continue with the Change-of-Command ceremony if this current threat was resolved tonight. He had to lay out his argument and speak with the director tonight as soon as she returned to the building.

CHAPTER SIXTY-SEVEN

SEPTEMBER 27, (Wednesday)

CIA HQ Operations Center

"We are patched into a conference call with all the other agencies, Zak. I want you to tell them what you just told me."

"Okay, Mr. Mattingly," Zak said with some hesitation. He halted for a moment, wanting to make sure he didn't fumble over his words. "I was just thinking about my approach plans to the USS Bush with Mr. Mattingly. He thought it might help give you an idea of how the drones might approach the carrier."

"Go ahead, young man," came the command from the Situation Room.

"I wanted to have as much back-clutter as possible while I maneuvered the drones to the ship in the event the defenses were using radar, infrared or even night-vision goggles. That would make it more difficult to pick out the drones from the background.

"Each time I sent drones into the carrier, I launched them down the James River, staying less than three feet above the water. I had video coverage for the path ahead that warned me of any obstructions. As the drones got closer to the carrier pier, I broke them into separate groups.

"One group would travel into Willoughby Bay and cross over the huge parking lot east of the pier, flying just above the vehicles. I almost lost a bunch of them one night when a motorhome was parked on the perimeter of the lot. The second group hugged the bulkhead and flew under the piers until reaching the Bush's berthing spot at Pier #14. I brought this second group all together under that last pier before proceeding into the ship."

"This is Karl Mattingly speaking," interrupted Karl. "Zak told us that all these flight paths were logged into the computer that the NCIS agents accessed on a regular basis. We can assume that they've studied those approaches and might follow a similar approach. Zak always entered the carrier through the hanger bay doors. If those doors aren't already closed, they should be!"

"We will get acknowledgement from the skipper," barked the CNO as he reached for a phone and asked the Watch Office to connect him with the USS Bush.

"It's possible that the drones launched from the barge at Willoughby Marina are programmed to come across the parking lot," Karl said as he swung his attention to the ARGUS live feed. "ARGUS is giving us an indication of movement near the fishing pier. Its algorithms are suggesting the movement is caused by a flock of birds."

"The Bush has the LaWS, doesn't it?" asked the DNI looking at the CNO.

"It does, but we've never tested it against objects as small as these drones," responded the CNO, shaking his head.

"Our key target is the relay drone. Unless the controller has line-of-sight to the drones," Karl said as he returned to the monitors but not finishing his thought, "That drone should be a large enough target for the LaWS. Am I correct?"

The CNO took a moment to remember the LaWS specifications from a recent briefing, "Yes. That should be a big enough target."

"Okay, we'll make adjustments to the collection algorithms on ARGUS and pass positional data as soon as it's available."

Karl walked over to the ARGUS control monitor and briefly explained to the operator what was needed. It took the operator less than a minute to feed the new requirements into the system.

Zak caught Karl's attention as he returned to his monitor. "Shooting down the relay will cause the controller or controllers to lose contact with the drones. The drones I flew all had a safety command to return to the launch point if a signal was lost and await reactivation."

"Did you have any indication of a lost signal on your control console?" asked Maddie as she tried to factor the various pieces of information, intent on discovering the location of the NCIS agents.

"I had three small LED lights, green, yellow and red, that told me the strength of my signal connection. If the relay is destroyed and the drones start to return to a launch point, they will search for a signal," Zak said excitedly. "If these guys followed my protocols, the command drone from each batch would leave the group and gain altitude. I set mine at 1,000 feet. If they didn't find a signal by the time they reached that height, they would return to the launch location."

"Let's hope they plugged in your procedures," said Maddie as she developed a plan. "Before we shoot the relay down, can we tweak the collection for the signatures showing up for that group of drones by the fishing pier?"

"Sure we can. What do you have in mind, Maddie?" asked Ken.

"This is all predicated on finding and destroying the relay."

Intrigued, Ken said, "Go ahead."

"The launch point for at least some of the drones was the Willoughby Marina. If we focus on anything that begins gaining altitude, we might get lucky and track the drones back to a controller."

"I like it!" Ken said with excitement. "Let's find that relay."

"Your request is answered," Karl said moments later as he highlighted the relay drone hovering above the Veteran's Hospital in Hampton.

Switching back to the conference call, Ken asked, "Is the Bush CIC online?"

"Roger, sir."

"Can you run a firing solution against the relay drone based on the ARGUS feed?"

"Working that now, sir."

Ken took a moment to update the rest of the members on the conference call concerning the CIA's plan. After a minute of questions and answers, the CNO gave his approval.

"CIA, this is Bush CIC."

"Go ahead, CIC."

"We have a firing solution and are prepared to destroy the relay on your command."

"We'll be with you in a moment. We're tweaking the system to follow the smaller drones."

"Copy that, sir."

CHAPTER SIXTY-EIGHT

September 27, (Wednesday)

Weigh Station at I-664

Agent Baxter was sitting in the cab of a Peterbilt truck that was attached to a trash hauler trailer. He was parked at the weigh station on I-664, just south of the bridge and the Monitor-Merrimac Tunnel. He already pulled back a portion of the canvas top meant to keep trash from blowing all over the highway, allowing an opening for his cargo. Over two hundred small drones were in a forward compartment, isolated from the trash that was used as a cover in the event he was stopped and his cargo inspected. Now all he had to do was wait for Reynolds's signal that the mission was a go.

A 'tally-ho' sound erupted from his phone informing him of an incoming text message. 'Kashteen Bush. Allahu Akbar!' Baxter slowly exhaled. The time had arrived. Years of planning were about to pay off. He could finally return to Chechnya as a hero. If the Americans placed a price on his head, so be it. He would be a martyr. 'Allahu Akbar' he texted back.

Baxter reached for the small control box sitting on the center console and activated the power switch. Moments later he pushed the programmed flight button, saying a quick prayer that the Virginia Tech kid knew what he was doing. He could barely hear the low buzz from the drones as they left the trash trailer and began their mission.

He started the timer on his watch knowing he had to stay put for five minutes as the drones approached the Norfolk Naval Base along the Elizabeth River. If he didn't get a signal from the relay drone confirming transfer of command, he was to wait an additional 10 minutes for all the drones to return to the truck.

CHAPTER SIXTY-NINE

SEPTEMBER 27, (Wednesday)
USS Bush and Norfolk Harbor
The USS Bush was at battle stations and all four laser weapons were activated. Marines, armed with shotguns and M-16s, were deployed on the flight deck and the four aircraft elevators.

Inside the CIC the tension was high but all those hours of training was paying off; sailors calmly reported to their duty stations as the Captain received the latest update from the Joint Forces Command.

"Sir. A probable control drone was located in position over the veteran's hospital in Hampton. A firing solution is ready for your approval," Lt. Krishton informed the skipper.

"Thank you, Lieutenant," replied the Captain as he gave a "thumbs-up" signal to his Weapons Officer indicating he could commence firing.

The LaWS platform on the aft port quarter of the ship quickly turned to the assigned azimuth and the firing tube elevated to the proper angle. The LaWS looked like a large telephoto lens mounted on a rotating platform. Ever since the successful tests conducted by the USS Ponce in the Persian Gulf, the Navy fell in love with the laser weapon.

The Weapons Officer initiated the firing sequence when he pushed the Fire button on his console. The LaWS generated a 30-kilowatt blast through a small, invisible beam. The very narrow beam burnt the central mass of the control drone in approximately three seconds. Crewmembers watching through binoculars saw a puff of smoke and a short blast of flame as the drone plunged to earth. ARGUS detected the blast and highlighted the location on the overview screen at Langley's Operations Room. Cheers were brief as Karl and the others began looking for indications the other drones were swarming to await re-contact and new orders.

Within a minute ARGUS detected two possible swarm locations. Karl focused on the area between piers 11 and 12 where his display showed small objects just above the water surface. As he watched, he could begin to make out individual softball-size drones just like those Zak built for the fireworks display at Virginia Tech. All the objects formed into a large ball-like shape and remained stationary. Karl knew the LaWS would be ineffective against this target because the pier blocked the LaWS' angle of view. Suddenly, one slightly larger drone broke from the configuration and began gaining altitude.

"I've got a control drone gaining altitude between piers 11 and 12," Karl said excitedly into the microphone. "If these guys didn't change Zak's parameters, it should ascend to 1,000 feet in search of a signal from the main control drone. Failing that, it should regroup with the rest of the objects and head back to the launch location. I suggest we let that process take its course."

"Copy that," responded the CNO, "unless they continue to approach my ship."

"I'm hoping that whoever launched the drones is sticking around in the event problems were encountered," Karl added.

CHAPTER SEVENTY

SEPTEMBER 27, (Wednesday)

Weigh Station at I-664

A quick look out the front window and a check in his side view mirrors told Baxter he was still the only truck parked in the weigh station lot.

His phone chirped causing him to suddenly panic. He picked the phone up off the truck's center console, answering it without looking at the caller ID. "Baxter," he said trying to keep his breathing under control.

"We have a problem," was all that Reynolds said before adding after a long pause, "with our control drone. I no longer have connection."

"How long since last contact?"

"At least 4 minutes. I think something has happened."

"Let's abort the mission. I'll leave for the safe house as soon as the drones are recovered," Baxter said trying to keep his composure. "We can evaluate our next move from there."

"Stay calm, my friend."

"Maasalam."

"Ilalika!"

"THEY'RE on the move and headed south," Karl blurted out to those sitting near him and into his mike. His gaze was stuck on a small blackish shape moving across his screen.

"Do you know where they are going?" asked the CNO in response to Karl's open mike.

"I don't, Admiral, at least not yet. All I can tell you is they are headed south, moving out and away from the base."

"Keep me appraised, immediately, if they turn back toward the piers. I've put the USS Arlington at General Quarters. She has one of the LaWS mounted above her landing platform and is berthed outboard on Pier 5. She has authority to fire at any returning drones."

"Thanks, Admiral. I hope it doesn't come to that."

Karl continued to watch the drones' flight path away from the naval piers. After a few moments, the mass changed direction towards the southwest on a heading of 230 degrees. Karl quickly traced a line along that azimuth and queried ARGUS history for any previous activity similar to that being displayed by the drones. What seemed to Karl like minutes was only a few seconds. A marker popped up on the screen just north of the Nansemond Treatment Plant.

Maddie looked at her dad and Ken before saying, "They launched a group of drones from that shipping container at Willoughby Bay. Do you think they would have done the same from the south?"

"That's possible. We can ask ARGUS to identify any objects that meet the criteria of a 20 or 40 foot shipping container. The options might be endless. Even a pickup truck could hold these things," Ken said sadly.

TEN MINUTES PASSED and Reynolds still didn't have an indication that the relay drone was working. He picked up his phone and sent a text to Baxter. 'No connection to relay. Shutting down. Going to Ahvaz.'

Baxter acknowledged as he reached over and turned the ignition switch. The Peterbilt's engine sprang to life. The first drone appeared above the truck just as Baxter engaged 2nd gear and started to pull out of the weigh station. He stopped abruptly and considered his next move. He could remain in place and recover the drones or get on the road. Leaving meant the drones would congregate at the weigh station until their batteries died. The alternate was to proceed to the safe house as indicated by the code word Ahvaz. He decided to stay.

ARGUS FOLLOWED the swarm of drones to the weigh station and watched as they entered the open area at the end of the trailer.

FBI's command center sprang into action. The commander asked for all unmarked cars in the vicinity and across the river in Hampton to stage at locations he would assign. No attempt would be made to stop the trash truck. FBI hoped the driver would lead them to a control center or fabrication building. Only then would they attempt to apprehend the driver.

Based on NSA's input from recently captured intercepts, there was a chance the other pseudo-NCIS agent was in the Greater Hampton area. All they had to do now was allow ARGUS to track the truck.

Karl was impressed with the choreography of police and FBI movement. ARGUS' parameters were adjusted to capture the GPS data sent by each unit. Once it went active, the FBI commander had a visual of the deployment and could manipulate movement to keep the trash truck always boxed in but never coming closer than two blocks.

"He's just entered the Monitor-Merrimac Tunnel."

"Truck acquired coming out of tunnel," said a calm voice sounding like an air traffic controller. The voice continued a turn-by-turn account of the truck's movement for the next ten minutes.

"Target remaining on Hampton Beltway.

"Turning west on I-64.

"Taking exit off I-64 toward Harpersville on Hampton Roads Center Parkway.

Without injecting any emotion the voice continued giving a turn-by-turn report. "Just took the northbound exit for Big Bethel Road."

"Looks like he's headed for the Hampton Dump," interject the FBI commander.

"Think you're right. He just turned left onto North Park Road."

Agent Baxter parked the trash truck among several others at the Hampton Dump and walked the 300 yards to his automobile parked in the employee lot. Setting up at the dump was good cover for their operations. Now he had an hour-long surveillance detection route to run before arriving at Ahvaz. His only consolation was that Reynolds was doing the same thing. Before heading out though, he needed to get some food.

"Target is making some aggressive moves in the Saunders neighborhood. He might be running an SDR?" commented the FBI commander. "Everyone, stay alert and listen closely to directives from the Center. We have eyes on the target and I don't want to spook him."

For forty-five minutes Baxter ran a route that took him through Hampton, across the Coleman Bridge, north on Route 17 to White Marsh, Gum Fork and Sassafras before returning north on Rte-17. He exited Rte-17 again and passed through Plain View and Cologne before turning left on Highway 33 headed for Shacklefords.

"What's he doing?" asked someone on the radio net.

"It's a classic Surveillance Detection Route. His turns and back roads are all meant to flush out anyone following him. Taking the bridge back over the York is meant to funnel any tails making it easier to detect if he's being followed."

Just before crossing the York River, he pulled into the unofficial truck parking lot adjacent to the west side of the Puller Bridge. He got out and urinated next to a group of bushes before returning to the highway and heading south. His last diversion was taking Farmer's Road into Barhamsville were he made another aggressive surveillance move by ducking into Barham Woods Drive at a fast rate of speed, drove around the cul-de-sac before making a left turn back onto Highway 30. ARGUS almost lost him when it appeared he took the exit for I-64 but instead he just pulled off the road under an overpass, waiting for a few minutes. He eventually left Highway 30 at La Grange Parkway for Mt. Laurel Road. He turned off at Ware Creek Road. About a half mile down this gravel single-lane road, he pulled into a driveway and parked in front of a singlewide trailer that had seen better days. He parked next to Reynolds' car and walked up to the trailer.

"We got 'em!" came the excited voice.

"Let's get set up. I don't want to give them time to collect their thoughts and get back on the road," said the FBI commander.

Two FBI SWAT teams, standing by at Langley Air Force Base, were immediately ordered airborne. As the crow flies, they were only 33 miles away. Their trip would be longer, taking them out over the York River to avoid air traffic around Newport News/Williamsburg Airport.

While the helicopters made a path up the river, local police were directed to lock down all the secondary roads leading to Ware Creek Road. The only chance for escape would be through the swamp and woods.

One of the ARGUS drones remained on station giving continuous live video of the trailer. As the helicopters approached and began Fast-Rope deployment, Baxter exited the trailer door and began shooting. He managed to wound one officer before crumbling under return fire. The team lead called for Reynolds to come out with his hands up. After a tense minute, Reynolds walked out of the door holding an AK-47. He began to raise the weapon but never got the barrel higher than his knees before being dropped by an FBI sharpshooter.

CHAPTER SEVENTY-ONE

September 27, (Wednesday)

White House Situation Room

Tony Tinsley, the Special Agent in Charge of the FBI's Counterterrorism Division, was wrapping up his briefing for the National Security Council with a summary.

"Today's coordinated activities resulted in the deaths of two probably deep cover Iranian agents who planned to destroy the USS Bush by blowing up the reactor rooms. Current assessments suggest their plan would have put the Bush out of commission and contaminated a large portion of the Greater Hampton Roads area.

"Analysts are scouring documents found in an apartment rented by the agents in Hampton. Downloads for their vehicle GPS revealed numerous trips to the Washington D.C. area that coincide with movements of Iranian Embassy personnel.

"The Virginia Tech student, Zak Hashemi, confirmed these were the two men who posed as NCIS agents and tasked him with 'helping the Navy.' Mr. Hashemi has been released on his own recognizance awaiting legal action."

"Thank you, Tony," said the president. "Did any of the recovered documents and digital records indicate that other carriers were at risk?"

"Nothing was noted after cursory checks but analysis is continuing, sir."

"Thank you."

"Mr. Secretary," the president said as he turned to look at Hollis Lundgren, the Secretary of State. "I want a démarche to go out today. Strongly worded to the Iranians demanding the immediate release of Pastor Hashemi. I also want them to arrest whoever planned and supported this effort to either assassinate me or destroy one of our aircraft carriers or both. They can start by extraditing the two lawyers. The US demands access to any and all perpetrators of this incident. Tell them that time is of the essence."

"I will take care of that immediately, sir."

POTUS turned to the other council members and asked if they had any further questions. When no one spoke he dismissed the group saying, "Mark, come with me to the Oval Office please."

"Certainly, sir,' he replied as he followed the president out the door.

As they walked down the hallway, Chester placed his hand on Mark's shoulder and said, "Great job getting those guys. Keep the pressure on all of the organization for a thorough review of the captured data. I want to be able to tell the CNO and DHS they can lower the alert levels."

"I understand, sir. Consider it done."

"One more thing. Work with Maggie and clear an hour on my calendar to meet with Karl, Maddie and Sam in my office." He paused a second and continued, "Without their bosses but with their immediate family members. I want to thank them for their excellent analysis and tenacity." Pausing for a split second, he added, "Add the drone kid to the list."

"Sir, do you think that's a good idea? The kid is possibly facing jail time for what he did."

"Okay. Keep his name off the list but still bring him here with the rest of them. His information was invaluable in saving the Bush."

CHAPTER SEVENTY-TWO

September 28, (Thursday)

Malacca Strait

Lt. Gibson held her course alongside the battle group. She was always impressed with the massiveness of the combat ships and the firepower each carried. From 1,000 feet above the water, she could barely see the two destroyers and the cruiser, spaced two thousand yards apart, in front of the carrier. When she made the turn down the port side of the group, she could see the small frigate behind the carrier, overshadowed by a huge container ship.

"Scramble 1 to Eagle's Nest," Patricia said into her lip mike, "we completed our first revolution and are preparing to pass alongside your starboard side. Will maintain 1,000 foot elevation and 50 knots."

"Copy Scramble 1. Starting second evolution."

Cmdr. Buehl stood on the starboard bridge wing and waved to Bosco as she flew by. He thought he may have detected a return wave but wasn't sure. He knew that she and her crew were busy scanning the water surface for suspicious objects and trying to make quick judgments about small craft movements. He doubted she had time to wave back.

With the Strait's pilot onboard and in command, Ben only had to occasionally check his charts to confirm the pilot's instructions. He stayed out on the bridge wing as long as possible to watch the bustle of activity in the Strait.

"Sir," the Quartermaster called to Ben, "*The Star* has approached within 5,000 yards."

"Thank you. Keep me informed if she gets closer, please."

"Based on her speed, she's projected to come alongside in about two hours near Raleigh Shoal."

Ben walked over to the chart table and highlighted the Raleigh shoal area on the electronic map. What he saw didn't make him feel very comfortable. The Raleigh Shoal area didn't allow any maneuver room outside the very narrow shipping channels. Getting passed by a huge container vessel in that section of the Strait had the potential for disaster. "Can we raise *The Star* on radio?" he asked, looking at the Commo Officer.

"We'll work on it, Commander."

"Try to get *The Star* to slow down a little bit and remain at least 5,000 yards back."

"Will do, Commander."

Ben went athwart ship to the port side bridge wing, picking up a pair of binoculars along the way. He brought them to his eyes and adjusted the focus before centering the container vessel in the field of view. He felt his heart skip and thought, *'that's one big ship.'* Counting the levels of containers stacked on the deck he came up with a total of nine full levels and a tenth that was partially filled. *'That ship must have ten thousand containers,'* he silently remarked.

AFTER THREE HOURS of flying circles around the battle group, Bosco and her crew gently landed on the Nimitz's deck and headed for the Ready Room. Their relief crew was already airborne and headed up the starboard side of the Battle Group.

"We've got a four hour break," she said to her crew. "Get something to eat and report back here at 1145. We'll do a walk around and then return to burning circles in the air. I'm going to check with the weather guessers about conditions for our next flight."

CHAPTER SEVENTY-THREE

SEPTEMBER 28, (Thursday)

Malacca Strait

On the gleaming red painted bridge of *The Star*, Captain Xiang handed the ship-to-shore phone to a nearby crewmember and mumbled under his breath, "How dare they threaten to report my actions as unsafe. I have just as much right to this channel as those Americans in their warships. I have a schedule to keep and won't slow down just to accommodate a nervous captain."

The crewman, dressed in clean, neatly pressed white overalls with the blue China Ocean Shipping Company's logo embroidered over his left front pocket, cautiously took the phone from the captain and returned it to its holder. He sheepishly looked at his fellow crewmember on the bridge and shrugged his shoulders. *'Was the captain going to explode?'* he asked himself. The crew knew that Captain Xiang had a quick and violent temper. They also knew he didn't like Americans. As a former Chinese naval officer, he'd been humiliated by them, forced to turn away from the Spratly Islands during one of the many naval shoving matches to prove dominance in the area. Now he was putting *The Star* at risk by attempting to pass the Americans in the narrow channel.

"Quartermaster, maintain current speed and position," growled Xiang.

The Strait's pilot objected, "Captain, we should reduce our speed to avoid any unsafe situations."

Everyone on the bridge turned toward the captain expecting a torrent of profanity.

Glaring at the pilot the captain raised his voice and said, "Mr. Ling, while you may work for the Malacca Strait Pilot Organization, you are employed by the China Shipping Company. My orders over-rule the Strait's policy."

CHAPTER SEVENTY-FOUR

S<small>EPTEMBER</small> 28, (Thursday)

Malacca Strait

Ten hours since leaving the Singapore anchorage, the Nimitz was just about ready to enter Section Six of the Strait. Activity on the bridge was heightened as two additional watch standers were added to the crew complement. Cmdr. Buehl, upon returning from a late lunch, didn't like the conditions shown on the latest weather satellite images. Two large swaths of smoke were coming off Sumatra. One completely covered the straits from Malacca to Port Dickson, almost 30 nautical miles of heavy smoke. The Strait's reports from other ships indicated visibility levels dropping to less than 500 yards.

Walking over to the Captain who was perched in his chair with binoculars poised in front of his face, Ben said, "Captain, I don't like the conditions ahead, especially with that Chinese container ship off our port stern."

"I don't like it either, Ben. Any suggestions?"

"Several, but none of them ideal."

"I'm all ears," said the Captain, turning his attention from the bridge windows to Ben.

"We could continue our current speed and have *The Star* close to our port side for the next 20 or so miles as she passes. We need to be mindful of course that this section of the Strait, while looking wide, has some of the narrowest channels. Secondly, we could reduce our speed to 10 knots and let her pass, putting her in close proximity for about 10 miles. Thirdly, we could ask the admiral to increase the battle groups speed to 13 knots and keep The Star on our stern and at least 5,000 yards away."

Glancing back at the window, the Captain rubbed his chin and adjusted his jaw. "Admiral Henderson will not increase the battle group's speed. He's a stickler for rules and the Strait's rules state no more than 12 knots for a VLCC, which is our category."

"I'm aware of the admiral's penchant for rules and regulations, Captain. I served under him in the past. I doubt if he would approve a slowdown either. However, he's sitting on that cruiser and never had command of a carrier. His experience is with ships that can maneuver quickly and have a shallow draught. We're stuck with this old sow that takes forever to stop or turn."

"I don't agree with your calling her an 'old sow', Ben, but I agree with the rest of your remarks. Let's continue steady as we are and be hyper-vigilant. If that Chinese ship gets any closer than a 1,000 yards, I'm filing a formal protest to the Strait's Commission."

"Aye, aye, Captain."

"GET THOSE HATCHES SECURED, SEAMAN CARSON," barked Chief Thomson as he walked along the fourth deck passageway. "We are underway and on a modified Sea and Anchor detail."

"Chief, I've got to get this passageway cleaned, waxed and buffed before the inspection. I need the hatches open to dry the floor quicker."

"How long will that take?"

"No more than an hour, Chief."

Looking down the long row of knee-knockers and freshly scrubbed deck, the chief understood. "Ok, but try to work faster."

THE 1MC SCRATCHED TO LIFE, "Lt. Gibson, Lt. Gibson, report to HS-7 Ready Room with your crew on the double. Repeat. Lt. Gibson, report to HS-7 Ready Room with your crew on the double."

"What the heck," *Bosco* said as she sat up in her bunk. "What do they want now?"

She quickly used the head, returned to her stateroom and changed out of her sweats into her flight suit. She was putting on her boots when she heard a knock on her door. "*Bosco*, what's up?" asked *Battleship* from the other side of the door.

She joined him in the passageway and started hopping over 'knee-knockers' as they headed aft for the Ready Room. It was a funny sight – *Bosco* was so short, she had to step up and stand in the hatch openings, while Battleship had to duck and turn sideways to get through them. They looked like a Chihuahua and a St. Bernard competing on a doggie obstacle course.

Lt. Gibson looked at her watch. It was 1710 hours. "We've already completed two surveillance missions and have one more to go. I sure hope it's not a mail run. Or worse, the admiral wants to play golf at Phuket while we transit the Strait. It's too late for a round but I'm sure he wouldn't mind a few rounds at the bar."

"I wouldn't mind an RON at Phuket," Sims said with a smile extending ear-to-ear.

"You sailors are all alike. That place is an evil and disgusting place."

"Lighten up, *Bosco*. They have bars with male strippers too."

"Not the way I want to spend an evening, thank you."

They entered the Ready Room and quickly scanned the Operations Status Board. All seemed in order. Their next mission was

Battle Group security patrol in three hours. "What's up, Chief?" *Bosco* asked.

"*Miner* and *Major* are having engine issues. We're putting you guys back out on security patrol while we try to fix the problem. They're just landing now." *Miner* got his nickname because he was from a small West Virginia mining town. He tried several times to get folks to call him Coal Digger but his short stature made *Miner* stick. *Major* on the other hand, didn't have a nickname when he was paired with *Miner* but made the mistake of revealing that his college major was in music. *Major* seemed the perfect fit.

"What's the weather look like, Chief?" Lt. Sims asked as he settled into one of the leather-covered crew seats. Sims couldn't understand why retired pilots wanted to buy these old seats. They might recline but weren't in the least bit comfortable. His uncle, a former Marine chopper pilot, had four of them in his man cave in Pennsylvania. *Battleship* had suffered through enough pain watching the Steelers lose without piling on the pain caused to his body by the chair. He just wanted the weather report and then be on his way.

"Doesn't look good." Gathering notes off the desk, the chief scanned over the sheets and said, "Winds are steady from the west-southwest at 10 knots below 1,000 feet, increasing to 12 knots at 5,000 feet. Heavy smoke off Sumatra in patches as wide as 30 miles here and here," the chief said pointing to a satellite photo.

"What's the visibility in the smoke?" Lt. Gibson asked as she leaned over Sims' chair.

"Not good based on ships passing through the stuff. Some ships are reporting less than 500 yards."

"Great. When's nightfall?"

The chief looked down his notes and said, " 1907 local."

"Any idea how long *Miner* and *Major* will be down?" asked Lt. Gibson.

"No ma'am. Didn't sound like it was catastrophic though."

"What do you think, *Bosco*? Should we ask for another set of eyes in the back?" Sims asked as he looked at the satellite image. "With darkness coming on and all that smoke, we're going to have our hands full."

"Chief, how soon can we get another operator for the FLIR?" Lt. Gibson asked, looking intently at the satellite image and the smoke streams crossing the Straits.

"I can have Petty Officer Westcott in your bird before you start rotation."

"Thanks, chief. We're headed up now. What's our spot?"

"Before you go, Skipper says you'll have company out there. Because of the smoke, you're only going to patrol the starboard side of the BG. *Dogbone* 2, off USS Chancellorsville, will patrol the port. Keep your eyes open and be safe. You're on Spot 4."

CHAPTER SEVENTY-FIVE

SEPTEMBER 28, (Thursday)

Malacca Strait, Cape Rachado

Anchored in the area of Port Dickson, two kilometers off of Cape Rachado, the Fatimah rocked gently with the waves of each passing ship. Some waves barely moved their craft while others, from those big super tankers, almost made them loose sight of the horizon as they dropped into the trough.

Mohammed and Junaedi stood on the bridge, each peering through binoculars, trying to make out the ship traffic in the sea-lanes seven kilometers further off shore.

"I can hardly see any ships," exclaimed Mohammed in frustration.

"Patience, my brother. Our source reported they departed Singapore at 0600 this morning. If they are maintaining 12 knots, they should be arriving within the hour. Our mission approaches completion. Allah be praised."

Mohammed scanned the deck forward of the bridge. Four of his crew sat on the top of the fixed cargo containers. They were passing binoculars back and forth. *This will be better than any Ramadan fire-*

works display,' thought Mohammed. 'We must get closer. This smoke is too thick and I want to see the Americans die.'

"Let's move closer to the channel, brother, to better see the show," Mohammed said aloud with an urge to lick his lips.

"I think it is too dangerous, Mohammed. We should not even be here. The mines are designed to work independently and will crush the ship. We will see the results on all the news broadcasts."

"But I want to witness the destruction; to tell my grandchildren how the Great Satan slid beneath the waves as I watched the dead bodies float to the surface."

"We should not be here!" Junaedi said with frustration. "The plan always stated we needed to be on the west coast of Sumatra near Ache, totally out of the way. I only agreed to your wish because we would be anchored and appear as any other small ship waiting for traffic in the Straits to subside. We need to stay here."

"I disagree and I'm in charge."

"We are both in charge, Mohammed."

Moving to one side of the bridge, Mohammed motioned to his crew to come aft. "My brother, you were in charge of the mines. You have done well. They are in place and ready to destroy. I will record that destruction to prove to our leaders we accomplished our goals."

Junaedi could hardly contain his composure; "They will see it in the news. We should remain here!"

"We will let the crew decide." Turning toward the stern, Mohammed asked the eight men standing on deck, "How many wish to remain anchored here instead of moving closer to the channel to see the Great Satan stabbed in the heart?"

Each crewman's hands remained at his side. "Excellent! Prepare to raise the anchor." A cheer went up from the stern. Junaedi shivered and pulled his open coat together thinking a cold breeze had just passed over him.

CHAPTER SEVENTY-SIX

SEPTEMBER 28, (Thursday)

USS Nimitz, Malacca Strait

The whine from the twin General Electric turbo-shaft engines could barely be heard through the crew chief's headphones. The noise-canceling feature was working fine and allowed him to communicate with Westcott as he climbed aboard. "Sit in the gunner's seat," the chief said as he pointed to the jump seat on the port side of the helo. "We're lifting off momentarily." The chief climbed aboard and tapped Lt. Gibson on the shoulder to let her know they were a go.

Lt. Gibson activated the microphone switch on her cyclic stick, "*Eagle's Nest, Scramble 1* ready for takeoff."

"*Scramble 1*, you are cleared for takeoff."

After a quick glance at her flight instruments, *Bosco* lifted her head and saw the Yellow Shirt with his two red wands crossed above his head. When he dropped them to his side and then pointed one to port, she slowly pulled up on the collective hearing the GE engines begin to whine louder. Five feet above the deck, she made a slight movement with the cyclic stick that shifted her sideways to the deck's edge before adding more collective and a forward movement of the cyclic.

Bosco always liked that feeling of leaving the deck. She looked down and saw the Nimitz getting smaller as she applied a forward motion on the stick and started her surveillance mission along the starboard side of the battle group.

Less than five minutes into the flight, the visibility dropped to less than 500 yards.

"Chief, get Wescott hooked up and monitoring the auxiliary FLIR. I want continuous coverage transmitted to Ops," ordered Lt. Gibson.

"Wescott's already set, ma'am."

"Wescott, can you hear me?" asked *Bosco*.

"Yes, ma'am, fivers."

"Good. I want complete coverage of anything moving. Use the zoom on each moving vessel and record activity. If you see something suspicious, even if it looks crazy, don't hesitate to record it and notify myself or Lt. Sims."

"Roger, ma'am."

"Chief, I want you to do the same off the port. I realize most of your field of view will be blocked by the BG but pay close attention to the gaps."

"Aye, aye, ma'am."

CHAPTER SEVENTY-SEVEN

September 28, (Thursday)

Malacca Strait

"Captain, that Chinese container ship is 600 yards off the port stern beam. She intends to pass us in this narrow channel, sir," the Quartermaster said with alarm.

"What the hell is that bastard trying to prove?" barked the captain. "There's not enough room to maneuver in this channel."

"Cmdr. Buehl, how much room do we have to starboard?"

"We've got about 1,000 yards, sir."

"Let's hug the starboard side of that channel and slow to 10 knots. If that idiot is so intent on passing, let him get it done quickly and not be a threat."

"Aye, aye, Sir. New track plotted and initiated."

Ben had an odd feeling all of a sudden, almost a feeling of impending doom. He reached under the plot table and pulled out his life vest, placed it over his head and secured it in place. As he walked to the starboard flying bridge, he contemplated removing the vest but instead cinched the straps a little tighter. He never wore the vest unless General Quarters was sounded. He was at odds with himself as to why he was wearing it now.

PETTY OFFICER 2ND CLASS BUTTERFIELD sat at the sonar console reading the latest National Geographic. His console was on automatic and his headphones slightly askew. His assigned duty was to monitor subsurface threats. Due to the narrow confines of the Strait and the huge amount of noise generated by the ship traffic in the channel, Butterfield had switched the system to automatic and let the computer sort through the cacophony.

Unbeknownst to the petty officer or the computer, four modified EM-52 rocket mines, 170 feet below the surface, just self-actuated after comparing the Nimitz's acoustic signature with that loaded into the mines' memory. The activation took less than a second as the rockets fired and launched at close to 80 yards a second, heading directly for the Nimitz.

Before the computer could sort out and identify the threat, four mines exploded along the keel at a spacing determined by Iranian naval analysts to create the best conditions for breaking the Nimitz's keel. The massive explosions barely lifted the 90,000-ton vessel. Six inch steel plates buckled and in several places the hull was breached. The major destruction took place as the Nimitz settled back into the void in the water and the keel split in several places. The EM-52 mines accomplished what they were designed to do. The effect is similar to standing on a 12 foot long 2x6" board. If laying flat on a solid surface, a person can walk back-and-forth on the board and no damage will occur. However, suspending the board between two sawhorses placed as far apart as possible creates a void under the board. Attempting to walk the distance on this board will most likely cause it to break at some point. Without the water under the Nimitz, it was suspended just like the two-by-six.

Cmdr. Buehl had just reached the flying bridge when the mines detonated. Before he could secure a firm grasp on the railing, he was tossed in the air and over the side. At least twenty other personnel were jettisoned from their watch stations along the rails and hangar decks. The explosion caused two F-35 Lightnings to move toward the stern, breaking loose from their attached tow vehicles. One of the F-35's punctured an F-18 Hornet. The explosion that followed instantly killed 30 flight deck personnel who were at muster near the Island. In a chain reaction caused by the explosion, four more aircraft burst into flame as hot shrapnel penetrated full fuel bladders.

On the bridge, the Officer-of-the-Deck was the first to recover. Picking himself off the deck, he pushed the General Quarters alarm. As the recorded message went out, he noticed blood dripping into his eyes and raised his hand to staunch the flow. Looking around the bridge he saw others struggling to their feet just as the force from the explosions on the flight deck knocked him off balance.

BEN AUTOMATICALLY TRIED to orient himself for a feet first entry into the water but was unsuccessful. The over 100-foot fall disoriented him and he hit the water in a cannonball position. His knees slammed into his chest forcing the air out of his lungs as his head made contact with his left knee knocking him unconscious. His life vest inflated automatically, turning him onto his back with his legs stretched out. He did not feel the explosions from the second set of mines.

Three of the four mines, modified to pierce several inches of metal, intruded into the now damaged underbelly of the Nimitz and exploded in the forward propulsion room. Seaman Carson, on the deck above, never experienced any pain as the steel floor plates crushed him into the overhead cable racks. Salt water surged over his body and down the fourth deck passageway, unhindered by the open hatches.

Less than 90 seconds into the attack, the Nimitz began to list to starboard by five degrees. The upward force and the list caused three more aircraft to break free of the tie-down chains and roll off the deck.

LT. GIBSON WAS AWESTRUCK as she saw the explosions on the flight deck. She had just completed a search rotation and was headed back up the starboard side of the battle group. Her helo was pushed sideways by the shock waves coming off the carrier and she concentrated on maintaining control and moving further from the ship. With composure she didn't believe she had, *Bosco* quietly spoke to her crew. "Chief, record all activity you can on the Nimitz. Wescott, conduct a sweep on your side and record everything. Concentrate on anything you deem unusual. Battleship, look for survivors." Her crew acknowledged the commands just as shock-waves from more explosions jostled the helo.

CAPTAIN XIANG'S jaw looked like it was disjointed. He peered out the bridge windows at the chaos engulfing the American aircraft carrier just to his right. He was about to tell the pilot to conduct an emergency stop when the stern of his ship was lifted from the water sending him and his crew slamming into bulkheads and equipment. One of the rocket mines, thrown off course by the explosions, detonated upon contact with *The Star's* propeller. The rudder was jammed to its fullest starboard extent, forcing the ship into a hard right turn. As the stern settled back into the water, several containers broke free from the tall stacks and smashed into the bridge, killing the captain, pilot and helmsman. Out of control, *The Star*, still running at 12.5 knots, headed on a collision course with the Nimitz.

WESCOTT HIT the record button and zoomed in on a small vessel with containers on its deck. His attention was drawn to the crewmembers that were jumping up and down in jubilation. It looked like some members were pointing phones or video cameras at the Nimitz. Wescott had difficulty keeping the vessel in the frame as Lt. Gibson swung the helo around to search for people in the water.

Battleship caught sight of the saltwater activated light on Cmdr. Buehl's life vest and notified Lt. Gibson, "Survival light located dead ahead approximately 800 yards. Do you think we can get that close to the Nimitz?"

"Copy that, eyes on target. Looks like it's aft of the Nimitz. Let's hope a person is in the vest and still alive.

"Chief, are you rigged for rescue?" asked Bosco.

"Getting the winch and pulley deployed now. Ready in one minute."

"Copy. I'm going to hover over the target. Get me a visual and report sign of life. We will have to triage our targets."

"Aye, aye, Lieutenant."

"Battleship, contact the Battle Command Center and request options for recovery and any change in orders. If BCC is busy, call the ship that's helo configured."

"Copy."

Lt. Gibson brought the helo down to 20 feet above the surface of the water as she approached the blinking light. "Lieutenant, I see a body in the vest and I think there's movement." Quickly shifting his selector off voice to the megaphone mounted under the helicopter, he called out to the person floating in the water, "If you can hear me, wave your arm."

Cmdr. Buehl couldn't believe his luck as he forced his arm above the water, waving at the helo. "Movement confirmed," the Chief relayed to Lt. Gibson. "Do you need help getting into the harness? If no help is needed, wave your arm."

Cmdr. Buehl again raised his arm and saw the helo begin to deploy the rescue harness. In less than five minutes he was hauled into the helicopter, untangled from the harness and directed to sit on the floor away from the door. "Party of one onboard, Lieutenant," said the chief.

"Well done, chief. Stand by. Battleship has two more targets spotted."

As Bosco added more collective to gain altitude, she and her crew glanced at the Nimitz when they heard a crunching noise loud enough to be heard over the rotor blades and engines. "Oh my God," mouthed Battleship as they all watched the containership strike the Nimitz broadside near Elevator Four. In what seemed like slow motion, the Nimitz shuddered and then began to list to starboard. Planes broke from their tie downs and rolled off the deck. Sailors could be seen either jumping or frozen in place trying to fight against gravity. *The Star* kept pushing forward and began riding up on the port side of the Nimitz until the carrier passed its point of vertical stabilization. The Nimitz slid sideways into the Strait.

MOHAMMAD WAS as ecstatic as the rest of his crew. He gave Junaedi a big hug and kissed him on both checks. "We did it! We did it!" Never had he believed they would sink the American aircraft carrier but, before his eyes, Allah had blessed them with a successful operation. He called to his crew to get underway and return to their camp in Ache. He knew he had to get out of the area before authorities started an organized search for bystanders. He could not afford scrutiny of his vessel. Within minutes, the little ship was heading north, lost in the flurry of activity.

CHAPTER SEVENTY-EIGHT

SEPTEMBER 27, (Wednesday)
Mattingly Home
"Dad! Dad!" Maddie yelled to her father who was downstairs in his study.

Hearing a tone in her voice suggesting danger, Karl charged up the stairs thinking someone had been hurt, only to be confronted by the large TV screen showing a picture of the USS Nimitz and a commentator talking above a title block displaying, "USS Nimitz reported attacked in the Strait of Malacca."

"What's going on, Shug?" he asked, not sure if he wanted to hear an answer.

"All the news outlets are reporting the Nimitz was attacked while transiting the Strait of Malacca. Early reports claim the ship capsized. I've pulled up Twitter accounts and YouTube already has video posted from ships in the area showing the carrier laying on its side and sinking. Dad, they think thousands of sailors are dead or trapped inside."

"Shug, do you think this has anything to do with the threat message?"

"I do, Dad. I've got to get to work," Maddie said as she got up to get her things.

"I'll go with you. I have a terrible feeling that the ship I found hiding on Sumatra might be involved," Karl said as his hand rubbed his beard.

As he stood up from the couch, Phillip touched Maddie's shoulder causing her to turn. "Don't you have a relative stationed on the Nimitz?"

"Oh, my!" exclaimed Liz, shocked that she hadn't remembered. "Maddie, *Bosco's* on that ship!"

Karl opened his arms and gathered Lisa and Maddie close to him. With a slight gesture toward Phillip, they all gathered into a close hug as Karl said a brief prayer for his sister's daughter and her crewmembers' safety. He concluded with a request for guidance for the Nation's leaders as they worked to respond to this unprovoked attack.

CHAPTER SEVENTY-NINE

(24 HOURS after attack)

White House Situation Room

The atmosphere in the Situation Room was tense as President Wolton entered and sat down. He looked exhausted and beaten except for the hint of anger in his eyes. "Situation, folks?" he asked.

In a room where most attendees jumped at the chance to speak first, silence greeted POTUS as he looked over the top of his reading glasses, scanning the room before stopping on the Director of Homeland Security. He was about to ask Angela for an update when the Director of CIA motioned to him. "Go ahead."

"Mr. President, I believe an update is available from the CNO by secure TV. He asked to go early in the discussion in order to focus on the ongoing rescue efforts."

"Certainly. Is it all cued up?"

"Mr. President," Admiral Harris said weakly. "Our latest data confirms 3,106 deaths. The Nimitz continues to settle in the 170 feet of water making rescue operations dangerous. Every Navy diver not on a vessel at sea has been directed to report for duty at designated staging bases. Thailand has agreed to unfettered access to Phuket airbase. Carrier Battle Group 11 has onsite command. Pollution control booms are deployed and radiation monitors are in place above and below water. Based on acoustic analysis, it appears the reactors scrambled and shutdown without further issue. CBG 11 is currently planning next steps. Indonesia, Malaysia, Australia and Myanmar have offered assistance."

"Thanks, Wilson. Don't hesitate to call if you need anything or the situation changes. The Joint Chiefs are all onboard for any material or transportation assistance you require."

"Thank you Mr. President. My condolences to your lost crewmembers."

"And to you, too," replied the president.

"Mr. President, if I may," injected the Director of CIA.

"Go ahead, Mark."

"I have several analysts sitting outside who are prepared to brief you on our idea of who conducted this attack."

"Bring them in, please."

Maddie, Karl and CTI2 Ives entered the room.

"Hello again, Ms. Mattingly and Petty Officer Ives. Who's the new member of your team?" he asked as the flat-screen blinked to the first slide in their presentation.

Maddie cleared her throat to answer just as Director Baker introduced her father. "This is Karl Mattingly, Maddie's father. He's a retired CIA imagery analyst, currently working for the commercial satellite firm GlobalWatch. He is cleared for TS/SCI and other tickets as necessary for this operation."

"I'm sorry that we have to meet under these circumstances," President Wolton said as he reached out and shook Karl's hand. I've been impressed with your daughter and the company she keeps," he said glancing at Sam. "I understand that's putting undo pressure on you, Karl."

"We will shoulder it, sir," replied Karl with a slightly shaky voice. The last president he had briefed was George W. Bush. The excitement and dread never seemed to diminish.

"Based on the close coordination between CIA and NSA," said Mark, "these folks have identified our best candidate for the attack."

Over the course of the next 15 minutes, Maddie, Karl and Sam outlined their information for POTUS. Maddie told him about the source she debriefed in Jakarta and his mention of something big going to happen. Karl outlined the discovery and activity surrounding the small vessel at Suak Seumaseh in Ache, Indonesia. He pointed out the unusual addition of the shipping containers on the vessel and the peculiar angle of the containers. He also highlighted the vessel's absence from its hiding place in the cove that correlated with movements reported by NSA. Sam completed the briefing with NSA's intercepts of a congratulatory phone call located in the Strait of Malacca at the time of the attack on the Nimitz.

CIA Director Baker closed with information on current actions taking place. He told the president that all overhead systems were tasked against the vessel. Video taken by the helo crew from the Nimitz helped confirm that the vessel had indeed been in the immediate area of the attack. Karl had located the vessel on subsequent imagery near the north end of Sumatra, exiting the Strait. "Estimated vessel speed is 8 knots giving them three days before it returns to its hiding place, if that is the ultimate destination," Karl added.

"We have an armed reconnaissance Australian Reaper headed to Christmas Island as I speak. It is tasked with standoff monitoring of the vessel," Mark said as concluded his remarks.

"Blow the son of a bitch out of the water!" said the Chairman of the Joints Chiefs as he slammed his fist onto the table.

"Settle down and control your language. I recognize tensions are high but profanity doesn't help," intoned the president.

Looking at the three briefers, POTUS asked, "How confident are you that this is the vessel that laid the mines?"

Maddie and Sam both deferred to Karl who leaned forward and placed his hands on the conference table to steady himself. "Mr. President, we are 90% sure that this vessel was involved in the attack. A close inspection of those shipping containers will probably show they are configured with rails used to deploy the mines. A review of all imagery, classified and commercial, put that vessel in the Malacca Strait in July. An NSA intercept from the same cellphone used to make the congratulatory call reported a mission success. We are assuming that refers to the deployment of the mines."

"So, an inspection of the ship is necessary?"

"It would confirm the involvement," replied Karl.

The president sat back in his seat and picked up the photo of the ship Karl had included in the briefing package. "Such a nondescript ship; a no threat vessel that has taken out a major man-o-war and killed thousands of sailors. It's hard to believe.

"How do we capture this ship and crew?" he asked of the members around the table.

The President's National Security Advisor broke the momentary silence. "Mr. President, we have Seal Team [redacted]'s, [redacted] Squadron at Darwin, Australia. They've been training with their Aussie counterparts, the SASRs. They have a full equipment load. If we can get approval from Prime Minister Ian Homes to conduct lethal actions from Australia, it would save us days of logistical effort. We would also need assistance getting the team to Christmas Island and probably onward transport."

"I will call Ian. He's an old naval officer who still owes me a few beers for beating him at darts," chuckled Chester trying to lighten the mood, if only for himself. "I'll take him up on that offer of assistance."

CHAPTER EIGHTY

SEPTEMBER 30, (Saturday)

Christmas Island

Pherball, as his teammates called him, a foreshortened moniker for Christopher, sprinted the last 200 yards to the hangar were his team was making preparations for deployment. LCDR Christopher McInnis, a US Navy SEAL, was the team leader of SEAL Team [redacted]'s [redacted]. He'd just finished five circuits around the runway to work the cobwebs out of his mind and body. The Squadron arrived on Christmas Island, a small lightly inhabited island 500 miles south of Jakarta, Indonesia and 1,600 miles west of Darwin, Australia where they had been the night before when the movement order set the current preparations in motion.

For the past six weeks, *Pherball* and his team were engaged in training exercises with Australia's equivalent of US Special Forces, the Special Air Service Regiment, more commonly known as SAS. The squadron had orientation and welcoming ceremonies at Campbell Barracks in Perth, moved to Bindoon training base for firearms checks and house-to-house or Close-Quarters Battle (CQB as the

Aussies like to call it) clearing exercises at the mock village just west of the small airstrip.

The Squadron split up with SAS team members to form two action squads of 10 men each. The exercises became very intense as the training pitted the teams against each other in several real-life scenarios like hostage control and recovery. LCDR McInnis was impressed with the Australian members. Once they got to Darwin and shifted to the sea insertion and ship-boarding exercises under hostile conditions did the gaps in experience begin to show. After two weeks of extensive operations, under real and controlled events in the sea-lanes of Timor Sea, the SAS team began to appreciate the unique skills and abilities of SEAL Team [redacted] members.

Pherball and his teammates, along with the Aussies, had been sitting at Fiddler's Green Bar, overlooking Kitchener Bay, tossing back a constant flow of Crown Lager from the tap when they saw the news report of the Nimitz's sinking. To a man, glasses were lifted in honor of those lost at sea. Preparations were immediately made to get the squadron back to their accommodations at Robertson's Barracks. Less than twenty-four hours after the attack, McInnis' cellphone rang with orders to pre-position at Christmas Island. He was to take both CCM Mk1 boats and all equipment necessary to board and secure the vessel *Fatimah* before it could land at its base on Sumatra. SAS offered any services required.

While his team and the Aussies began inventorying and packing equipment, *Pherball* and his SAS counterpart set up a command center in the Communications Operations Center. They established direct links to the Pentagon, NSA, CIA and the White House. LCDR McInnis was able to ask Karl, Maddie and Sam questions about the *Fatimah* and the perpetrators of the Nimitz's destruction. By 0600 hours the next day, a plan was in place. The Two C-17a Globemaster III's on assignment from the 36th Squadron were parked at RAAF Darwin. After the last two weeks of training, the pilots were proficient at deploying the CCM Mk1 boats and the assault teams. Within hours they were airborne for Christmas Island, 1,600 miles to the west.

AS MCINNIS WALKED toward the small hangar, the high level of activity encouraged him. The SAS commander yielded operational control to *Pherball* even though eight of his soldiers made up part of the assault teams. Commander Pittaway would have his hands full anyway. He and a small assault team planned to conduct a HALO insertion at the camp located at Suak Seumaseh.

Timing of both operations was critical to maintain the element of surprise. Pittaway's eight-man team would conduct a parachute drop from the C-17's while enroute to dropping the ship boarding parties. Two helicopters from the USS Antietam, currently positioned near the northwestern entrance to the Malacca Strait, will exfiltrate the team once they've completed the mission. After dropping Pittaway's team, the two C-17's will descend to 3,500 feet and drop the two CCM Mk1 boats, along with the two assault teams, about 30 miles in front of the *Fatimah's* expected route.

A RAAF Reaper was already on station monitoring the *Fatimah's* movements, transmitting real-time data to McInnis' team. A second Reaper repositioned from Guam to Phuket and was approaching the terrorist camp.

All available intelligence indicated that *Fatimah* took a wide path around Pulau We and Sabang City rather than the short cut between the island and Banda Aceh City. CIA and Pentagon analysts believed the *Fatimah* was attempting to stay outside local shipping lanes to reduce any possibility of recognition. Owing to the fact that *Fatimah* had once plied those water as the *Warapi*.

CHAPTER EIGHTY-ONE

SEPTEMBER 30, (Saturday)

Off the west coast of Sumatra

"Team One clear! Team One clear!" came the call over the aircraft's intercom. McInnis already knew that as he watched the last man step off the C-17's ramp. The rear ramp slowly closed as the aircraft began to loose altitude. Pittaway's team had exited the aircraft at 25,000 feet 20 miles off the coast. If all went well, six of the eight SEALs and SAS members would land in a rice paddy 300 meters north of the camp while two would land on a sandbar about the same distance south of the camp. The surrounding countryside was mangrove swamp and no one wanted to chase terrorists for long in the thick undergrowth. The task was to capture any male personnel in the camp and recover any electronic equipment. Once accomplished, two SH-60 helos, flying at tree top level down the Krueng Aceh river valley, would rendezvous with the team for pickup.

"FIVE MINUTES. Repeat, drop zone in five," the copilot called out over the intercom.

"Copy," acknowledge *Pherball* as he gave a thumbs up and an open hand with five fingers extended.

Both C-17's made wide descending circles until they approached 3,500 feet and the drop points. The small panel above the cargo ramp folded upward and inward as the ramp began to lower. The load-master was positioned to deactivate the pallet brakes on the Mk1 boat that took up almost all of the 84 feet of cargo space. The sleek, low-radar observable hull, painted a dull grey, looked ready for action. Four SEAL Special Warfare Combat-craft Crewman (SWCC – pronounced 'swick') stood near the ramp, ready to jump out of the aircraft as soon as the boat cleared the ramp.

"Go, go, go," shouted the loadmaster just as the C-17 started a slight nose-up angle. He released the brakes and the boat began to slide out of the cargo bay. Seconds later, the Swicks jumped, followed by McInnis' team of 10 men. They stepped off the ramp into the cool morning air. It was 0230, October 1st.

So far, the plan was going without hitch. Both boats landed in good condition. Crews de-rigged the boats and assault teams climbed onboard. A final weapons check was completed and contact was made with Pittaway. His team landed safely with only a minor cut on a team member's hand.

As the *Fatimah* steamed toward the assault teams at 6 knots, McInnis and company approached *Fatimah's* position at 40 knots. In less than 30 minutes, both boats were positioned four miles abreast the vessel. The darkness, late hour and low profile of the boats made them invisible to any guard on the *Fatimah's* deck. As *Fatimah* passed their position, the Mk1's would fall into a position one mile behind the terrorists' vessel. McInnis received and evaluated the Reaper's live video feed of activity on the ship before giving the command to commence final approach and boarding.

CHAPTER EIGHTY-TWO

SEPTEMBER 30, (Saturday)

White House Situation Room

The Situation Room was crowded as President Wolton entered. He waved everyone to remain seated. He was afraid someone would get injured as they all tried to stand to attention.

"Status, please," he said softly while settling into his chair.

Paul Albrecht had arranged for primacy of the meeting. He stood up and pointed to the large flat-screen monitor at the end of the room. "We are viewing a live feed from the Reaper, sir. Two assault teams are positioned one mile astern of the terrorist's vessel awaiting a final review of activity on the ship." He paused, looked over his notes and continued. "On the screen to your left, Mr. President, is a wider view of the activity from a second camera on the Reaper. This FLIR image highlights the 'hot spots' and you can make out the heat coming from the *Fatimah's* stack. One crewman is on the bridge, one crewman is on the forward shipping container and at least five crewman are on the afterdeck."

"Are those guys on the deck sleeping?" asked the president.

"Based on observations over the last hour, we believe that's a good assumption," piped in the CNO.

"It's not unusual for a crew to sleep topside for the fresh air and coolness of the evening. Most of these tramp steamers don't have any air conditioning and can be unbearably hot below deck," continued Mark.

"I realize this is a little late in the game to ask but are we sure this is the right ship?"

"Sir, Mr. Mattingly at CIA confirmed the identity earlier today and is available on the conference call connection if you wish additional background."

"No need, Paul. When does this all begin?"

"We're awaiting the SEAL Team [redacted] commander's approval now. It's expected shortly."

CHAPTER EIGHTY-THREE

October 1, (Sunday)

Off west coast of Sumatra

Junaedi stirred in his sleep, rolled onto his left side and opened his eyes. It was dark. He tilted his head toward the sky and saw star-filled patches between the clouds. He closed his eyes, wanting the slow repetitious thumping of the engine to lull him back to sleep. A cool breeze passed over him and he curled into the fetal position to keep warm. A minute later he sat up and made the decision to get a coat or blanket, whichever he could quickly find. As he stood, he noticed movement alongside the ship. Jumping to his feet, he rushed across the deck toward the AK-47 braced against the deckhouse bulkhead. Before he could reach his weapon or cry out in alarm, two bullets entered his back, about four inches below his collar bone, and exploded inside his heart.

Awakened by the crash of Junaedi's body on the deck, three crewmen abruptly scampered from their sleeping mats and reached for weapons. Two SEALs quickly neutralized the threat as the third crewmember dropped his weapon and put his hands over his head.

Meanwhile, McInnis climbed the ladder going to the bridge with his weapon trained on the man standing at the controls. Surmising he had no chance of escape, the terrorist stepped back from the wheel and placed his hands on his head. McInnis pointed to the man and the ladder, indicating he wanted him to climb down. When he reached the bottom rung, a SEAL quickly secured his hands with flexi-cuffs and pushed him down on deck. He was quickly joined by two more of the crew that had been on the forward deck.

McInnis activated his lip mike, "All clear topside."

"Berthing, se..." came the unfinished reply followed by an explosion.

"Keep an eye on these guys, Crane," *Pherball* said as he turned toward an open hatch leading below deck. He was followed by one of the Aussies and another SEAL.

"*Keeper? Keeper*, are you alright?"

A long pause, followed by the sound of slow heavy breathing, filled McInnis' earpiece. "Hang in there, *Keeper*. We're coming for you."

McInnis motioned to his teammates that they would conduct a CQB through the three small cabins before doing the same in the engine room.

The smell of cordite filled the air in the second cabin. Lying just inside the doorway was Sgt. Orman, the best goalkeeper in the Australian Army. His mate quickly made an assessment, determining that *Keeper* had some non-life threatening shrapnel wounds and probably suffered a concussion. McInnis left the two of them with instructions to contain bleeding.

"Medic 1, Medic 1. If able to disengage, proceed to Cabin Two. Acknowledge."

"Disengaged and proceeding," came the quick reply.

Slinging his MK13 CQBR over his shoulder and pulling his Sig Sauer P226 from his holster, McInnis started down the passageway to the third cabin.

"Pay attention, *Frosty*. Looks like we might have booby traps," Christopher said in a hushed voice to the SEAL from Minnesota.

"I'll take the point and go high," he said as they approached the cabin door.

Mohammed crouched behind the slightly open door waiting for the attackers to enter. He had a grenade in one hand and an AK-47 in the other. How ironic he thought, '*I am attacked by pirates on a ship I pirated.*'

Through the space between the door and jam, *Frosty* could only see the grenade in Mohammed's hand. Raising his P226 with the laser sight he placed the dot on Mohammed's hand while holding his other hand up to stop McInnis from entering the room. He fired his weapon, expecting an explosion to follow. Instead, only a painful scream emanated from the compartment.

Both men charged into the room as Mohammed struggled to raise his gun. *Frosty* kicked it to the ground and quickly applied flexi-cuffs to the terrorist.

"Cabins secured. Need someone to come get a hostile so we can clear the engine room," McInnis barked.

———

THE LIVE FEED to Washington was delayed about four seconds, but no one seemed to care. When McInnis returned to the weather deck, a cheer went up in the Situation Room. Backs were being patted and hands shaken around the room. The less uptight attendees even hugged.

"When will we have a report?" asked the president.

Paul Albrecht didn't hear his boss ask the question. He was still watching the monitor trying to fully grasp the capabilities of the US military.

"Paul! When will I have an after action report?"

Startled by the sharpness in the president's tone, Paul turned to him and said, "I'll check, sir." He followed up by telling the president he would bring the report to the Oval Office as soon as he got feedback.

It would take two hours but it was worth the wait. Preliminary reports confirmed six terrorists captured, three dead. A computer, several cellphones and a small book with possible coded entries were recovered. Digitized copies of the book and a download of the computer's hard drive were already in the hands of techs at CIA and NSA. NSA confirmed that one of the cellphones matched the intercept acquired near the Nimitz in the Malacca Strait just minutes after the attack.

President Wolton reviewed the report and pulled his immediate staff together for a prayer of thanksgiving. He then sat with his speechwriter to compose a message for the American people and the world-at-large. He knew the news of captured terrorists would raise the country's spirit but it would not go far in relieving the tremendous loss felt by the family members of the over 4,000 sailors and marines dead or unaccounted for still aboard the sunken remains of the USS Nimitz.

EPILOGUE

OCTOBER 1, (Sunday)

Maddie's apartment

Maddie rested her head in her hands and looked at the *Washington Post* headline again, *Worst Loss of American Life Since 9/11*. She could almost write tomorrow's headline herself, *"House and Senate Intelligence Committees Demand Investigations."* She also knew there would be little sleep until Congress got their pound of flesh. What could she tell them? Like so much of the public, Congress didn't understand the murky world of Intelligence or the difficulty of putting pieces from disparate puzzles together to create a new puzzle. Who could have predicted that two unrelated events would have such a significant relationship? Maddie was visualizing a power point slide's bullets –

•Naturalized US citizen, Pastor Hamid Hashemi, arrested by the Islamic Republic of Iran

•Small coastal steamer *"Warapi"* pirated from Sabang Port

UNTITLED

The End

ACKNOWLEDGMENTS

Most importantly, I thank God for the inspiration, timing and opportunity He planned and for which I am now aware. To my brother-in-law Rick Talbot, an author in his own right, who continually encouraged me to write – even if it was terrible. I owe a great debt to the many friends and family members who read approved drafts, giving me their unbiased opinions and suggestions for improvement. Special thanks to Dan Schofield for information on the FBI, my neighbor Ken Buell for helicopter operations and Don Mann regarding Seal Team [redacted] activities.

Writing this first novel was a joy, as are the follow-on adventures of the Mattingly family currently in work. Working titles include *"Terraglyph"* and *"90 – K"*. Look for them in coming years on Kindle Books.

I say years because I'm required to submit everything I wish to publish to CIA's Publication Review Board, even before letting friends and family see a draft. Writing under those conditions is difficult. Each subsequent edited version must be approved by the PRB. Elapsed time from first submitted draft to approved draft was 11 months. An additional 2 months was required for requested changes so, please be patient. I have every intention of answering your questions in the second book and providing some backstory in a third book.

My family offered tremendous support and opportunities to disappear and write. My wife, Gwen, allowed me free passes from numerous "honey-do" items when inspiration was active. She put up with my long stays in the hot tub where ideas seemed to flow the hotter I got. She helped breathe life into several of the characters. Any errors are truly mine and I encourage my readers to contact me with questions and comments about this book at mattingly.series@gmail.com.

Made in the USA
Middletown, DE
14 May 2019